WHEN WE WERE LOST

KEVIN WIGNALL

Foreword by James Patterson

JIMMY PATTERSON BOOKS
LITTLE, BROWN AND COMPANY
New York Boston London

Copyright © 2019 Kevin Wignall
Foreword copyright © 2019 by James Patterson

Hachette Book Group supports the right to free expression and the value of copyright. The purpose of copyright is to encourage writers and artists to produce the creative works that enrich our culture.

The scanning, uploading, and distribution of this book without permission is a theft of the author's intellectual property. If you would like permission to use material from the book (other than for review purposes), please contact permissions@hbgusa.com. Thank you for your support of the author's rights.

JIMMY Patterson Books / Little, Brown and Company
Hachette Book Group
1290 Avenue of the Americas, New York, NY 10104
JimmyPatterson.org

First paperback edition: June 2020

Originally published in hardcover by JIMMY Patterson Books, Little / Brown and Company, June 2019.

JIMMY Patterson Books is an imprint of Little, Brown and Company, a division of Hachette Book Group, Inc. The Little, Brown name and logo are trademarks of Hachette Book Group, Inc. The JIMMY Patterson Books® name and logo are trademarks of JBP Business, LLC.

The publisher is not responsible for websites (or their content) that are not owned by the publisher.

The Hachette Speakers Bureau provides a wide range of authors for speaking events. To find out more, go to hachettespeakersbureau.com or call (866) 376-6591.

LCCN: 2019938308

ISBNs: 978-0-316-41779-2 (hardcover); 978-0-316-41781-5 (trade paperback)

10 9 8 7 6 5 4 3 2

LSC-C

Printed in the United States of America

For George and Rafael

FOREWORD

As someone who loves to tell stories, I've found that the best ones take you in a direction you never expected to go. I started reading *When We Were Lost* thinking that it would be a straightforward survival tale of kids whose plane crashes in a remote jungle. Kevin Wignall certainly packed it with all the nail-biting suspense and wild thrills of a terrific disaster narrative, but I was delighted to find it ends up being much more than that.

We see the catastrophe unfold through the eyes of Tom—a friendless kid who just wants to be left alone. I think we all have a little bit of that in us, a part that makes us feel like we never quite belong. This story has Tom fighting to survive unexpected situations—the savage jungle *and* high school social hierarchies—and finding them both vicious to contend with in their own ways.

In the end, this story is about being lost in more ways than one, and what it really means to be found.

—James Patterson

PROLOGUE

It's called the butterfly effect, and it's the part of chaos theory that everyone loves. The idea is that a butterfly flapping its wings can cause a hurricane on the other side of the world. Not directly, of course. It's not like the wings disturb some air and that disturbance disturbs more air and so on until it grows into a hurricane—that would just be stupid.

What it really means is that everything is incredibly complex, with millions of tiny factors built into almost every occurrence, and if you remove just one of them (the beat of the butterfly's wings), then it might happen differently, or even not at all.

So, years ago, some jerk named Matt Nicholson thought it might be funny to spike a girl's drinks by slipping in vodka shots without her noticing. Unlikely as it seems, Matt Nicholson is the butterfly, and the spiking of the drinks is the beat of his wings.

The girl was Sally Morgan and soon enough she was reeling. These were their first weeks at college, so when Sally went staggering out of the bar looking green, no one paid much attention— no one except Matt Nicholson, who thought it was hilarious.

Outside the bar, a girl named Julia Darby spotted Sally, and though she didn't know her, she knew this girl was in trouble and needed help. Julia stepped in, and managed to get her to a bathroom stall just before the inevitable happened.

They were in different schools, studying different subjects, so if Matt Nicholson hadn't spiked Sally's drinks, Sally and Julia wouldn't have met, not then, maybe not ever, and they wouldn't have become best friends. And then Julia wouldn't have introduced Sally to her friend from back home, Rob Calloway.

So Sally and Rob wouldn't have fallen in love, gotten married after college, had a child. And when the time came to make their wills, they wouldn't have chosen Julia to be the guardian of their child should anything happen to them.

And one night when the child was nine, if the cab they'd ordered hadn't failed to pick up Sally and Rob from the restaurant outside Hopton, Connecticut, where they'd been celebrating their tenth wedding anniversary, they wouldn't have decided to walk home along the road instead.

And if the girlfriend of someone named Sean Hodges hadn't dumped him for being a loser, he wouldn't have gotten drunk and cried and driven over to her place. And if she'd taken him back or let him in, he wouldn't have driven home again, angry and still drunk, and he wouldn't have hit two people walking along a dark and quiet country road, killing them.

So as much as they'd never really imagined it happening, Sally and Rob's child, nine-year-old Tom Calloway, ended up in the guardianship of their oldest friend. But, it has to be said, she was someone they hadn't really had much to do with in recent years. In truth, they'd tired of her woes and her flakiness, but even if it had ever crossed their minds to amend their wills, death had caught up with them first.

And being landed with the responsibility of looking after a child had little impact on Julia's lifestyle. So it didn't matter eight years later that a school trip to Costa Rica for a special environmental project was completely *not* the sort of thing Tom would usually do, because Julia wanted to go on a yoga retreat in Italy, and the dates fit perfectly. So in the end, to escape her pleading, Tom agreed to go to Costa Rica, a place he didn't want to visit, with people he didn't want to be with, to do things he didn't want to do.

And that's the butterfly effect. If a jerk named Matt Nicholson had not spiked the drinks of a girl named Sally Morgan, Tom Calloway, if he'd been born at all, would not have been boarding a plane more than twenty years later, a plane that, unbeknown to Tom or any of the other people in his school party, would never reach its destination.

CHAPTER 1

It wasn't that Tom didn't care about the environment. He recycled and he liked those David Attenborough documentaries on TV, but he couldn't help thinking there was a lot of hypocrisy out there too. Hypocrisy like burning a ton of fuel to fly a whole bunch of schoolkids from the richest country in the world to look at plants and butterflies in Costa Rica. He just didn't buy it.

That was one of the reasons he didn't want to be on this trip—because it was fake, a vacation dressed up as saving the world, a vacation without the fun, paying resort prices to stay in some insect-infested eco-camp.

Then there were the people—thirty-nine other kids, three teachers, one teacher's wife. He supposed the other kids were okay, interesting in their own ways, probably friendly, certainly friendly enough that they were friends with each other. It was just that Tom wasn't really one of them.

Once, when he was a little kid, he was given a jigsaw puzzle as a gift, a complex picture of a castle, and one wet weekend he'd completed it, only to find there was one piece left over. It wasn't a duplicate, either, but an odd piece that had crept in from some other puzzle.

Tom had kept it, and still had it at home. At the time he hadn't been sure why he'd kept it, but in the years since, he'd come to think that he *was* that jigsaw piece. He was shaped right. He looked right. At first glance, most people might have imagined him a perfect fit. But he didn't fit.

Whichever picture he belonged in, it wasn't this one, the one that was his life right now. And he was fine with that, because he realized that the spare piece he'd found in his jigsaw had probably been a missing piece from some other person's jigsaw, and somewhere—maybe at college, maybe later—there'd be a picture that he *would* fit into.

It wasn't just Tom who thought this way about him, either. The other kids knew that he was different, detached, playing the game by his own rules. Even the teachers saw it, and unfailingly mentioned it in his school's uniquely lengthy report cards (which Julia never read), the most recent one being no exception.

> Tom's academic record speaks for itself and I
> have to commend him on it. I only wish he would
> make more effort to become an active part of our
> homeroom group. As it is, he's aloof to the point of
> being unfriendly, which is a great shame because I

feel he could contribute enormously to the group if he chose to do so.—Mr. Glenister, Homeroom.

Well done, Tom, on an impressive junior year! As you know, I've urged you to throw yourself just a little more into the life of Hopton High and I hope your involvement with the forthcoming trip to Costa Rica is an indication that you've heeded my advice and will take the chance to bond with your peers!!—Principal Rachel Freeman.

Tom is a puzzle. His work is of a consistently high standard, and his comments in class are always incisive and to the point. I only wish he would give a little more of <u>himself</u>, both to his studies and to his fellow students.—Miss Graham, AP English Literature.

Miss Graham was a puzzle too. She was young enough and attractive enough that it sometimes felt a little weird being alone with her, and she'd told Julia this year in a parent–teacher conference that she was "desperate" for Tom to become more involved with his classmates.

She was here now, one of the teachers on the trip, and she was currently doing one last head count before boarding, slowly working her way across the group, her mouth moving as she counted in silence. But she reached Tom and stopped dead, a look of amazement or confusion, followed by a strange smile, as if she still couldn't quite believe that he was on this trip.

She cursed under her breath then and went back to the beginning, her mouth forming a silent and labored *one, two, three...* and perhaps that summed up as well as anything how Tom didn't fit in, how unlikely it was for Tom to be part of a trip like this, that his very presence was enough to leave Miss Graham incapable of counting to forty.

CHAPTER 2

"I'm glad you chose to come on this trip, Tom." It was Miss Graham, sitting next to him on the plane. "Hopefully it'll give us all a chance to get to know you better."

"Miss Graham, it's only two weeks."

She laughed, as though he'd made some clever joke, which hadn't been his intention, then turned to say something to Barney Elliott, who was sitting on the other side of her.

Tom had flown a lot with Julia and, while he had to admit she'd been more like an unreliable roommate than a parent, he could at least say she knew how to travel. They always turned left as soon as they entered the plane, heading for business or first class.

On this trip, though, he was at the back, as were most of them. Mr. Lovejoy and his wife were sitting in the middle section, near the door, with Jack Shaw, who was 6'7" and needed the legroom, and Maisie McMahon, who was tiny, but who, for some undisclosed health reason, also had to sit up there.

The rest of the party took up two blocks of seats at the back of the cabin. Coach Holdfast, the gym teacher and football coach, sat at the front of the first block with the members of his team who were making the trip—he was laughing and joking and occasionally chanting *"Go Hawks!"* like he was still a kid himself.

Miss Graham was in the other block at the very back of the plane, with Tom on the aisle next to her. Boarding was almost finished now, and she turned to Tom and said, "Can I make a confession?" He wasn't sure he wanted to hear it, but he made a show of looking interested and she smiled, a little embarrassed, before saying, "I'm kind of scared of flying. Always have been. Turbulence—that's the worst."

"So why did you come?"

She shrugged, as if to ask what other choice she'd had.

Barney, on the other aisle seat, who was the same age as the rest of them but looked smaller and younger, said, "You know, Miss Graham, it's almost impossible for a large aircraft to be brought down by turbulence."

She turned to him and said, "Really, is that true?"

"Absolutely. The structure's never compromised and pilots really don't have a problem with it."

"Oh. But how come planes crash then?"

"They don't, statistically. I mean, yes, of course planes crash, but it's so statistically improbable that your plane will crash, it's really not worth thinking about. I mean, you don't go to sleep every night worrying your house will burn down, but it's more likely you'll die in a house fire than in a plane crash."

"How interesting." She turned back to Tom. "Did you hear that, Tom?"

He nodded. He was actually thinking that the statistics probably weren't much comfort to people sitting on a plane that was hurtling in a ball of fire toward the earth. But he was saved from having to say anything because a girl named Olivia stood up a few rows ahead of them and looked at Miss Graham.

"Miss Graham, can you tell Chris to stop annoying us?"

Miss Graham gave a knowing look to Tom, as if they were both adults, a look he actually mistrusted in some way, and then she said, "I'll be back in a minute."

He let her pass and as he sat again, Barney said quietly, "I think Miss Graham has the hots for you." Tom looked at him, and Barney added defensively, "It does happen. You see it in the news all the time."

"Do you have a statistic for it?"

Barney wasn't sure how to react, but settled for saying again, "It happens, that's all I'm saying."

Tom noticed movement up ahead and, although he didn't believe Barney was right about Miss Graham, he was fairly relieved to see she'd decided the best course was to swap seats with the oafish and apparently annoying Chris Davies.

He came clumsily down the plane and said, "Graham said I have to sit here. Can I have the aisle seat?"

"No." Tom got up to let him in, then sat down again.

Chris shook his head. "Olivia—what a bitch. I can't help it if I had a dream."

Chloe, sitting in the row behind them, said, "Not the dream again! Chris, just shut up about it."

He didn't turn in his seat but raised his voice slightly for Chloe to hear, sounding too loud as he said, "You won't be saying that if I'm right and the plane crashes."

Barney said, "What?"

"I dreamed it. And it was exactly this plane."

Joel Aspinall was sitting across the aisle from Tom—student rep on the school council, son of some local politician—and he leaned forward now and said, "Chris, bro, you need to keep it down or we'll get thrown off the plane."

"Maybe we *should* get thrown off. *Then* you'd all be thanking me when it crashes."

There was a murmur of voices in response, the talk clearly getting to some of them, but then from somewhere behind, possibly the back row, a very clear voice sounded, not raised, but deadly serious.

"Christian!" It was Alice Dysart, who'd known Chris since kindergarten and whose family was close to his. They were nothing alike, but the connection, whatever sort of connection it was, obviously carried some weight, because Chris yielded instantly and slumped down into his seat.

He still couldn't resist turning to Tom and whispering, "This plane *will* crash. We're all gonna die."

He was such an attention seeker that it was hard to tell whether he'd really had a dream and was genuinely nervous, or whether it was some poor attempt at causing a stir.

Either way, Tom looked at him and said, "I don't care."

Chris kept eye contact for a few seconds, then seemed to give up and faced forward again. Tom did too, staring at the seat in front of him, struck by a strange realization.

He didn't believe for one minute that Chris Davies had been having prophetic dreams, but he also realized he'd been telling the truth, that he actually didn't care. Whatever was going to happen would happen anyway, and one day or another they would all die. The way Tom saw it, there wasn't any point worrying about whether that day might be today.

CHAPTER 3

The first time Tom flew in a plane he'd been really excited beforehand, but also bored and impatient in equal measure. He'd been excited boarding, and really excited and a little scared for the first ten minutes. After that, it had been really boring and he'd fallen asleep.

He'd never really enjoyed flying since, because the little peaks of excitement he used to feel had flattened out and the boredom had swept over them. Just about the only thing he did enjoy was the dream. He always slept on planes, and for at least the last five years he always had the same dream, or more or less the same one.

And it was the only time he had it, never at home, never sleeping anywhere else. He'd wondered a few times if it was something particular about the cabin pressure or the engine noise, but he was none the wiser—it was just his airplane dream, and this trip was no exception.

It was one of those strange dreams in which he still felt partly conscious, aware of the seat he was sitting in, vaguely aware of the low engine whine in the background. But rather than being strapped in, he felt like he was floating in the darkness, still in the seated position, but free of the seat and the plane, adrift in the open air.

And then, all at once, he seemed to become acutely conscious of the entire world around him, of the air and the cold and the moisture, of the land below and the stars above. He was aware of countless people living and dying, and could see them all within that moment, some in daylight, some in the depths of night on the other side of the world, children playing games in a dusty street, lovers kissing in a twilight park, an old man surrounded by family as he rattled through his final breaths, images swarming around him from every part of the planet, oceans and deserts and hushed-breath forests and forlorn streetlights and empty amusement parks.

It was as if his mind had opened, fully opened, but what he really loved about these dreams was that he felt connected, to everything. He spent so much of his life feeling like he didn't have a place in the world, and yet here he felt he completely belonged, an integral part of all those lives and non-lives, of all those places and non-places.

Finally, as it always did, the dream ebbed away from him, but one last vision crashed into his mind from the void. He was on a rough ocean at night, feeling almost a part of the waves, conscious of something seething beneath him, and then he realized it was a whale, gliding and crashing through the heavy swells, dark within darkness, a massive mournful muscular presence, and for those few moments Tom was part of that too, pulsing through the darkened ocean, a black abyss below, an endless sky above, and he felt at peace there.

He was woken by a jolt, thrusting him upward against the restraint of the seat belt. He opened his eyes, saw the strangely half-lit cabin, took a second to remember where he was and immediately understood.

Turbulence. He thought of Miss Graham, but also thought of Barney's reassurance. He heard a couple of mumbles from here and there, guessing everyone had been sleeping, that they'd all been woken by it.

The oxygen masks had dropped down, as if they'd been knocked loose by the turbulence, and they danced around now above the seats. Tom had seen that happen once before on a flight and he knew it was nothing to worry about—

Another thud came, so hard that it jarred through the seat and up his spine even as he took off and his body yanked against the restraint of the seat belt. People were awake now and cried out, some even screaming, and Tom felt the adrenaline run through him and a sickly clench in his stomach. This was no ordinary turbulence.

The next jolt was bigger still, juddering through the structure of the plane, and there was a strange wrenching noise that he could hear even over the screams, which were everywhere now. Things fell from the overhead bins, and somewhere up ahead, maybe ten rows in front, someone catapulted into the roof before crashing back down.

There was noise all around them, but Tom realized there was one sound missing—he could no longer hear the engines. Tom wondered again if this could really be just turbulence, or if they were no longer flying at all, if they were actually in the process of crashing.

He was tilted backward in his seat, but it didn't feel like they were climbing. He tried to look toward the window but could only see darkness beyond, and then another wrenching crash shook through them and more screams filled the air and Tom felt a pain in his arm and realized Chris had grabbed hold of him.

A bigger thud, Chris released his grip, Tom was lifted out of his seat, grateful for the fierce restricting pain of the seat belt. Then a shearing of metal that he could feel in his teeth, and somewhere through all the noise, the sound of someone in front crying softly.

An odd, violent tug threw him forward before the incline increased and he flew back and down into his seat, the incline steeper again, another wrench, sounding this time as if the entire body of the plane was about to rip apart.

Then a percussive jolt, almost like an explosion, and the floor seemed to buckle under his feet, and the air filled with debris and the roof above him tore open and before he could even see what was happening, the seats in front of him were hurtling away into the darkness, air was rushing in, and for the briefest moment it seemed they had stopped, but the seats in front—the rest of the entire plane—had kept going and vanished into the night.

Barney was screaming, his voice surprisingly deep, not the

scream of someone injured, but of someone in shock, repeating some formless and desperate syllable over and over. And he didn't stop as they instantly started to move again, backward, gaining speed.

They were sitting on the edge of all that remained, their feet hanging into space, and Tom could see and was sure for the first time now that they were moving not in the sky but on the ground, could see some sort of vegetation in the darkness beyond the snowstorm of debris that trailed in their reversing wake.

They were sliding downhill, and he was bracing himself, knowing the real impact was yet to come, and Barney was still screaming, more screams behind them, Chris scarily silent next to him. How far did they slide, how quickly? Tom could only see the cluttered green darkness hurtling past before his eyes.

And then they seemed to level out a little, and more, and with one last unexpected snap and grind of metal, the plane, or what was left of it, seemed to shift slightly on its axis and came to an abrupt stop, thrusting him back so hard into his seat that he felt he might go right through it.

The silence was immediate and total, and so unyielding that Barney and the others briefly hushed too. Only now could Tom feel his heart thumping along in his chest, and all at once he was aware of the night open in front of him, the blanket of warm air, the strange noises of insects and animals like a constant background interference.

And he understood. They had been in a plane crash. Their plane had *crashed,* torn itself apart, and they had survived.

For now.

CHAPTER 4

Everyone started talking and shouting at once. There was no screaming now, no crying, just manic and garbled conversations. Chris said to Barney, "I told you we'd crash."

"You said we'd all die too. Didn't he, Tom?"

Tom turned from the compelling darkness of the night in front of him and looked at Barney. "We still might."

Chris laughed nervously as he said, "Jesus, I was just joking around. I didn't dream anything." He had blood running down the side of his face from a small gash on his forehead.

Tom said, "You're bleeding."

He nodded, apparently pleased for the change of topic. "Something hit me."

Tom glanced up, curious that he could see anything at all. Some sort of emergency lighting system had come on, filling the cabin with half-light, even though the wiring must have been torn to shreds.

Barney said something else, but the noise of the other voices drowned it out, and then above them all, Joel shouted, "Quiet!" The voices fell away, the silence almost as full of shock as the babbling had been. Tom looked across the aisle to where Joel was also half-dangling over the drop, like they were on some particularly extreme roller coaster.

He had everyone's attention now and Joel turned awkwardly in his seat and said, "Okay, is anyone in this section hurt? Check the people next to you. Or if you're hurt yourself, speak up."

There was a flurry of responses as they relayed what seemed incredible, that no one had gotten any serious injuries.

The noise seemed once again in danger of building into a barrage of conflicting voices, but Joel put his hand in the air, silencing them. "Okay, quiet again. I think we've crashed in the rain forest or jungle, so it could be a while before a rescue party arrives, but that means we have to stay calm and organized."

Chloe's voice came from behind, saying, "Where's the rest of the plane?" It was as if she'd only just noticed it was missing.

"Gone," said Chris, no longer sounding like much of a joker. "It just tore off."

"So there could be other survivors."

No one answered her. Then Joel said, "Me and Chris'll climb down and see what the ground's like below."

Chris was quick to say, "Why? I think we should stay on the plane."

Barney leaned forward to look at Joel. "We should all get down, if it's safe." He looked up at the dull glow of the safety lights. "There's still electricity coming from somewhere, maybe the auxiliary power unit, which means there could be an electrical fire—until we're absolutely sure there isn't, we should all be out of the plane."

Shen was sitting across the aisle from Barney and said, "It's strange that the lights are working at all."

Barney started to reply, but Joel cut in, saying, "Okay, you're right. But I still want to check the ground out first."

He released his seat belt and looked forward, like a nervous kid on the edge of a diving board, but Barney said, "Whoa, don't even think about jumping down there." Joel looked at him. "The cargo hold's below us, so that's a ten-foot drop, onto a fuselage that's just been torn apart. There could be jagged edges, all kinds of debris."

"So I'll climb down," said Joel.

"Or you could use the doors behind us. If we can get one open, we'll be able to engage the emergency slide."

"Okay. You come with me." He swung out of his seat onto the safety of the aisle floor. "I'll check outside. But everyone turn your phones on. You never know, one of us might just get a signal."

Joel seemed to be taking on the role of leader and they all did as they were told. Tom and Chris both switched on their phones in unison, but there was no signal on either of them, and the mumbled comments from around the cabin suggested it was the same for everyone.

Chris held his phone up in the air, moving it around, trying to find a stray signal. Tom simply turned his off again, figuring it was probably best to save the battery power for some time they might need it.

Here and there behind him, people were starting to mention their parents, how worried sick they'd be when they heard the news of the crash. The irony was, Julia had flown out to Italy a few hours before Tom's plane had left, and the yoga retreat was a tech-free zone, so she might not find out about the crash for two weeks, anyway.

He was pleased about that, although a little part of him was curious to know how she'd have responded to the news if she had been at home. She'd be shocked, of course, but he wasn't sure how much deeper her feelings would go.

He remembered as a little kid that he'd always talked to his mom about the school day, what they'd done, what he'd enjoyed, who he liked, who'd annoyed him, all the petty triumphs and grievances of being in elementary school. Then the accident had happened, and he only remembered fractured moments of the months that followed.

One of those moments was the day Julia had arrived and said she'd be coming to live with him. *Live with him,* not, *look after him.* And even as a nine-year-old, he'd known somehow that Julia didn't want to hear about his day at school, about the things that excited him or bothered him, so he'd stopped talking about them, and in time, not much had bothered or excited him anyway.

He didn't blame Julia. It was just the way she was, and he'd reached the point of admiring her and being grateful that she'd been willing to take on a responsibility she'd never foreseen and for which she wasn't well suited. It was no one's fault, and no one was to blame, except maybe the guy who'd killed his mom and dad.

He saw a light appear down below in the darkness and

realized it was Joel, using his phone to show the way in front of him. Barney had been right about the drop and it was a shock to see Joel so far beneath them.

Joel called up now, saying, "Okay, there are some branches and stuff to climb over on the side, but it's pretty clear here in front of the plane. We could smell burning near the back—it doesn't mean anything's on fire, but I think we should all come out front for now."

It was only then that Tom saw Barney standing right next to Joel, so deep was the darkness and so weak the light from the phone. People started moving, a controlled rush to disembark, as if they'd simply arrived at their planned destination and everyone was eager to be on their way.

Tom undid his seat belt and Chris finally gave up on his phone, turning it off before releasing his own belt. Tom watched him as he shuffled over onto Barney's seat, then into the aisle on that side.

Tom didn't move himself, but sat there listening to the sounds of the others making their way out of the plane, down the emergency slide, the gentle ripple of voices moving away from him and then back toward him as the first people appeared below.

There was silence then in the cabin behind him and he readied himself to move, stopping only because something appeared to be happening in the area around the plane. It was getting lighter, not a creeping dawn, but the urgent daybreak of the tropics.

Suddenly he could see the trees rising up on either side, the hill in front, the same hill they'd so recently slid down. Within a minute or so he could see Joel and the others clearly, the daylight flooding across the sky so quickly that it was disorienting.

And now he could see the reality of what had just happened. Stretching uphill from where he sat was the path that had been swathed by the back of the plane, trees torn up and thrust aside, the earth gouged, debris littering the slope, so much debris that it was once again hard to believe that the small group of people gathering below him had managed to walk out of it completely unhurt.

CHAPTER 5

Tom made his way to the back of the plane. The emergency slide had twisted a little, but it was still workable. He slid down and clambered over the few strewn branches to the area at the front, skirting around the group so that he was on the far side of them.

They all seemed to be looking up at the remains of the cabin from which they'd just emerged, all talking again, trying to take in what had happened now that they could actually see it. Barney and Shen were even studying the tear in the fuselage body like professional air accident investigators.

Tom looked up the hill. Farther up the slope he could see some of the large metal containers that had spilled out from the hold—a couple had burst open and the hill was also littered with suitcases and what looked like their huge hiking backpacks.

At the top, the rise seemed to end in a fairly sharp ridge, and though there were still trees on either side of it, the plane had opened up a pass where it had collided. He guessed it was the ridge that had torn the fuselage in half, the front section presumably crashing down onto the other side of it.

He looked up into the sky, already a faultless blue, but he could see no signs of smoke. He looked at his watch then, still set to the time back home, and for the first time he became truly confused. He checked to make sure it was working, then set off up the slope.

Joel's voice interrupted Tom's train of thought, calling out, "Hey, uh, Tom." He sounded uncertain with the name, and actually, had never spoken directly to him before. Tom turned as everyone else fell quiet and looked on. "Where are you going?"

"Up there."

"Well, you know, I think we should all stick together, until the rescue party arrives."

Chris added, "Yeah, you know, it's like in *Lord of the Flies*—we should all stick together."

"Exactly," said Joel. "We need to be organized."

Tom nodded, smiling at Chris's wobbly analogy. "So organize. If I see anyone arrive, I'll come back."

Joel nodded, perhaps sensing that Tom would do his own thing no matter what. "Okay. I guess you can check if there's any more wreckage."

Tom was already walking even as the voices started up again, Joel's vaguely audible above them all. He hadn't gone far when he noticed a carton full of bottled water lying by the side of the newly flattened path. The heat was already building so he bent down and freed one of the bottles, slipping it into his pocket before continuing on his way.

A little farther on, he reached the first of the open containers. There were backpacks strewn around on the ground, but a handful still inside it too, and even without going over to look, he could see one of them was his own.

He continued to climb and, though the slope got no steeper, he found himself breathing hard, his T-shirt sticking to him in the dense humidity. He kept getting buzzed by insects too. This place would be unbearable within a few hours.

He noticed a piece of paper on the ground and bent down to pick it up—a boarding pass for someone named Miguel Fernandez, someone who was now presumably dead. Tom folded it and slipped it into his pocket without thinking, then looked around, wondering why he couldn't see any bodies.

He'd seen that one person fly out of their seat and hit the roof, but he had to assume the split in the fuselage had been pretty clean and the bodies had remained strapped inside. It was even possible some of them had survived, but that seemed one miracle too many.

He glanced behind, surprised by how far he'd already climbed. And seeing the rump of the plane from this vantage point, and the cluster of people standing in front of it, he knew for sure that none of them should have survived. It would go down in the books as a freak occurrence, like that flight attendant who'd survived a plane being blown up at thirty thousand feet and had landed safely in deep snow.

He pushed on, increasingly conscious of the wall of noise around him, the birds and other animals, but mainly insects, that filled the jungle they'd crashed into. For all those creatures, nothing had changed, and sooner or later—starting with the bodies first and then the wreckage—all evidence of this crash would slowly be absorbed back into the landscape.

Finally he reached the top, but it didn't provide him with much satisfaction. The other side of the ridge descended into a deep, forested ravine before rising up to even steeper hills beyond. He took a quick look behind at the landscape beyond the tail of the plane, undulating and densely jungled, more low hills in the distance, a vast expanse of green stretching as far as he could see.

Then he turned back to the valley and it took him a short while to see the rest of the plane, far below and far enough away from the ridge to suggest it hadn't simply slid down the slope but had catapulted away from it and belly-flopped onto the valley floor. It looked flattened and crumpled, the paint charred as if a swift fire had engulfed it before burning out.

He wasn't sure how easy it would be to get to the wreckage from there, but he knew without moving from the ridge that there was no one still alive in it. Miss Graham with her fear of turbulence, Jack Shaw with his long legs, Maisie McMahon with her undisclosed health problems—they were all dead. So was Olivia, who'd complained of Chris annoying her, and in so doing, had saved his life and cost Miss Graham hers.

In a way there was something wondrous about it, the random movements that had determined who would live or die, including the movements of the plane—if it had traveled just one yard more before hitting that ridge, Tom would have been down there in that blackened wreckage with them.

He remembered a family he'd seen during boarding, probably Costa Rican, with two daughters. One had been about his own age and Tom had noticed her first because of how pretty she was.

Her sister had been much younger, maybe only eight or nine, clutching a soft toy.

He wasn't sure why, but the thought of those two girls being down there among the dead was hard to accept. He hadn't known them, would probably never have seen them again, yet in some way it was harder to comprehend they were dead than it was Miss Graham or the others.

A seed planted, that maybe they weren't dead at all, that they were trapped down there hoping to be rescued. Maybe that was why he'd thought of them, why he'd climbed this ridge in the first place, because this was what he was meant to do, he was meant to find them.

The feeling was so strong and filled him with such urgency that he took a step forward without meaning to, then another, down the slope, sensing there was no time left to lose. He glanced quickly at the distant wreckage, meaning only to remind himself of the direction he was heading in, but the sight of it stopped him short and brought him back to his senses.

The wreckage. Nobody was alive down there, not the two sisters, not Miss Graham, nobody. That truth hit him harder the second time, seemed more shocking somehow—how could all those people simply be gone?

He thought of Miss Graham and the way she smiled encouragingly when someone was making a point in class. He thought of others, kids he'd only known as faces around school. All of them were gone.

He didn't want to think about them at all, didn't want to imagine the final terrifying moments that had left the wreckage pancaked against the valley floor like that. So he turned away from it, staring blankly at the trees off to his left instead, staring for some time before he realized he could see a body.

It was wedged in the branches of a tree a short way below where he stood, checked blue shirt, blond hair. Having spotted one body, Tom scanned the trees for more, but there weren't any others that he could see.

He set off toward the boy but the descent was trickier on this side and the trees had not been flattened. By the time he got to the tree he was aiming for he was lost in the dappled half-light of the jungle and the body was almost out of sight above him. He recognized him—Charlie Stafford, a kid Tom had known a little, looking unhurt but too much at peace.

There was no way Tom could reach him, but even at that distance, looking at the strange angle and pose of Charlie's body, there was no question that he was dead. Even if Tom got him down, he couldn't bury him. And with the insects swarming around, he guessed nature would take its course whatever he did.

Charlie had once borrowed a pen from Tom, and had said hello every time he'd seen him after that. So they'd hardly known each other, but still enough to make Tom wonder how Charlie could be suspended up there now, present and absent at once, still possessed of that clean, healthy look, but the easy smile and the likability and the friendliness all gone.

Charlie had often looked deep in thought, a dreamer, and yet whatever had occupied his mind, it all seemed pointless now. Here he was, thinking nothing, and he would never think or dream or plan again, never again snap out of his own little world as they passed in the hallways and say, "Hey Tom, how's it going?"

Slowly, sadly, Tom turned away and made his way back up

onto the ridge. He sat there, looking down at the crash party and the wreckage and at the scattered trail of debris and the unyielding jungle stretching out beyond. And with the thought of Charlie still lodged in his mind, he felt an odd relief that he had not gone to find those sisters.

He reached into his pocket for the bottle and took a small swig. The water was already warm and yet felt incredibly refreshing running over his tongue, down his throat. He didn't think a simple drink of water had ever felt so good.

It wasn't just the water, either—as hot as he was, as exhausted by the climbing, bruised by the thrust into the seat belt, as troubled as he'd been by the sight of the wreckage and of Charlie suspended in that tree, he was suffused with a strange sense of restfulness and well-being. Maybe that was a reaction to the shock too, but right now he felt he could have sat contentedly on this ridge forever.

He wouldn't be able to stay, of course. He'd have to join the others, as much as he sensed he'd be better off on his own, and as ill-equipped as he felt about being part of a group.

With that in mind, he wondered if they had a plan of action yet, or if they'd even thought about it. Maybe they were just killing time until the rescue party arrived, but judging by this landscape, it would be a long time before that happened.

With that thought in mind he looked at his watch again, knowing they could not be where they were meant to be, but he was once more distracted by something below. It still seemed Joel was holding court with all the others standing around him. Or all but one. Because someone had left the group now and was walking up the hill to where Tom was sitting.

She stopped where he had and also picked up a bottle of water, and then continued on toward him. It was Alice Dysart, who was actually in all the same classes as him, though he didn't think he'd ever spoken to her. And he wondered if she'd just broken free like he had, or whether Joel had sent her to bring Tom back, because to people who thought *Lord of the Flies* was a survival manual, it was probably vital that they all stick together...

CHAPTER 6

Alice seemed to climb without much difficulty, an easy balance
about her, as if she found walking up the slope no more taxing than
a flat path, yet it seemed to take her a long time. And the effort of
doing anything in this humid blanket of heat was apparent in the
damp patches already appearing here and there on her T-shirt.

She threw glances at the debris as she walked, but didn't look
up at him at all. It meant he was able to watch her progress. Until
recently she'd always worn her fair hair long but she'd had it cut
short, perhaps specifically for this trip. She was pretty, although
he didn't think he had any more in common with her than with
any of the others.

She'd almost reached the top before she stopped and finally
looked at him and smiled. "You must work out. You flew up here."

"You made it look pretty easy yourself."

"Didn't feel like it." She opened her bottle and drank some water. "They're already driving me crazy, and I think it'll be a while before anyone comes." She looked around at the dense growth surrounding them.

Reminded again, Tom looked at his watch, checking that it was working. It had been his dad's watch, and it had never let him down in the couple of years his wrist had been big enough to wear it. But if it was right, it really didn't make any sense at all, not unless they'd been through a wormhole.

"I saw you check your watch earlier—what's wrong?" He was surprised that she'd noticed, in the same way that he was surprised when anyone really noticed him at all. But before he could answer, she said, "No, tell me in a minute. I want to see what's over that ridge first."

She climbed the rest of the way to where Tom was sitting and then he stood to join her as she scanned the canopy beyond and spotted the wreckage.

"Oh," was all she said, the word little more than a sigh, and she looked depleted now, exhausted by the sight in a way that she hadn't been by the climb up the hill. Tom remembered she had a boyfriend—Ethan—on the football team. Maybe that was why she'd climbed up here. "Well, it must've been quick—that's something, I guess." If she'd been trying to comfort herself, it clearly hadn't worked.

Tom nodded. "Sorry about your boyfriend."

She turned and looked at him. She looked on the verge of tears and her throat was tight but she pushed through it, saying, "*Ex*-boyfriend. I thought everyone knew we'd broken up." He didn't respond and she nodded, acknowledging that Tom wasn't everyone. And perhaps because Tom wasn't everyone, she stared out at the landscape again and said, "I'm not even sure why I went out with him in the first place. I mean, we didn't have anything in common, but..." She ground to a halt.

But. That about summed it up. "I'm sorry anyway."

"Thanks." She sighed deeply and turned away from the wreckage in the same way Tom had. Likewise, she let her vision drift across the view in front of them before stopping with a double take. She pointed and said, "Oh, my God! Is that a body?"

"Yeah, it's the only one I could see. I went down there but he's high up in the branches—I couldn't get to him."

"Who is it?" She sounded nervous, like someone who didn't really want an answer.

"Charlie Stafford."

He thought he saw relief in her expression, perhaps because it wasn't someone she knew, even though there was no doubt that they were all dead anyway.

"I didn't know him. How weird." Even without her spelling it out, Tom felt he understood what she meant, that it was strange to think she hadn't known him and would now never get the chance.

He thought about Charlie himself, wondering why he'd never bothered to have a proper conversation with him. Maybe they really did have only that borrowed pen in common, but they might have become friends if Tom had made an effort. Either way, he'd never know now.

Alice turned her back on the body and said, "I'd rather not think about it. Do you think that's selfish?" Tom shook his head but she still frowned, not looking convinced. Then she pointed at his arm. "Why do you keep looking at your watch?"

He glanced at it again, not even really taking in the time

shown there. "We crashed about half an hour ago, and the sun just came up, so it's around six in the morning." Her eyes opened wide, perhaps remembering when they were supposed to arrive. "Exactly. We were supposed to arrive last night at ten p.m. local time, eleven p.m. our time, but we only just crashed, which means we kept flying for another six or seven hours." He pointed at the wreckage far below them. "I'm guessing that's why the fire burned out so quickly, because there was no fuel left."

"But if we reached Costa Rica and kept flying for seven hours…"

"We'd be somewhere in the Pacific Ocean. The pilot must have changed course."

"Like that Malaysian plane."

"Like that Malaysian plane. That's why I was checking my watch, because it's set to the time back home. It's just getting to be time for breakfast."

She looked distracted by that final detail, probably thinking that her family would know by now, would be distraught and waiting for news.

Quickly, to take her mind off it, he said, "It means we're somewhere in South America. Costa Rican time is an hour behind us, but I guess my watch is just about right for where we are. So we're some place in the same time zone as back home, and looking at this landscape…"

"So we're in South America. But if the plane flew for an extra seven hours, we could be anywhere—Venezuela, Brazil, Colombia…" He nodded when she paused. "We could be anywhere," she said again, her voice full of resignation and all the things that didn't need to be said.

If the pilot had changed course on purpose, he'd probably turned off the plane's transponders, just like in that Malaysian plane. If they'd flown for seven hours off radar, they could be anywhere within hundreds of thousands of square miles, and even with satellite data to help narrow down the search, the rain forests of South America were probably as tough a search zone as any ocean.

There would be no rescue party, he was certain of that now. He'd already sensed they might have a long wait, but unless someone had actually seen or heard their plane cutting through the early morning dark, they might as well have vanished off the face of the earth.

Right now, they would have become a mystery, filling news bulletins all over the world. But this was the reality of that mystery—most of them were dead, and the survivors would have no choice but to find their own way out of this vast and undoubtedly hostile jungle.

She sat down, almost where Tom had been a few minutes before. He looked back down the hill. They were still all just standing in a huddle, their focus on Joel, who seemed to be above them on a box or something.

Tom sat down near her and took a small swig of water, conscious now that they would need to conserve their supply. He'd always imagined Alice being talkative, perhaps only because she was normally with a group of other girls who were more than talkative, but she seemed happy to sit in silence.

The two of them watched as nothing happened below, as the landscape whispered and hummed around them, as the sky remained relentlessly empty.

They'd been there a few minutes before she finally said, "What do you think we should do?"

It hadn't really occurred to him until now. He'd already accepted that a rescue wasn't likely, that they'd probably have to make their own way out, but he hadn't given any thought to how they might do that or if it was even possible.

"Make a camp, I guess. Wait here for a day or two, maybe three, just in case. Then make a plan for getting out."

From the corner of his eye he could see her nod, then she said, "Think the others will see it that way?"

As she asked the question, Joel's raised voice reached them, apparently bringing order after one of those brief crescendos of noise from the group.

Tom shook his head. "I don't care what the rest of them do. I'll give it three days tops and I'm heading out."

"If you do, I'll come with you." He turned and looked at her, surprised that she would want to go with him. She shrugged, looking embarrassed in some way, though he wasn't sure why. "It's just... we have to get out."

"Okay. It's a deal. Three days."

"Three days."

Chris emerged from the group down below, not drifting away as they had, but walking with purpose. After about twenty paces he stopped and looked up before waving for them to come back.

Alice waved in acknowledgment. She stood then and turned, waiting. Tom stood too, but for some reason he felt the need to let her know that he was deadly serious.

"Three days, no more."

She nodded, and they set off down the slope.

CHAPTER 7

They stopped on the way down and Tom retrieved his backpack from the burst container. Alice's was one of those that had fallen onto the slope and she picked it up, checking it for insects before slipping it over one shoulder. Tom stopped a second time, scooping up the carton of bottled water.

The rest of them were still all talking more or less over one another, but they fell silent as Tom and Alice approached, and they were still a few paces away when Chloe said, "What happened to the rest of the plane?"

Her tone was so urgent that Tom wondered if she'd had a close friend or boyfriend in the front section, or whether she just wanted desperately for everyone to have survived.

Alice said, "It's wrecked. They're all dead."

Chloe looked stunned and there were gasps and stifled

outbursts from some of the others too. A couple of people simply broke down and started to cry. Tom found it hard to believe that any of them could be totally stunned by the news—sad, maybe, but not shocked. *This* was the real shock: all of them, standing here, breathing. They had to have guessed what had happened to the rest of the plane, but the confirmation of the fact seemed to hit them harder than the crash itself.

Once again, Joel rose above them, saying, "Did you check the wreckage?"

He'd always seemed to have that debate-society, future-politician tone, but his voice had developed an extra edge of authority now, leaving no one in doubt that he'd taken on the mantle of group leader.

It irked Tom in some way, and perhaps Alice too, because she sounded defiant as she said, "No, we didn't. It's a big valley, and the plane's way down in it."

"Even so..."

Her fire was up now, and before he could finish, she said, "Anyway, there's something more important."

Chloe sounded outraged, saying through tears, "More important than helping the others?"

"There are no others, so yes, more important. There probably won't be any rescue party—no one's coming for us."

The babbling started again, smothered at once by Joel, who raised his voice above them all, shouting, "Quiet!" They did as he said, the whole group apparently just as happy to accept his adopted role. He turned to Alice and said, "What are you talking about?"

"Tom figured it out." He was conscious of them all looking

at him briefly before giving their attention back to Alice. "We should have arrived in Costa Rica about seven hours ago. But we didn't, we kept flying, and the only way we could have done that without landing in water is if the pilot changed course. We think we're in South America, but nowhere near where we're supposed to be."

The babbling started again, and this time Joel seemed disinclined to stop it.

Barney walked over to Tom and Alice and said, "I tried to tell them the same thing, but they didn't listen. That's why the oxygen masks had deployed and why everyone was asleep, like the Malaysian plane. If you fly at a high enough altitude, all the passengers pass out. Probably wasn't for long, just long enough to knock us out. Or maybe he tampered with the air supply in some way." He pointed at the slope. "But the pilot did this on purpose, I'm sure of it. Maybe he tried to glide it in, or maybe he wanted the whole plane to crash into the valley. We shouldn't be here."

Tom nodded and looked up at the seats high above them. The lights in the cabin had gone out now, and it didn't seem any sort of fire had developed, not yet anyway.

"Okay," said Joel. The conversations stuttered to a halt. "You're right, of course, so we need to be even more focused and coordinated. And I hear what you're saying about the wreckage, but we still have to check, just in case." Alice started to shake her head, but he ignored her. "Chris, you and Toby go and take a look."

Toby was one of Joel's friends, athletic and bland but the kind of person who'd probably get down to the wreckage without a problem. Chris was too bulky and solid, and Tom could already envisage how much he'd struggle with the climb alone. Even so, they both stepped forward eagerly, willing lieutenants to Joel's leader.

Kate, who was in Tom's English class, said, "I'll go too."

Joel smiled at her. "I don't think—"

"You should let her go," said Emma. She was also in Tom's English class and so inseparable from Kate, and looking so like her with the same slim build and long dark hair, that it had taken Tom months to tell them apart. "It's totally her thing."

Tom wasn't sure what she meant by that, and clearly Joel wasn't, either, because he said, "Look, everyone will have their part to play."

He pointed at Barney then. "You should go with them. You'll know if there's anything we can salvage from the plane, radio equipment, anything like that."

Barney didn't seem convinced, and he especially didn't seem like the most natural candidate for a trek through the jungle—he was small and looked a good three years younger than the rest of them. But he shrugged his acceptance and the three of them set off as Kate and Emma exchanged an exasperated look.

The three boys had only walked a few paces when Tom shouted, "Hey!"

They stopped and he pulled three bottles free from the carton, throwing one to each of them. They thanked him, Toby with little more than a nod, and walked away.

Chloe looked reassured by the departure of the three boys, as if simply going might be enough to bring some other people back alive, but she turned to Joel then and said, "What do we all do now, Joel?"

"We have to organize. It looks like we might be here for a day or two so we need to get hold of everything that could be of use. First off, collect all our backpacks and all the suitcases, even the ones that belong to the other passengers. There could be useful stuff in a lot of them."

Shen said, "Shouldn't we build a fire first?"

Joel shook his head, nonplussed, and sounded vaguely patronizing as he said, "I hardly think we need to worry about getting cold, Shen. That can wait until later. In fact, if you find some, you should all apply sunscreen. We'll burn easily out here."

"Even me?" Everyone turned to look at George.

Joel looked uncertain how to handle the question, the future politician stumbling over his words as he said, "Uh, well, you know, uh, even black skin... I mean..."

George smiled broadly. "Relax, I'm just messing with you."

"Oh, okay, well... I guess there's always a place for humor." Joel turned his attention back to the wider group. "Okay, everyone, let's get busy."

There was an immediate burst of activity, and the people who'd been desperately huddled together before were now dispersing across the narrow slope, searching purposefully through the debris.

Alice put her backpack down and said to Tom, "Could you keep an eye on this for me? I'll help the others find theirs."

He nodded, and she walked off to join her friends farther up the slope.

Joel was the third last to leave the imagined base camp. He glanced over at Tom but, probably sensing his authority didn't extend in that direction, he nodded, the meaning of which was lost on Tom, and simply walked away. A moment later, his voice started carrying back as he answered questions and gave instructions.

Shen was the only one left, and he looked at Tom now and said, "A fire is more important than luggage." He frowned. "Lots of things are more important than luggage."

It was pretty weird that both Barney and Shen seemed to choose Tom as the person they could complain to. If they thought he'd step up as an alternate leader, someone who'd challenge Joel, then they'd thought wrong. It was true, Joel struck him as someone who liked to lead rather than someone who was actually any good at it, but Tom had no desire to take his place.

He slipped his backpack off his shoulder, then took another bottle of water out and handed it to Shen.

"Thanks." He opened it and took a swig.

Tom put the carton down on the ground and said, "What would you do first?"

"Build a fire, make the area safe. There are lots of things here that could kill us, big things, small things." As if to prove Shen's point, something buzzed at Tom's ear and he shooed it away. "And we need to check how much food and water we have."

"So let's take a look in the galley." Shen glanced in Joel's direction and Tom added, "Unless you want to check with Joel first."

Shen smiled and shook his head, and they headed to the back of the plane.

CHAPTER 8

Climbing an emergency slide, even from a reduced height, wasn't quite as easy as sliding down it. Tom went first, and then helped pull Shen up.

Once inside, Shen said, "The slide could come in handy for something else, but we'll need to make some steps or find a ladder."

Tom nodded, understanding immediately that the inside of the plane, or all that remained of it, was probably the safest place for them, particularly once it got dark again.

Shen pointed then. "The toilets need electricity to function, but we might be able to adjust them so they're usable, for a couple of days at least. We don't want people going outdoors. Urine attracts rodents, rodents attract snakes." He smiled uncertainly, perhaps afraid he was coming across as a know-it-all.

"It's great that you know all this stuff. I don't think we've ever spoken before."

"Well, we have different classes, so . . ."

There was a hint of nervousness in Shen's voice, as though he felt he was talking to someone dangerous, so Tom smiled a little and said, "Actually, I don't really speak to anyone."

"I know." Shen smiled too. "You wanted to look in the galley."

They walked through, checking the food stocks, the water, soft drinks, alcohol. Shen looked at the equipment and the utensils as well, with the air of someone working out what he could salvage, what might be used for other things. When Tom found the emergency and medical kits, Shen was transfixed, looking through the items carefully, showing more interest in the hand pump and the medical supplies than he did in the flare gun or the knives.

They carried out their entire survey in silence, and then finally stood facing each other in the cramped quarters of the galley.

Shen seemed more relaxed with him now, and appeared to be busy calculating as he said, "A lot of this food will have to be eaten today—the meat, the rice—and even then, we'll need to heat it, which means we need that fire. Some of the vegetables, potatoes, they could be kept until tomorrow, the pastries and things in plastic maybe longer. Water might be a problem. Maybe if we're careful we could make it last a few days, but nineteen people is a *lot* of water. Of course, if it rains, we could collect it, boil it, and use the purifying tablets if we have to."

Tom nodded toward the cans of soft drinks. "And we have those."

"Sure, but we should keep them in reserve, in case we decide we have to leave—they're portable. And the alcohol we might need for cleaning wounds."

"You know about stuff like that?"

"My mom and dad are both doctors. I'm hoping to be a surgeon."

"Cool."

"Yeah. I'd still prefer it if my medical career didn't start just yet."

Tom laughed a little, then looked around the galley and said, "So we can survive on what's here for two or three days."

"If we're careful."

Tom thought of the endless green jungle he'd seen from the ridge, wondering how long it would take to walk out of it, how many more days they would need to feed themselves before reaching safety.

Shen seemed to study him and said, "You don't think anyone will come."

"Do you?" Shen shook his head and Tom said, "I think the pilot put a lot of thought into this. I don't think he expected anyone to survive, and I don't think he wanted anyone to find the wreckage."

"That's what Barney said." In response to Tom's quizzical expression, Shen added, "You think I know a lot—trust me, Barney really knows a *lot* of stuff. Like I said, I'm hoping to become a surgeon, but Barney, he'll probably become some billionaire inventor."

Tom thought of Barney struggling to get down into that valley to reach the wreckage. It was a pointless mission anyway, and probably dangerous, but Tom hoped nothing happened to him because he had a feeling Shen and Barney would play a big part in keeping them all alive.

"Walk up the hill with me, Shen. Let me know what you think of the terrain."

With a hint of curiosity, Shen asked, "You're already thinking of leaving?"

"Thinking about it, yeah. I'll give it two or three days, but that's all. Alice wants to come too."

"And the others?"

"I'm not with the others."

Shen grinned, but then grew serious again, and said, "If you go, I'll come. So will Barney."

"Sure. But keep it between us. You can tell Barney, but no one else. I just don't want it turning into some kind of...debate."

"Of course."

"Good. Let's check out what we're up against."

To his surprise, Shen reached out solemnly, and shook Tom's hand, as if they'd made some sort of pact. And maybe they had. Tom knew one thing—if he was going to walk out of a jungle, he'd rather do it with a scientist than with someone who wanted to run the school council.

CHAPTER 9

By *the time they got* back outside, a collection of suitcases and other luggage was building up in front of the plane and people were still coming and going, dripping with sweat. Most of them were laughing and talking too, so maybe Joel's plan had served some purpose in keeping morale high.

Tom retrieved his and Alice's backpacks from the edge of the stack and placed them inside the remains of the luggage hold. He left the carton of water where it was, though he couldn't understand why no one else had taken a bottle yet.

Tom and Shen set off up the slope, apparently unseen by most people. Alice walked past carrying a backpack and threw a half-smile at Tom, nothing more.

Suddenly Joel called out, saying, "Hey, Shen!" Shen stopped and turned. "Where are you going?"

"With Tom. We're going up the hill."

Joel glanced at Tom, then back to Shen, and said, "That's good. Maybe you can help the other three."

Tom hadn't stopped walking and after a few seconds Shen caught up with him and they climbed in silence. It was the second time Tom had made this climb in an hour and it was already harder, the heat more intense and constricting, the buzzing of insects relentless.

When they reached the top, Shen immediately searched the valley beyond until he spotted the wreckage. He nodded when he saw it.

Without looking at Tom, he said, "Barney would have told them that they're wasting their time."

But they had gone anyway, Chris and Toby too eager to notice what should have been obvious to anyone, that there were no more survivors. Briefly, Tom tried to listen for their voices or sounds of their progress, but there was nothing beyond the wall of noise and the stray sounds coming from behind them.

Tom looked to the left, nonplussed that he couldn't see Charlie's body now, but after a few seconds he noticed the blue of his shirt, just visible among the branches. Maybe some movement had caused the body to drop a little and he wondered if it had been an animal or if the others had tried to reach him.

Turning to Shen, he said, "Which way would you go?"

Shen glanced behind before pointing at the hills rising up high on the other side of the wide valley where the wreckage lay. "Not that way. The hills are higher there, so it's possible we could get a better view, but it could be a day's hike just to get a better view of even higher hills." He turned slowly, getting a full panorama, then pointed off to the right. "See that line over there?"

Tom stared. It took him a while to see it because it was barely a line, little more than an irregularity snaking through the tree canopy. Once he'd spotted it though, it was unmistakable.

"You think it's a river?"

Shen nodded. "I guess it'd be too much to hope it's a road. But if it's a river we can see which way it's flowing and then we can follow its course. It's no guarantee, but it's our best chance of finding a way out." His eyes fixed on a slight cleft between the distant hills. "It's probably heading that way, running down from the bigger hills behind us, through the gap in those hills over there."

"So that's our escape route. Follow the river and hope the pilot didn't drop us a thousand miles from anywhere."

"Follow the *course* of the river." Shen smiled. "There are lots of things in and around the water that might want to eat us. So we follow the course, but keep our distance."

Tom smiled too, but before he could say anything they heard Chris's unmistakable voice shouting, "Hey, you two, come and give us a hand."

It took a few seconds to see them down among the trees. Tom wasn't even sure how Chris had spotted them, but he started down the slope.

They'd gone pretty far before finally seeing them ahead. Chris was struggling up the slope carrying someone on his back. Tom's first thought was that he'd been wrong and they had found a survivor, but he quickly discounted that idea. His next thought was that Barney had been hurt, and he felt an odd sense of relief when he noticed Barney walking behind Chris.

It was only then that he realized it was Toby on Chris's back—Toby, whom he'd imagined the healthiest and most able of the three of them. Even before they got close, Tom could see Toby's stricken face resting floppily on Chris's shoulder, and it didn't look good.

They were close now and Chris said, "Barney, help me get him down." They lowered him from Chris's back onto the ground. "He slipped and something bit him on the arm."

Shen said, "What was it?"

Barney said, "He thinks it was a snake. The bite looks like a snake."

Chris added, "But we need to get him back. He's in a bad way."

Tom looked down at Toby lying on his back on the forest floor, and was moved in some way that Chris had carried him this far, because he didn't seem in a bad way at all—he seemed to be dead.

Shen crouched down next to him and checked his pulse, then his eyes, then his pulse again, waiting longer than before with his fingers probing Toby's neck. The rest of them watched, Chris's face full of confusion and horror, as if he couldn't quite accept that the person he'd struggled to carry had already embarked on a much longer and much simpler journey.

Shen looked up at Chris. "He's dead." He turned to Barney then. "Could it have been a viper? It looks like he went into shock."

Barney seemed lost in thought, and sounded distracted as he replied. "We didn't see it, but maybe, yeah—the fang marks look deep. He...yeah."

Shen studied the wound on Toby's lower arm as Chris turned to Tom and said, "How crazy is that? I just carried a dead guy." His face was all nervous tics, his eyes blinking rapidly.

Tom didn't respond but glanced at Toby and understood that it could have been any one of them, that none of them had definitively *survived* yet. All it took was a stumble and fall, or to be bitten by something, or any number of other things that could kill them in this environment.

As if he'd heard Tom's train of thought, Barney said, "Joel needs to understand how dangerous it is here."

Chris seemed to think the comment had been addressed specifically to him and said, "Yeah, I'll talk to him." He looked at the body. "We'll have to take him back and bury him."

Shen raised his eyebrows. "With what, and where? We don't have tools, and this soil..." He stamped on the ground. "We won't be able to dig deep enough."

"We can't just leave him."

Tom said, "You left the people in the plane."

"That was different. They were all charred and..."

"Not all of them," said Barney. He looked at Tom, his voice wavering as he added, "I mean, they were all dead. Absolutely. But they weren't all burned. It might have been better if...if they had been."

Chris nodded, agreeing with him, and it was clear both of them had been left disturbed by the sight of all those broken bodies, that seeing Toby die had only magnified it.

Tom said, "It doesn't matter. You left them because you had to, and we're leaving him. If we get rescued we can tell them where to look."

"You're right," said Chris, though he didn't sound sure of it. "Should we say a few words?"

Tom looked down at the body, angered that this had happened. Toby had been so eager to follow Joel's orders that it had made him careless and disrespectful of the jungle, to the point of succumbing to an entirely avoidable threat. And now he was dead, for no good reason, and Tom felt a sudden, almost physical urge to be away from him.

"Up to you." He didn't wait for an answer, but turned and walked back up the hill.

CHAPTER 10

He guessed no words were said because Chris and Shen and Barney were right behind him by the time he regained the ridge. What use were words anyway? He remembered lots of words at his parents' funeral, people talking about what amazing friends they'd been, how they'd never be forgotten, and even at that young age he'd wondered what the point of it all was.

Tom stopped on the ridge. The rest of the group was still busy but most of the luggage had been cleared off the slope now.

Chris stood next to him and said, "I think I should be the one who tells them."

He seemed to think Tom might object, as if there were some glory in being the one who broke the news, but Tom said, "Fine by me."

Chris nodded, then glanced at Shen and Barney, perhaps

fearing they might try to steal his thunder, and set off down the slope, gaining speed as he went, his bulk and his eagerness to share the news propelling him downward.

Shen and Barney were talking quietly as they looked out at the jungle. It was clear Shen had mentioned the line of the river, because Barney studied it before pointing at the low hills in the distance and the cleft that suggested the river might run between them.

Then Barney said to Tom, "Shen told me about your plan."

"It's hardly a plan."

"All the same, I want to come, if you don't mind."

"I don't mind at all."

Chris had almost reached the tail of the plane and the people higher up the slope dropped what they were doing and followed after him, the crowd quickly gravitating to hear what he had to say. Distressed responses rose up to them on the heavy, still air.

Apparently ignoring the commotion, Barney focused his attention on the small mountain of luggage that had built up in front of the open tail section. "What are they doing? That's exactly where we'll need to build the fire."

"I said that, but Joel doesn't think a fire is important right now."

"Idiot."

Tom said, "Maybe we just need to give him a good enough reason to build one. Come on."

He set off down the slope and the other two followed him. The whole group was gathered together, Joel and Chris at their center, surrounded by too many voices, too many questions, not enough answers.

As Tom and the others approached, Joel was saying, "Look, there's nothing we can do about that for now. We just need to stay calm and be vigilant."

Alice was standing near the back. Tom gestured for her to follow and she peeled away from the others and followed him to the back of the plane.

"What's going on?"

Tom said, "We need your help. Do you know Shen and Barney?"

"No. Hello." She reached out and shook their hands, which seemed to amuse Barney. "I'm Alice."

Barney's amusement grew all the more. "We know who *you* are."

Tom said, "We can climb up again now, but Barney, could you get some boxes or hard suitcases to use as steps up to the door?"

"Absolutely."

Tom climbed up the slide, then reached down for Alice's hand, pulling her up, then the same with Shen.

As soon as they were inside, she said, "Lara wants to come too, when we go. I told her not to tell anyone else." She looked at Shen with concern, maybe wondering whether she should have said anything in front of him.

Shen smiled. "I'm coming too. So is Barney."

Tom pointed at the galley. "We did a check on the food. If we use it in the right order, there might be enough for a few days."

"Good. I think people are beginning to get hungry."

"That's even better. Shen thinks we need a fire and I think he's right."

"So do I." Alice turned to Shen. "Joel was wrong to put you down like that. A fire's obviously more important than collecting luggage."

Shen smiled appreciatively.

Tom said, "So tell Joel that you and Shen are taking over the galley, that you've found food but you need a fire to heat it. You need to act possessive about the galley—I don't want Joel or the others coming in here."

"Why?"

"There's an emergency kit, other stuff we'll need, and I don't want them wasting it."

She nodded, but Shen said, "There's something else. The fire should be exactly where all the luggage is right now. We'll need to stay in the plane at night, so the fire should be in front of it."

"Okay. I'll see what I can do." Alice was about to leave again, but she stopped and said, "Joel's a complete jerk, but Chris and the others think he's got all the answers."

"So did Toby," said Shen.

"So we have to work as a team, stick together, back each other up, that kind of thing."

Tom was about to say he wasn't part of any team, that he was his own person, but he knew she was right, and in truth, he probably couldn't do this on his own, anyway. He even sort of liked the idea of being part of a group.

As long as it was the right group.

CHAPTER 11

Shen started to sort out the food, separating the things that would need to be eaten first from those that would keep for a day. Tom stashed the emergency kit at the back of one of the bins just as Barney finished making his impromptu staircase and appeared in the doorway.

"What should I do next?"

Tom didn't have an answer for him, but Shen came out of the galley and said, "See if you can do something so that the toilets work without electricity."

Barney immediately looked intrigued. "Of course, it's a vacuum system. Now there's a puzzle—I'll see what I can do. Unless you wanted me for anything, Tom?"

"No, go ahead. Besides, I'm not in charge."

Barney walked through to the bathrooms and Shen went back

into the galley. Tom drifted through into what was left of the cabin. He could already hear Barney getting to work inside one of the bathroom cubicles, presumably working out how it all fitted together. Tom was impressed that anyone could get excited about being asked to adapt a toilet.

He walked the few remaining paces to the torn edge of the tail and was even more impressed as he looked down. Because there was still a hive of activity but it had changed and he knew Alice was responsible for that change.

Some of them were moving the stack of luggage so that it formed two semicircular walls on either side of the space where the fire would be. The others were on the slope, carefully collecting branches from the edges, their caution no doubt driven by what had happened to Toby.

Joel was looking on, but when he saw Tom he waved a little and walked over so that he was standing below him.

"Tom, bro, could I have a quick word?" Tom didn't answer but looked down at him expectantly. "Maybe if I come around to the side of the plane?"

"Sure." Tom walked away and down the boxes and cases that Barney had stacked.

Joel was waiting at the bottom and pointed at the steps. "That's a good idea."

Tom glanced back at them briefly. "What did you wanna talk about?"

"Nothing really, it's just...actually, the steps. Barney said you told him to do it." He seemed to be waiting for a response and looked uneasy when Tom remained silent. "Like I said, it's a good idea. I just think, if we're gonna get through this, we need to stay organized. You know, otherwise we'll end up working at cross purposes. So, maybe if you have an idea, it might be better to run it past me first."

Tom had never really had any direct dealings with Joel before, and now, face-to-face, he was struggling to comprehend what a complete fool he was.

A hundred different responses ran through his head, but in the end he said only, "I don't think so."

"Hey, bro, I don't mean I'm telling you what to do, it's just... we need someone to take control, and I've stepped up. Now by all means, if anyone else wants to be leader, if *you* want to be leader, just throw your hat in the ring."

"I'm not sure what it is you think you're leading, but I don't want any part of it, not as a leader, not as a follower."

"I hear what you're saying, but I don't think you...look, obviously, I don't want an argument, it's just—"

"Good." The unmistakable sound of Chloe raising her voice and Chris's obstinate response reached them. "Sounds like you're needed."

Joel nodded and walked away, clearly unsatisfied and confused by the way his quick word had turned out. Alice came in the other direction and thanked Joel as their paths crossed. She probably had it right, letting Joel think moving the luggage and building a fire was all his idea. Tom had just been on his own for too long to adapt this quickly to dealing with the Joels of the world.

She smiled at Tom. "He's scared of you."

"I doubt it."

"I'm telling you he's scared. He can't figure you out, and that scares him. I think it scares a few people."

"But not you?"

"I'm not scared of anyone." He could believe that, but then she smiled and added, "Doesn't mean I can figure you out, though." She shrugged and climbed the steps up into the plane.

CHAPTER 12

Within an hour they'd made some progress. Barney had managed to make one of the toilets operational. They'd collected enough dry branches to get the fire going after a few false starts, using a lighter found in the luggage. And between them, Shen and Alice had managed to heat plenty of chicken and rice to feed everyone.

The whole group, eighteen of them remaining, sat on the suitcases, which formed almost a complete circle around the fire and for the first time, there was more silence than conversation. With full stomachs, even Chloe and Chris had made their peace.

For Tom, the only jarring note came at the end of the meal when Joel stood and said, "I think we should give Alice and Shen a round of applause—that was fantastic."

Dutifully, everyone clapped, even though most of them had

already thanked or complimented the two cooks. Alice looked slightly embarrassed by the attention, but Shen looked mortified.

Once Joel had sat again and everyone had settled, Chloe said, "Is there anything we can do? I mean, to help them find us? They have to be searching, right?"

"Of course they're searching," said Joel. "Who knows, someone could see the smoke from our fire."

Chris nodded, even though he'd seen the scale of the jungle they were lost in. Tom noticed Chloe's friend, Mila, taking in Joel's words as if they were nothing but the gospel truth. Nick and Oscar, both friends of Joel's anyway, looked equally convinced by his assurances, as did Sandeep.

There were others, though. George was on the football team, so Tom wasn't sure why he'd been sitting at the back of the plane rather than with the rest of his teammates, and he actually smiled to himself at Joel's comment about the fire. He had the face of someone who wasn't buying Joel's air of confidence. Kate and Emma from Tom's English class glanced at each other in that telepathic way of theirs, looking equally skeptical.

Tom wasn't sure why it mattered to him that they weren't all lining up behind Joel, except that he sensed Joel wouldn't get them out of this. And Tom still wasn't convinced they needed a leader at all, but Alice or Shen would have gotten his vote.

"What about a flare? There must be a flare gun." Tom tuned back in to the conversation. He wasn't even sure who'd said it, though it might have been Nick.

But with impressive certainty, Barney said, "They're generally kept in the forward galley, for obvious reasons. But even if we found a flare gun, we couldn't afford to waste it out here."

Nick shook his head, perplexed, and sounded impatient with Barney as he said, "How would it be a waste?"

Barney held his ground. "Chris has been up the hill, he'll tell you—there's absolutely nothing but jungle for as far as you can see in every direction. And we've been here all morning, but there hasn't been any sign of another plane."

Joel said, "He's right. If we find the flare gun, we'll save it until we know they're close." And there it was—Joel still believed if they waited long enough, a rescue party would come and find them.

Chris looked into his empty plastic dish and then at the fire, a sudden idea almost visible on his face.

"Was there any alcohol in the galley?"

Nick leaned forward and pointed at him with a smile. "Good call!"

Joel didn't seem sure how to react to that one, but Alice was in no doubt. "There is, and no one's touching it." Everyone looked at her. "We'll keep it for treating wounds, and if we have to, as an anesthetic." The implications of her words were grim and Tom could see the unease settling in people's faces—Toby's random and sudden death was probably still playing on their minds and it was too easy to envisage the sort of medical emergencies that Alice was hinting at. "There's something else. It'll be tough for Shen and me to make the food and water last, so if we're handling it then I don't want anyone else going in the galley."

Tom wondered if one or more of them might object, but when Alice spoke out, she was a force to be reckoned with. So instead, they looked to Joel and he nodded his consent.

"Alice is right, about the alcohol and the galley." He looked pointedly at Tom. "We all need to play our part. We'll never survive if everyone just does what he wants."

Tom held his gaze, and Joel looked slightly relieved when Shen said, "So should we collect some more wood for the fire?"

The fire was burning steadily at the moment, though there was no more wood to put on it when it burned low, but Joel said, "I think that can wait until a little later. For now I think we should finish going through the luggage. Every backpack should have a flashlight and insect spray, and there could be things in the luggage of the other passengers too. Let's get everything we can find before it gets dark."

There was an immediate flurry of activity, but again, Tom couldn't help notice that some were quicker than others to jump up and get busy. Alice, Shen, and Barney all headed off to the steps at the back of the plane, and after a minute of sitting in the middle of the luggage-rifling, Tom got up and followed them.

CHAPTER 13

As he got to the top of the steps he could hear Alice and Shen discussing the food, mentally sorting it and dividing it up. He walked the other way and found Barney working on the second toilet.

Tom looked in on him and then turned and noticed the compartments behind the back seats that held the cases for the life rafts. An idea struck him and he smiled with the simplicity of it.

It was so simple that he began to doubt himself and said, "Barney, could you come out here for a minute?"

He stepped out of the bathroom, looking expectant. "Yeah?"

Tom pointed. "Life rafts."

"Of course, all planes have them. The emergency slides double as life rafts too, but there has to be enough capacity for everyone on board. Not that it's much use in a jungle."

"Unless there's a river nearby."

"Of course!" His eyes lit up. "Yes! Even if it doesn't take us all the way, it's safer and easier than trekking through the jungle. I mean, there are risks, but..."

He stopped at the sound of someone climbing the steps. They both turned to look as Naomi came in. She was tall, incredibly beautiful, and played tennis at the semi-pro level. Principal Freeman never failed to brag that one day she'd be Naomi Kang, Wimbledon champion. But despite all her gifts, she didn't seem to have many friends, either.

She smiled when she noticed them staring and said, "I need to pee."

"Be my guest." Barney gestured with a flourish toward the toilet he'd already worked on. "There's no flush, but gravity will be your friend."

Tom couldn't help but laugh. Naomi smiled uncertainly and went into the bathroom.

They hadn't heard him approaching but George appeared then and looked at Tom and said, "Can I have a word?"

Tom shrugged. He'd never had so many people want to talk to him.

Barney took that as his cue to leave. "I'll get back to work."

George watched Barney go, puzzled, as if he'd never noticed him before, and once they were alone, he said to Tom, "I overheard Alice and Lara talking. If you're gonna get out of here, I'd like to come, if you don't mind. Joel's okay, I guess, but staying here, it's not an option."

Tom shrugged again, though he was beginning to wonder who wouldn't be coming with him.

"Sure. We'll be going day after tomorrow, if there's no sign of a rescue."

"Great. I know we've never spoken before, but I really appreciate this." Tom nodded and George started to walk away. But before disappearing he turned back to Tom. "I quit the football team a month ago. They weren't happy about it. It's why I wasn't sitting with them."

"Okay. I'm not sure why you're telling me, but...okay."

He smiled, a touch of humor as he said, "I know. I guess I just needed to tell somebody—leaving the team's the only reason I'm alive." Tom nodded, and George walked away.

The bathroom door opened then, and Naomi stepped out and said, "I'll come too. If I can. I want to come with you guys."

"Okay."

She seemed thrown that he'd said yes so easily, and as if feeling she still needed to persuade him, she said, "Thanks. I'm... well, I guess I'm kind of an outsider here."

"You and me both, but don't worry, I won't leave you behind."

"Thank you."

She tried a smile, but looked on the verge of tears. He didn't know her at all, but in that moment he saw how vulnerable she was beneath the veneer of confident athleticism, and he felt sorry for her.

More than that, he pitied her. He pitied *all* the people who wanted to come with him. They were relying on him in some way, counting on him, and that showed how desperate they had to be—because Tom had never helped anyone in his life.

CHAPTER 14

The activity below continued for an hour or so, but people started to flag as the heat of afternoon grew and the insects defied the spray they were all using. The drop in energy levels was almost visible and within a short while, most people were sleeping, lying on their backpacks around the fire.

Tom yielded in the end too, sitting in one of the cabin seats. As his thoughts fell away he briefly hoped he might have the flying dream, but no dream came, none at all, and perhaps that was for the best.

When he woke and saw the back of the seat in front of him, it took him a moment or two to remember where he was and that this plane was going nowhere.

He heard Alice's voice and walked to the front of the plane and looked down. She was just adding some branches to the fire, which was dangerously low. The others were stirring too and Joel, who'd obviously been roused by Alice, was trying to regain control.

"Everyone, spread out, find more wood for the fire. Old and dry is better, but anything you can find. And remember to watch out for snakes—no more accidents." Most of them were struggling to shake the heat-induced drowsiness and he sounded more urgent, more forceful now. "Come on, people, we have about an hour before it gets dark and we need this fire!"

Finally, people started to move, dispersing into the surrounding trees. Tom looked at his watch, then at the sky. By his best guess, it would be nightfall in much less than an hour, and darkness would come quickly.

He made his way out, stopping to let Alice come up the steps first.

She shook her head, furious. "People should've been collecting wood earlier, not sorting luggage.... What a jerk!"

Shen appeared in the galley door, and seeing Tom, he said, "Oh, hi. Barney told me about the boats. It's a good idea. I don't know why I didn't think of it."

Alice's anger fell away. "What about boats?"

Shen said, "Come and help me with the food and I'll tell you while we're working."

Tom headed into the trees to help collect wood. It was the first time he'd been under the canopy since coming down off the ridge and he was struck now by the eerie peacefulness of it.

Yes, he could hear the voices of the others as they clattered about among the trees, and nearby he could hear the general whirr and whisper of a thousand different creatures, of the trees and the earth itself. But within all of that there was still, somehow, a sense of peace and order.

It reminded him of the way he felt in his flying dream, of being connected to the world and to everything in it. That was how he felt here with the jungle breathing around him and through him. It was as if he'd always been meant to be here, as if a part of him had been here all along, waiting for the rest of him to catch up.

He drifted along a natural path and then noticed that ahead of him, a tree had fallen some time ago. He walked toward it, scanning the ground and the plants around him for snakes and spiders.

The tree lay across the path, but there were branches that had dried and were easy enough to break free. He snapped a few, dropping them back onto the path, quickly creating a decent pile of firewood. It was a satisfying exercise, except for the noise of the snapping branches, which seemed too alien, too destructive, against the natural wall of sound that surrounded him.

When he'd collected enough, he stopped and listened, the other voices distant now, as if he'd walked into another jungle and left all of them behind. He became acutely conscious of how alone he was, how far from everyone else.

And then, without warning, he became fearful, sensing that he was *not* alone here. No one from the crash was nearby, he knew that. But he also knew that someone else—or some*thing* else—was watching him, and he had walked too far from safety. Exactly the kind of carelessness he criticized the other kids for.

As hot and humid as it was, a shiver of cold ran through him. His fists clenched, the muscles in his legs tensing, ready to run, and he wanted to run but couldn't, his feet planted. And he didn't even know what the danger was, but there was something here, he could feel it.

He turned slowly to the right and flinched, almost jumped, seeing the shape of the figure above him on the fallen tree, feeling the danger even before he realized what it was, even before he met the piercing golden eyes that were locked on to him, full of a tense and tightly focused menace.

A part of his brain stubbornly identified it, a jaguar, even as his eyes started to water and his stomach clenched and he felt the sickening acceptance seep through him, that this was it, that it didn't just happen to other people—his own luck had run out.

Still he wanted to run, but couldn't, and that same stubborn part of his brain was telling him that he shouldn't turn his back on it, that his only hope was to remain face-to-face. And he couldn't believe how big it was, how intimidating.

He took a half-step backward, thinking it might put him in a position to grab a branch from the pile he'd collected. But even that slight movement brought a response from the jaguar, a visible coiling of its muscles that Tom sensed was dangerous, a readiness to pounce.

He wasn't sure what use a branch would be anyway. This thing was too large, too powerful, and Tom knew his only chance now was to charge toward it, to scream, to confuse the cat enough that it might run. He knew that was what he had to do, but he couldn't commit himself, fearing it wouldn't work, that death would only come quicker.

And he *wanted* to live, he understood that sharply for perhaps the first time, that he wasn't ready to die. But he would only have one chance, and the sweat was cold on his back, his body telling him the brutal truth, that it wasn't much of a chance at all.

He thought of his phone, how bright and loud and brash it was. He slid his hand into his pocket and pressed the button to switch it on. A second passed, seeming too long, and he could hear the deep growling purr of the jaguar above him, a tension that seemed in danger of snapping at any moment.

He kept staring, and his eyes were still watering and he wanted to blink away the tears that were filling up there but he was afraid to blink, afraid to break the contact between them.

At last, the phone buzzed against his palm and his heart lurched again, an overload of adrenaline. He pulled it free and held it out, afraid of dropping it, no longer fully in control of his own hand.

The phone lit up, dazzlingly bright here in the jungle deep. The familiar jingle sounded, loud and jarring against the stillness surrounding him. And in that moment he saw his one slim opportunity. Whether it was the light or the noise, the jaguar's head twitched, the tiniest movement, but it seemed like uncertainty or even fear, and another pulse of adrenaline burst into Tom's body in response.

He didn't hesitate. He threw the phone as hard as he could now at the jaguar's head. The cat sprang from the fallen tree, and Tom jumped back involuntarily. But it had leapt away from him, not toward him, a graceful flight of such speed, it only reinforced that he wouldn't have stood a chance. The cat was gone, tearing through the undergrowth. The phone, never coming close to its target, clattered somewhere beyond the tree.

For a second, Tom froze, his heart hammering, taking a

moment to catch up with the facts, with his survival. He glanced down, saw the woodpile, and that brought him back to his senses. He bent down, scooped up the wood and ran, ran faster than he'd ever run, loose-limbed and weightless, lungs on fire, muscles electrified by all that built-up energy. He stumbled a couple of times as he looked behind, refusing to believe that the threat had gone, that it wouldn't come after him, but he never fell, just pushed on faster.

Even as he saw the plane he kept running, even as he saw Joel and Alice, clearly in the middle of a disagreement, a heated exchange but with their voices low. Joel looked in his direction and seemed relieved to have a reason for changing the subject.

"Good job, Tom. Just put it with the rest of the wood."

Tom reached them, struggling to stop, looking back one last time. He dropped the wood with a violent clatter.

"Whoa, what's—"

"Call everyone back!" He was troubled by the sound of his own voice, how shaky it was, how hoarse. The words burned in his throat. "Call everyone back."

He noticed Alice look at him with shock, even a little fear.

"Bro, you're not making any sense."

"I just saw a jaguar, big." He shook his head, remembering just how big it had seemed, particularly standing above him, and how close, the dangerous intensity of its gaze.

Alice said, "Oh, my God! Are you okay?"

He looked at her, started to nod, but Joel said, "Tom, are you sure? You know, in the jungle—"

Tom grabbed hold of Joel's T-shirt.

"I threw my phone at it! Now call everyone back!"

"Okay, I will, I will!" Tom let go, stepped back. Joel raised an eyebrow, as though to express his disapproval of Tom's lack of control, then glanced up at the sky. "I'll call them back, but we'll give them a few minutes. They're probably starting to come back anyway."

Alice looked at him in amazement. "Did you hear what he just said? Call them back."

"Or I'll call them back myself," said Tom, his anger building again, coming in waves.

"And create a panic? That's the way we'll get another accident." Alice shook her head, exasperated, and headed to the steps at the back of the plane, hurtling up them with almost as much grace as the jaguar leaping from that tree. Joel nodded at Tom, before adding, "Look, the others are all in groups, so they'll be okay. I don't want people freaking out, possibly for nothing."

"I know what I saw."

"I'm not doubting you. All I meant was, the jungle, you know, it's confusing sometimes."

Tom wanted to hit him, wanted it so much, but he wouldn't sink to that, particularly after what had just happened.

He bent down, picked up the wood and walked away, leaving Joel standing there. A couple of other people had already come back, including George, who was using one of the branches to work on the fire, pushing the burning material into a more stable shape.

He nodded to Tom and said, "Are you okay?"

"Yeah, I just... it's nothing."

George didn't look convinced, but he shifted his attention to the branches Tom was holding. "They look pretty dry—I could use them."

"Sure," said Tom, and put the branches next to the fire instead of on the larger woodpile. He noticed his hands were still shaking.

He helped George add them, calming down now, even though he kept looking toward the trees, watching for signs of the others coming back, trying to remember how many more were still out there.

Then George said, "What's that kid's name, the one who fixed the toilets?"

"Barney."

"Barney, that's it. I don't really know him, but he seems okay."

Tom thought of Barney, and of Shen, and perhaps because of the scare he'd just had, he felt an odd attachment to both of them. He felt good too, that this kid George, whom he'd never spoken to before today, was talking to him now like they were friends. For once, he liked the thought of not being alone, of not having only himself to rely on.

"If I'm honest, I don't know him, either, but he's a good guy."

"Yeah." He smiled, the look of someone who'd come to a realization, maybe just that there were people worth knowing beyond the narrow world of his former friends on the football team.

George started to say something else, but appeared to change his mind as Joel strolled over. Joel looked ready to speak too, but a faint scream sounded from deep within the trees to their right. All three of them looked in the direction of the cry, but a few seconds later it was followed by the sound of people laughing.

Joel looked at Tom. "They're just fooling around."

Tom didn't answer, but turned slowly back to the tree line.

The two sounds had come from more or less the same direction, but it seemed to him that the scream had been farther away, the laughter nearer. As if to prove that point, Chloe, Mila, and Chris emerged from the shadows, laughing, carrying a few small branches between them.

"I'll speak to them," said Joel, and walked over to meet them, and Tom wondered if Joel had come to the same conclusion as him about the location of the scream, because he looked rattled in some way. He spoke to Chris, who turned back to the trees and shouted for everyone to come back, his voice bellowing and briefly drowning out the jungle chorus.

CHAPTER 15

Tom sat by the fire and watched as the others came back with the wood they'd collected. When darkness fell and the last of the stragglers emerged from the shadows, he tried to do a mental count, making sure everyone had come back. That in turn reminded him of Miss Graham, dead, probably still strapped in her seat in the burned wreckage of the plane on the other side of that hill.

There was another distraction then as Alice and Shen and Barney emerged from the plane and the business of preparing food got under way, set against a backdrop of bustling conversation and lame jokes and "helpful" advice to the cooks.

The volume only decreased slightly once they were all eating, but there was still an odd excitability about the entire group, as if they thought this was exactly the trip they'd all signed up for. Although, now that he looked around, Tom saw there was a divide in the mood too—the people who wanted to leave with him were quieter, more subdued, George and Alice in particular, Lara and...

His thoughts stumbled and fell away from him. He looked around the circle of people, their faces glowing and only half-shown by the firelight. He shook his head, angry with himself for not noticing before, even angrier at Joel.

"Where's Naomi?"

Joel said, "Naomi?" He sounded confident, though it was clear he wasn't sure who Naomi was. "Has anyone seen her?"

Chloe said, "We saw her, didn't we, Chris? She was in the same area as us."

"Yeah, but she walked farther. Maybe she got lost."

There was a sudden flurry of talking before Joel said, "Okay, we need to organize a search."

"No," said Tom, and everyone stopped talking and stared at him. He stood and said, "I'll go."

Joel stood too, his face half-lost in shadow, the other half dancing with the firelight, and he looked queasily paternal as he said, "Tom, bro, this isn't your fault."

Once again, Tom felt like hitting him. "No, it's yours, but I'm still going."

Nick said, "What's he talking about?"

But before Joel could respond, George stood up. "I'll come with you."

Then a girl's voice came from the other side of the fire. "So will I." She stood and Tom saw it was Kate, stepping up again. This time she didn't give Joel the chance to overrule her. "She might want a girl in the group that finds her, and we used to play tennis together years ago."

"Sure," said Tom, and the three of them got flashlights and each selected a branch from the woodpile, with Joel all the while talking in the background, giving instructions as though they were going on his behalf.

Tom wasn't listening to him and guessed the other two weren't, either. Joel only stopped when George pointed into the trees with his flashlight, saying, "That's the direction the scream came from."

They set off as one of the other girls said, "What scream? Who heard a scream?"

Tom was focusing on the beam illuminating a narrow sliver of ground in front of him, but he heard Alice say, "Why don't you tell them, Joel? Tell them about the scream."

Their small party moved into single file. Tom was at the front, George at the back, and as they edged carefully onto the straggling path, which seemed to have become even more hemmed in by vegetation now that night had fallen, Kate said, "What was Alice talking about as we left?"

Tom kept his eyes fixed forward as he spoke. "I came face-to-face with a jaguar when I was collecting wood." He paused, using the branch he was carrying to dismantle a spider's web that had been thrown across the path. "I threw my phone at it and it ran off, but I told Joel to call everyone in."

"And he didn't?"

"Not right away. Then we heard the scream."

George cursed under his breath with what sounded like a mixture of fury and frustration.

"Oh, my God." Kate sounded horrified, perhaps thinking of what might have happened to Naomi rather than dwelling on the reasons for it happening. And the reasons, it seemed, didn't even need spelling out. "Why is everyone listening to him?"

George said, "Because he's the only one talking. Tom should be the leader."

Tom couldn't help but be flattered, particularly when he'd never spoken to George until a few hours ago, but he was angry with himself too, because he could have called out and hadn't. He'd left it to Joel, and for all Tom knew, something had happened to Naomi because of that failure.

He said, "I don't think we need a leader. But if the others like him being in charge, I'm fine with that."

"Yeah, I guess I can live with it for one more day."

Kate was always pretty sharp in their English class and she was no different out here in the dark of the enveloping jungle, jumping on George's comment as she said, "Why, what happens after that?"

George didn't answer, perhaps fearing he'd spoken out of turn, so Tom said, "A group of us are walking out of here."

He'd hardly finished talking before she cut in. "I'll come. So will Emma. We've already talked about it anyway, but we'd rather come with you."

"Okay." It sounded like they were intent on leaving anyway, and since Kate had volunteered to go to the wreckage and had stepped up immediately to search for Naomi, he guessed she'd be a good addition to the escape party. "I'm thinking early morning, the day after tomorrow."

"Great, what's the plan?"

"Don't get too excited. There's a river nearby so we'll head for that. There are two life rafts in the plane, so as soon as we can we'll get them onto the water and head downstream."

"That sounds like a plan to me. It's better than sitting here waiting for a rescue that isn't coming."

"Maybe." He was about to tell her to keep it quiet, even though half of the survivors were now part of this secret group. But just as he was about to speak, his light picked up something on the ground in front of him. The words dried instantly in his mouth. He stopped walking.

Kate crashed into his back, knocking him forward. "God, sorry."

"My fault," said Tom.

"What is it?"

He moved to one side and pointed with his flashlight so that they could see.

A single white sneaker lying on the ground.

CHAPTER 16

Kate rushed forward, crouching down, picking up the sneaker.

She looked up at them, startled and horrified, her face caught in their flashlight beams like an animal on a nighttime road. "It's hers." She didn't wait for a response but called out, "Naomi?"

The wall of noise around them seemed to shudder and quiver briefly, as if all those creatures were trying to take in this new sound and adjust to it. But the soundscape returned to normal and no one called back.

Tom spotted a small bunch of twigs and branches scattered on the path just beyond where Kate was still crouching holding the shoe. So this was where the attack had happened, and he could imagine, looking at the pitiful pile of kindling, that she'd been determined to find more, heading farther into the jungle without realizing the danger.

He thought back to that brief moment of acknowledging they were both outsiders in one way or another, and it was true, but it had cost Naomi her life. He remembered telling her that he wouldn't leave her behind, and he felt like a liar now for making that promise.

George pointed his light off to the right where some of the undergrowth looked as if it had been recently flattened. "I guess it dragged her through there."

Kate moved toward it and studied the leaves, finally raising her fingers to one broad leaf and rubbing it under the light.

"It's dried a bit, but it's blood."

Something about the way she carried herself made Tom see that she was comfortable in this kind of environment. Emma had said as much when Kate had offered to go to the wreckage of the plane.

"You know about this kind of thing, Kate?"

"I guess so, because of my dad."

"But isn't your dad a lawyer?"

In fact, he knew that only because it was her father's firm that had handled Tom's affairs for him since the death of his parents. It was odd to think of it now, the little connections he had with people he'd never felt connected with at all.

"Yeah, but he grew up in the woods. So we spend most summers up at a cabin my grandpa built in Maine, and we vacation in places like this. I'm no expert, but I know my way around."

George said, "You're more of an expert than the rest of us."

"Don't feel like one, not right now." She glanced back at the shoe.

George turned back to Tom and said, "So you think that's what happened, the jaguar you saw..."

"Or another one, but it seems likely. I think it might have gone in this direction after I spooked it."

Despite her familiarity with the wild, or maybe because of it, Kate shuddered. "How horrible."

George shook his head. "I read about them last week. They attack from behind, kill with a single bite to the back of the neck. I know it's not much, but at least she wouldn't have known what was happening."

"But it's out there now, tearing her to bits, eating her. It's just horrible." Her voice seemed to get more agitated as she spoke, a volatile mix of anger and emotion. "How can we stand here calmly discussing it, and Naomi's dead?"

"We've got no choice, Kate. Stay calm or freak out—that's not a choice."

Resigned, she said, "I know, I know that. It's just..." They fell into silence, the jungle closing around them.

Tom thought back again to Naomi asking if she could go with them when they left, how fragile she'd seemed, how afraid. He wondered whether, at some subconscious level, she'd known something would happen to her here and that was why she'd been so eager to leave with him and the others.

Maybe all of them, at some deep-seated level, buried beyond all their conscious thoughts, knew how and when their deaths would come. It made him want to look into the eyes of each one of them to see if he could detect it. It made him want to look into his own eyes to see if it was there too.

And if it was, then, quite possibly, the jaguar had seen it and understood as only a wild animal could understand, that he was not its prey, that their encounter out there in the jungle might have been predestined, but it was not meant to end with death for either of them.

Or maybe it had just been spooked, giving Tom the time to react and throw his phone.

Kate looked at him now and said, "What are you thinking, Tom?"

He shook it off and shrugged, though he wasn't sure if either of them saw the gesture in the dark. "I was just thinking about how it didn't attack me right away but could've. And maybe this stuff about fate is true, you know, that it just wasn't my time."

As he spoke he realized it was the kind of philosophical discussion they had in English class, and true to form, Kate said, "No, Tom, because that means it *was* Naomi's time, and I know she wasn't meant to die like this." Her voice was shaky, but the anger was never far away. "She died for the same reason Toby died, because Joel's an idiot."

He smiled, not so much because of what she'd said, but because the conversation was even taking place. He often wondered during English class, what use conversations like that would ever have in the outside world, and yet here they were in the middle of the jungle, investigating the death of one of their classmates, and they were having precisely one of those conversations.

George chimed in now. "I think Tom's right. I've been thinking a lot about that, me quitting the football team."

Kate gasped and said, "I didn't know that! Of course, that's why you weren't sitting with them."

"Exactly. Coach kept telling me it was the worst possible timing and couldn't I just stick it out for a while longer. And I couldn't explain it to him, not any way that made sense, but I felt so strongly that I had to quit right away. So that's it, maybe I just wasn't meant to die in that plane." He turned to Tom. "But Kate's right too. This was still Joel's fault."

"Listen, I don't like the guy, but you can't blame him. I could've called people back, but I didn't. And if he'd called people back right away she might still have been taken. If the pilot hadn't crashed, none of us would've been here. If Naomi had any close friends she wouldn't have been looking for wood on her own." Kate bowed her head in response to that, and he remembered her saying she'd played tennis with Naomi years ago—perhaps they'd been friends once but had drifted apart. "It's nobody's fault. I'm not saying I believe in fate—I don't know whether I do—but look at all these random chances, one step to the left or right decides if you live or die. George quits football, Chris annoys Olivia, some kid survives an air crash but falls onto a snake—it's just all so random, and that's why it doesn't make any sense to blame Joel or anyone else."

Kate sighed heavily, then shooed away some flying insect that Tom couldn't even see, before she said, "Okay, maybe you're right. But our decisions matter, and that's why it matters who's making those decisions."

"It's true, Tom, it should be you."

"You're crazy. None of you knows me."

"I do," said Kate.

And before he could challenge her, that a year's worth of half-baked discussions about books hardly counted as knowing him, George added, "And I know enough."

Suddenly, Chris's voice boomed through the night from behind them, "Tom!"

He couldn't see Kate's face clearly, but her voice betrayed a smile as she said, "See, even that moron thinks you're the leader."

"They can pick leaders all day long. When we leave, we leave as a group, simple as that."

"Whatever you say, boss," said George with a laugh, and started back along the path.

Tom laughed a little too, and said, "After you," and Kate followed in George's shadow.

Tom brought up the rear, conscious of the deep black of the jungle on his back. One jaguar had done its hunting for the night, but there would be other creatures out there, all looking for food, this entire nocturnal landscape bristling with danger. And sensing that jungle around them, he could think of one more reason he wouldn't want to swap places with Joel, because no matter what decisions they made, he doubted Naomi would be the last to die out here.

CHAPTER 17

Chris shouted for them once more as they headed back, but none of them felt inclined to reply to his call. When they emerged from the trees, they found him standing in the shadows on the near side of the circle, his silhouette making him look even bigger than usual.

But as George's flashlight beam, then Kate's, caught Chris's face he seemed full of genuine concern and he was quick to say, "Didn't you find her?"

It was Kate who answered. "We found her shoe, and we found blood."

George added, "And we saw where it dragged her off."

Chris shook his head, upset, perhaps thinking he was responsible in some way because he'd been the last to see her. At the same time, a clamor of voices broke out around the fire, high-pitched and angry and urgent, people who wanted to believe something could still be done, that she couldn't be lost, this girl whose absence they hadn't even noticed. Tom thought Joel might intervene in his usual fashion to restore order but he was talking to Nick and Chloe, their voices just a part of the general hubbub.

They walked back into the camp and Kate went to sit next to Emma, the two of them immediately falling into conversation, Kate wiping away tears as she spoke, Emma putting her arm around her.

Tom nodded to Alice and sat next to her, and then she said, "Things were a bit tense after you left." He looked at her and she smiled. "I just wanted Joel to tell the truth."

"And did he?"

Her smile broke down, grudgingly. "Yeah, I have to admit, he took the blame. By the way, Jess and Freddie want to come—hope you don't mind."

He looked across the fire. He didn't know them or anything about them, except they'd been an inseparable couple for the last year. They were both slightly odd looking, irregularly featured, but somehow looked good together. At the moment they were holding hands and both gazing down at their intertwined fingers, as though they were able to communicate through that contact alone. He envied them a little, their understated intimacy, their completeness as a couple.

"I don't mind if they come. It's not up to me anyway."

The smile came back and she said, "Any more thoughts on when to leave?"

"I was thinking daybreak, day after tomorrow."

"Good, I was hoping you'd say that. Three days might be too long."

Joel cleared his throat and said, "Everyone?" The voices died down, and without standing he spoke, sounding more subdued than he had earlier. "Firstly, I want to apologize. I knew we needed to organize, and I took on the role of leader. I was just trying to do the best for everyone, and I'm not sure what I could have done differently, but it's obvious some of you think I took my eye off the ball, and that we've lost a couple of people as a result. I'm willing to take full responsibility if that's how you feel." There was a brief chorus of dissent, reassuring him that he wasn't to blame. He ignored it. "I know some of you believe there's no need for anyone to take charge, and I don't agree with that, but I accept I might not be the best for the job, so if anyone else wants to step up—" The chorus became more agitated, Chloe being particularly vociferous in Joel's defense.

Tom didn't trust Joel at all, seeing that the apology and the offer to step aside were both designed to elicit more sympathy and support, at the same time disarming any further criticism. Some of it had even been directed specifically at Tom, and Tom got the feeling everyone knew that and they were waiting to see if he'd respond.

Joel put his hands up now to quiet them, like some great political orator, and said, "Okay, but the offer stands, and if anyone isn't happy with anything I say, let me know. It's better we discuss it than have any more accidents. You know I'll try my best, but I can't cover every base without everyone working together." There were more encouraging noises, and he nodded in response, sucking it all up. "Good, now, does anyone have anything to say, any questions, anything at all?"

They fell silent, and Tom was conscious again that a reasonable number in the group were looking at him, not necessarily staring, but glancing repeatedly in his direction, expectant.

As a result, the silence only intensified when Tom said, "I have a question. Two questions." They were all staring now, but all of them would be disappointed in some way, because Tom had figured out how to play Joel, how to flatter him into doing the things that needed to be done. He'd learned from watching Alice. "I was just wondering where we're all going to sleep tonight, and how we make sure the fire keeps going."

Joel nodded, apparently acknowledging that they were good questions. "I'm glad you asked that, Tom, because I've been thinking about it. I know it won't be comfortable, but I think it's best if most of us sleep in the seats on the plane."

That seemed to go down well, particularly now that everyone accepted there were animals here that could kill them.

Shen said, "I'll sleep on the galley floor."

"So will I," said Barney.

"Great," said Joel. "That frees up another couple of seats so we can spread out a little more." Tom smiled, because he knew exactly what Shen and Barney were up to—making sure no one could get into the precious supplies. "We also need to have a roster of people to watch the fire and keep it burning, maybe two or three at a time."

Alice said, "I'll take first watch. I'm a night owl anyway. Tom?" He nodded.

Then George said, "I'll stay up too."

"Perfect. So you guys keep the first few hours. Then wake Chris, Chloe, and Nick. Then me, Mila, and Sandeep." He stood up. "I know it's been a tough day, but we got through it, and I have a good feeling about tomorrow."

Chris nodded, saying, "We're going to get rescued tomorrow, I can sense it."

Tom smiled, knowing that the eyes of nine kids were on him, those who'd claimed their place in the escape party. All people who were convinced that Chris's moment of predicting the future had come and gone.

CHAPTER 18

Preparations for sleep started almost immediately, and became almost immediately chaotic. Someone said something about mosquito nets, then Oscar remembered that he'd seen some earlier in the day when they'd been sorting luggage, but hadn't thought them useful and couldn't remember where he'd seen them.

So a flashlit search followed, interspersed by odd yells and screams as the searchers encountered any number of deadly creatures that turned out to be beetles or moths or, in one case, a bat. Eventually the nets were found and a group set about trying to fix them like a veil across the torn-open fuselage.

They failed each time, with laughter at first, then frustration, until finally Alice said, "Why don't you ask Shen and Barney to do it?"

Nick said, "Who's Barney?"

Chris said, "The little kid—the geek." He seemed to anticipate a rebuke from Alice and added quickly, "He's a good guy."

Shen and Barney were called from the galley, though Tom noticed that Alice drifted back there herself at the same time, ensuring the supplies remained off-limits. And within ten minutes the two boys had managed to attach three mosquito nets stretching across the open front of the fuselage.

People started to settle then, and after a short time, the only people left around the fire were the three on first watch, and Joel.

He stood, looked up at the flashlit activity behind the gauze of the nets, then turned his attention back to Tom, Alice, and George. "Thanks for this, guys."

Neither Tom nor Alice replied, but George said, "No worries."

Joel nodded, and said, "Sure, but you can wake me anytime if there's a problem."

It was Alice who spoke now. "I'm sure we'll be fine."

He nodded again, and Tom almost felt sorry for him, because it was clear he didn't have the first idea how to deal with any of them.

"Well, good night." He walked off to the side of the plane and the steps. A few seconds later, Shen emerged from the gloom and sat with them.

"Barney's using the other two nets to cover the door at the back. You'll still be able to separate them and step through."

Alice smiled and said, "Shen, if there's ever a zombie apocalypse, I want you and Barney on my team."

Tom looked at her. "I have no idea what that means, but me too."

"You know, a zombie apocalypse?"

"Yeah, Alice, I understand what the words mean, but..."

George started laughing, either at Tom's confusion or the fact they were having this conversation in the first place.

Then from above, they heard Chloe say disapprovingly, "Well, I'm glad someone's enjoying themselves."

That set them all laughing, but then Shen bid them good night and the three of them sat in silence and the cabin slowly quieted above them. And for a while there was only the crackling of the fire and the relentless noise of the jungle and the more distinct sounds of various creatures moving and sometimes crashing through the branches and undergrowth that surrounded them.

When they spoke again it was after a particularly loud rustling followed by a grunting of some sort and Alice whispered, "What was that?"

George turned his flashlight on and pointed it out toward the trees, though the beam only seemed to make the wall of darkness even more opaque.

"Some sort of pig, maybe. What are they called? Peccaries?"

"Yeah, I think I read something about that."

Tom smiled. They'd all been encouraged to do their research before coming out here, and most of them had, even though "here" wasn't exactly where "here" was meant to be—he guessed most of the wildlife was still more or less the same, and equally dangerous. He hadn't really wanted to come, of course, so the only knowledge he'd brought was the stuff he'd already gotten from nature documentaries on TV.

George and Alice talked on, their voices low, mainly discussing different people, some of whom had died at the beginning of this long day. At first Tom was confused to hear them talking in a tone that suggested they knew each other and had met socially, when they hardly seemed similar types, but then he remembered that Alice had briefly dated Ethan from the football team and had probably met George as a result.

After about twenty minutes, Alice said, "Sorry, Tom, we're talking about people you don't really know."

"I don't mind."

George glanced up at the cabin high above them, in darkness now, the sound of someone quietly snoring just audible above the more general noise of the jungle, then he said, "I thought you handled that really well earlier—he was obviously trying to push your buttons."

Alice nodded in agreement, but Tom said, "It's pretty stupid, really. But at least we only have to put up with it for one more day."

"When will you tell them?"

"That we're going?" She nodded. "Tomorrow afternoon, I guess, before it gets dark. We'll want everything ready so we can head out first thing the next morning."

She walked over and picked up a branch, placing it on the fire, saying, "I wonder how he'll take that."

Tom thought about it, how more than half of the survivors were now in the escape party, how he'd accepted every addition, pretending it had nothing to do with him. He realized now that there was only one way to deal with the inevitable disagreement the following afternoon.

"Look, if they all want to come, there's nothing stopping them. But there's nothing stopping us from leaving, either. They can argue all day, but we're going, so it's a simple choice: come with us, or stay behind and wait to be rescued."

He noticed that Alice looked relieved by that, and he felt like telling her again that it wasn't up to him, that he wasn't leading the escape party, but she surprised him by saying, "I hope they decide to come. I couldn't face Chris's parents if..." She brushed her hair back with both hands, something he'd seen her do often before, but she must have forgotten that her hair was short now and there was nothing to sweep back. "But I know I couldn't sit here and wait. I keep thinking about my parents and my little brother, what they must be going through."

"Me too," said George. He looked at her in amazement then. "I don't know why it never occurred to me before. You're Harry Dysart's sister! He plays baseball with my brother."

She smiled at the mention of her brother's name, an affection that left Tom feeling hollow.

"I know. Dylan's been to our house a few times. He's a cute kid."

"In small doses! But yeah, he's okay, I guess." He looked down at the fire for a moment or two, then back up at Tom. "Do you have any brothers or sisters, Tom?"

Tom noticed Alice's face drop, tinged with embarrassment, but Tom only shook his head. "No, I'm an only child, and my parents died when I was nine, so..."

"Oh, sorry."

"You didn't know. Makes it easier anyway. At least I know there's no one out there worrying." He thought of Julia, and for once, he felt he had to say something else. "I have a guardian, Julia, but she's in a tech-free yoga retreat in Italy, so she probably doesn't even know the plane's missing."

Alice smiled. "I saw her at a parent–teacher conference.

Actually, I've seen her a couple of times. It sounds terrible, but I was always a bit envious—she just seems so cool. And you know, she's on a *yoga* retreat—who does that?"

"Julia does that." He laughed. "Yeah, she's pretty cool, but, she's...more like a really high-maintenance friend than a parent. It's okay now, but when I was younger I just wished... Well, the envy cuts both ways, that's all I'm saying."

He realized that in those few seconds he'd said more about himself than he ever had before, and he felt instantly vulnerable, on the edge of a precipice, his heart beating faster and with a strange rhythm.

But Alice said, "Of course. I can only imagine," and Tom relaxed a little, some unseen danger averted. He guessed this was how people spoke to each other, that it was okay to tell people that he'd rather have parents than a roommate, that he missed them, even without really being able to remember what it had been like to have them there in the first place.

George was watching, transfixed. He said, "Do you think that's why you're the way you are?"

Tom looked back at him. "You mean unfriendly, doesn't play well with others, a little bit of a freak?"

George laughed, a mixture of shock and embarrassment playing out across his face, as if he couldn't believe he'd asked the question. Alice laughed a little too, looking more relieved that Tom had responded in that way, and that in turn made Tom wonder how she thought he might have reacted—were people really afraid of him?

Tom smiled too, making clear there were no hard feelings, though he wasn't sure how there could be because he knew that was how people saw him.

"Honestly, I don't know. Julia's always telling me how laid-back and friendly and funny my mom and dad were, so maybe I was like that too. I don't really remember what I was like before the accident."

For a moment there was no response, but then Alice smiled warmly and said, "The way you are in English, that's the real you. It amazes me the way you'll argue something really passionately in English, then I see you outside and just get a blank. Seriously, I think today's the first time you've ever spoken to me outside of class." She shook her head and laughed a little. "I was even a bit nervous walking up the hill. I thought you might not speak to me." He was amazed, because he'd seen no sign of her unease as she'd walked up the hill to him. But he was shocked too, that people thought of him as being that hostile. "So, yeah, AP Lit—I like to think that's who you really are."

Tom was touched in some way. But he was also thinking, hoping, that she might be right, that a bit of the happy-go-lucky little kid he'd been was still there, and that books brought it out of him, even if people didn't—or hadn't, until now.

Then George said, "While we're on the subject of envy...I've always envied you guys who take AP Lit." They both looked at him and George shrugged. "I don't know, you seem to have all these amazing discussions about books. It's like you're all sitting in some café in Paris being really cool."

Alice laughed too loudly, shushing herself, and Tom laughed too, because only someone who'd never set foot in an AP Literature class could think it was cool.

CHAPTER 19

It had started slowly enough, but they kept talking through the night. They sat in silence too, at times, comfortable enough in each other's company, tending the fire, listening to the jungle. Tom didn't talk as much as the other two, but he talked more than he usually did.

And when Alice first asked him the time, they realized they'd already been on watch for five hours, and still they weren't tired, so they stayed. At some point in the early hours they made the decision that they wouldn't wake the next watch but would remain until daybreak.

Occasionally someone stirred in the cabin above them. Once or twice people got up, sometimes turning on a flashlight, stumbling into one of the bathrooms. Several times during the night there were sounds of disturbed sleep too, maybe even nightmares.

As one person mumbled in their sleep, a distressed litany that sounded like a plea for help, Alice said, "That's Lara. She has nightmares even when she's not in plane crashes."

Tom was mesmerized that she could recognize Lara from such a faint and garbled cry, and he was briefly full of wonder at this world of friendship he didn't really understand, a world of sleepovers and knowing each other's hopes and fears and eating and sleeping patterns and any number of other things. He wasn't sure he'd want that world for himself, but he was intrigued and astonished by it all the same.

It was during one of their more talkative phases that they noticed the first sluggish blue tinge in the air around them. There was some movement farther up the slope and they looked as a large peccary emerged onto the gouged path of the plane. It seemed to root around amid the debris, then glanced at them, looking unfazed, before disappearing back into the undergrowth.

George said, "Think it tastes like bacon?"

Alice gave him a playful thump on the arm, but then they fell silent again as, within minutes, the sickly light transformed, taking on the hue of the day to come.

"Twenty-four hours," said Alice, and George nodded.

Only after a moment or two did Tom understand that they were talking about how long they'd been here, that twenty-four hours had elapsed since their plane had broken apart and they'd found themselves in this jungle. Tom's confusion arose out of the fact that he was thinking of a different twenty-four hours, the time that would pass before he set off to find a way out.

They heard some noise from the side of the plane, and looked to see Shen and Barney emerge carrying two trays full of foil cartons.

Barney said, "You stayed up all night?"

Alice smiled and stretched. "Didn't mean to. We weren't tired."

Shen reached the fire, saying, "Then you should eat before you go to bed. I think we'll have to frontload on food today—a lot of this won't keep for another day."

Tom said, "What about dry food, or the plastic-wrapped stuff?"

Shen looked noncommittal. "If we're careful we could stretch it over two more days, not much more. When are you thinking of setting out?"

"Tomorrow morning."

That seemed to satisfy him. "Good. Much longer and we'd have to start finding food here."

George smiled, probably thinking of the peccary.

Tom said, "What about water?"

"Again, a couple of days if we use all the soft drinks and things. If we're near the river we can use the water from there."

Alice looked horrified. "We can do what?"

"Filter it through mosquito netting, boil it if we can, or use the purifying tablets in the emergency kit. Hopefully we won't need to, but we have to be ready."

Tom said, "Good." He looked at Alice. "Shen's being realistic. Even if we take the river, it could take days to get out of here."

Barney was sorting out the cartons on the ground next to the fire but he looked up with a bright smile and said, "Or there could be an amazing beach resort on the other side of those hills." He pointed at Alice. "There could be a deck chair with your name on it, waiting for you right now."

Shen added, "And if there isn't, he'll build you one, won't you, Barney?"

They laughed and talked as they prepared the food. People

started to stir in the cabin above, and it was soon clear from the overheard conversations that no one was happy about waking up on their first new morning in the jungle, about feeling grubby and unable to shower.

Tom smiled to himself as he heard their gripes, amused by how quickly it set in. They'd had an astonishing deliverance from one of the biggest universal fears, a plane crash, and already they were forgetting how lucky they were to be alive.

Joel was the first to emerge from the plane, looking incredibly fresh and polished. He did a double-take as he saw the three of them sitting there, and looked ready to make some appreciative statement.

Alice jumped in quickly, saying, "We just weren't tired."

Joel smiled, nodding. "You'll probably sleep all day—we'll have to make sure not to disturb you."

Involuntarily, he glanced at Tom, perhaps giving away his true feelings, that he was relieved Tom would be out of the way. Tom didn't get it because he'd made it about as clear as possible that he didn't want to challenge Joel's position. It was ridiculous anyway—they were just a bunch of kids stranded in the jungle, not some kind of militia.

Shen made sure to feed them first and then once everyone had come down to the fire, Tom, Alice, and George made their way up the steps to the cabin. It was already hot in there, but the mosquito netting produced a feel of twilight and Tom found it unexpectedly easy to settle down.

As he drifted into sleep he could hear Joel talking about collecting more wood, but for once, even that sound and the subsequent chatter was oddly relaxing. One more day of this, he thought as he drifted into sleep—just one more day.

CHAPTER 20

He was woken by the sound of cheering. He stirred, rubbed his eyes, and immediately thought that the impossible had happened and a rescue party had arrived. Yet the commotion had sounded distant. He climbed out of the reclining seat, just as Alice and George did the same.

Alice said, "What was that noise?"

"Someone cheering," said Tom.

They went to the mosquito net veil and looked through. The camp in front of the plane was empty except for Barney, who was carefully positioning more branches on the fire. Everyone else was high up the slope, and as Tom craned his neck, he could see why and what they were cheering.

There was a bonfire on top of the ridge, burning erratically but producing a thick pall of black smoke that drifted straight up into the still air. He looked at his watch—it was early afternoon.

Quietly, Alice said, "Well I guess if anything's likely to attract attention..."

"It's luggage." It was Shen, who'd come into the cabin behind them. "All the things they don't think we'll need, people's suitcases, clothes, things like that."

"But why?"

Shen shrugged. "People were complaining, saying they should be doing something to attract rescuers, so Joel came up with that idea. And I suppose there's a possibility it'll work."

"But?"

"But they've been working in the full heat for the last few hours, carrying it all up the hill, and that means they've been drinking more. The water might last until the end of tomorrow if we're lucky, but..."

Alice said, "Did you mention that to Joel?"

"Yes. I did. Apparently we won't need water if we get rescued."

George cursed under his breath. Alice grabbed her backpack and headed into one of the bathrooms. Shen was still looking at Tom as if waiting for him to respond or come up with a decision on what to do next.

On the one hand, Tom could almost appreciate why Joel had come up with the idea of building a bonfire. For one thing, Joel thought the skies above were full of planes searching for them, and maybe they were. For another, he'd been responding to disquiet among the people he thought he was leading. But it was still an insane decision to have people doing hard labor during the hottest part of the day, and to use up the water like that.

"Shen, you and George start separating the food and drinks, half to leave behind, half to take with us. Start going through the equipment too, figuring out what we'll need, what we won't. Once everyone's back down I'll tell them."

George nodded with what appeared to be relief, and Shen smiled—both with the air of people who'd been waiting for Tom to take control. He felt like telling them that he was doing nothing of the sort, but in a way he was—he wasn't stepping up as leader, just taking control of his own escape and trying to insulate himself against Joel's stupidity.

Most of them were back around the fire by the time Tom made his way down from the plane. The euphoria had worn off, and up close, he could understand all the more why Shen had been so annoyed, because most of them looked terrible.

Chris had gotten sunburned, his face bright red. Nick looked the opposite, deathly pale and as if he was about to throw up. Jess lay with her head on Freddie's lap and he was stroking her hair. Everyone was listless, and even Joel kept looking up at the bonfire, probably as a way of reminding himself that this had been worthwhile.

Those who hadn't been involved seemed startlingly fresh in comparison. George and Barney were by the fire, apparently talking about the way different materials burned. Alice and Shen joined them after a few minutes, both of them looking across at Tom.

He turned to Joel and said, "A few of us have made a decision." Joel looked at him, curious, confused. "Your bonfire's burning up there, so if there's a plane in the area we should at least get a fly-past by the end of the day. But if we don't, a few of us are heading out first thing in the morning."

Joel responded as if Tom had said something impossible. "But you can't. We have to stick together. And there's nowhere to go."

"There's a river," said Shen. "And two life rafts. We can follow the course of the river until it becomes navigable, then use the rafts."

"Oh, my God." Joel's expression suggested someone who'd been stabbed in the back by his most loyal supporters. "So, you've obviously discussed this but you didn't think of sharing it with the rest of us?"

"We're sharing it now," said Tom. "This isn't a challenge to your leadership, Joel. We're just a group of people aiming to get out of a jungle. Anyone who wants to come can come."

Joel shook his head, making a show of being wounded by their unexpected treachery, and at first it seemed he wouldn't respond at all, but then he said quietly, "Who else is part of your group?"

Alice, George, Shen, and Barney all put their hands up, and Joel nodded, perhaps the people he would have guessed as being part of it. Lara, Kate, and Emma did too, then Jess from her prone position. Freddie made a weak attempt to raise his own hand, but couldn't, and let it rest on Jess's hair again.

"I see. I was going to suggest putting it to a vote, but since more than half of us are planning to leave..."

"There's nothing to vote anyway," said Tom. "We're going. If you're staying we'll leave half of the food and drinks, and if we make it, we can tell them where you are."

Chloe laughed, a single unpleasant laugh. Her face was red, not with sunburn but with the heat, and her hair was matted with sweat.

"You seriously think we can walk out of this jungle, with snakes and jaguars and who knows what else. And that's before you even get to the river. You'll all die."

"Chloe's right," said Chris.

"Maybe," said Tom.

Chloe became even more outraged. "Maybe! That's all you can say to defend such a stupid plan?"

"This isn't a debate. A group of us are walking out in the morning. Stay or come, your choice."

"It's not a choice, it's ridiculous!"

Tom didn't answer this time, determined not to get into a discussion about it.

Barney was willing, though, and said, "There's something else you should consider—"

Chloe interrupted. "Uh, when we want your opinion we'll ask for it."

Barney was silenced, looking stung. But with a flash of anger, Alice stood and stared directly at Chloe as she said, "Hey! Barney's walked to the wreckage, built the stairs, got the toilets working, helped put up the mosquito netting. What have *you* done?" Chloe tried to answer, her mouth moving but forming no words under Alice's fierce glare. "Exactly. Now if Barney's got anything to say, anything at all, I suggest you listen."

She sat down again, her face set, the fury barely contained. Tom noticed Chris nodding a little to himself, suggesting he'd been on the receiving end of that anger a couple of times in their shared childhood. Barney was blushing, almost as red as the people who'd been working on the bonfire, and appeared disinclined to speak ever again.

But Joel said, "Alice is right, of course, and if we don't listen to each other we won't get anywhere. Barney, everyone's hot and tired, but I want to hear what you were going to say. I guess it was something about the problems of staying here."

Despite everything, Tom felt like shaking Joel's hand for that intervention, and didn't only because he didn't want to embarrass Barney even more. He looked at Alice instead and smiled when he caught her eye. She smiled back, embarrassed herself, and having just seen her in full fury, he felt like he was seeing for the first time that she wasn't just pretty but really beautiful.

Barney cleared his throat. "All I was going to say was, it could be dangerous to leave, I mean, it will be, but I think our chances of surviving more than a few days here are pretty slim. This is a hostile environment, and forget the risk of starving or dying of thirst, forget the dangerous animals, there are parasites and insect-borne diseases, just too many ways of getting sick."

"But it'll be worse in the jungle," said Chloe, sounding afraid now, the fight gone out of her.

Barney looked at her more sympathetically than she deserved and said, "This *is* the jungle. We're in the middle of it. And it's true, we'll be exposed to all those same things after we leave, absolutely, and it's likely to be really difficult terrain, but at least we'll be heading somewhere."

"That's true," said Joel. He glanced up at the bonfire, the smoke still snaking upward but already looking less pronounced against the vast blue of the sky. "But I'm going to keep us together, so if we haven't seen a plane by the end of this afternoon, we'll all head out. Everyone should empty their backpacks of everything but the most essential things. And Barney, you and Shen should be in charge of the supplies, making sure we have everything that's useful."

They both looked at Tom, but he only smiled. They got up then and headed back to the plane, but none of the others seemed in any hurry to empty their backpacks, or to move at all.

CHAPTER 21

Tom followed Shen and Barney into the plane, but noticed they fell silent as he climbed the steps.

Barney said, "It's okay, it's Tom."

"Good." As Tom reached the top, Shen said, "Tom, once you've emptied the things you don't need from your backpack, leave it here and we'll load it up. I think it's better if you have the flare guns and things like that."

"Sure, I'll do it now."

Barney said, "I'm glad they're all coming. The chances of staying alive out here aren't good, and worse with Joel running the show."

Tom nodded, but in truth, he had mixed feelings. Their party, as big as it had already become, had been a fairly cohesive unit and he figured they'd have a pretty good chance of making it out of the jungle in one piece. Now, with nearly double the number and Joel back in the mix, he was less confident.

"Joel's still running the show." He could see both of them ready to object. "It's just not an argument worth having, and as long as we're moving, what does it matter? Let him be the leader, but we follow our own plan."

That seemed to please them, and Tom went off to empty some of the clothes out of his backpack. Alice came in and started doing the same with hers, in silence at first.

Then, without looking up at him, she said, "Do you think I went too far, with Chloe?"

"Not at all." She looked up now and he added, "You were sticking up for someone."

"Actually, I think some of that was guilt. I hardly noticed Barney before this—he was just some geeky little kid."

"I think geeks are pretty cool nowadays."

She smiled, but it waned quickly and she said, "I think Joel still sees himself leading everyone out of here."

"Let him." She looked puzzled, maybe wondering why he was so willing to defer to Joel. "It's like I just said to the boys, as long as he's taking us where we want to go anyway, let him lead."

"I like that." She smiled again. "I'll go and make up with Chloe."

She walked out and Tom took his half-empty backpack to the galley, then followed Alice outside. A lot of them were still sitting exhausted by the fire, but a few were scavenging for wood along the edges of the gouged path up the slope.

Tom joined in, taking it easy in the intense heat, watching everyone else as they drifted about, packing their backpacks with essentials as they'd been told, helping to collect wood. He noticed Chloe speaking to Barney at one point, what appeared to be a friendly conversation.

On the surface of it, things seemed no different from the way they'd been since they arrived, and yet there was something strange and expectant about the atmosphere. Tom couldn't pinpoint it, but it felt like something was wrong, some distortion in the air or in the background noise of the jungle, like a held breath, waiting.

It was late in the afternoon when he heard a puzzled and panicked, "Freddie?"

He turned and saw Freddie kneeling on the ground in the middle of the slope. Jess was standing above him, trying to pull him up by the arm. It was Jess whose voice he'd heard and it occurred to him now that he'd never heard either of them speak.

Freddie started to stand but there was something troubling about his face, flushed red, his expression that of someone who was locked away in some other place. He got to his feet but immediately staggered and fell forward again.

Jess cried out with more anguish, "Freddie!"

Tom dropped the wood he was carrying and started over to them but stopped after just a couple of paces, grateful that other people were nearer and got there first. Very quickly there was a small group surrounding the pair, a chorus of encouraging but increasingly frantic voices, and Jess's in the middle of it, reduced to a series of anguished and garbled cries, her distress so intense that it was difficult to listen to.

Tom picked up the wood again and carried it back to the fire. By the time he turned, they were carrying Freddie back. Mila rushed past, crying silently, and Tom noticed she was limping slightly, which made him think in turn about the number of minor injuries that might slow their progress the next day. She was calling Shen before she got to the plane and he came out, followed by Barney.

As soon as Shen saw the stricken Freddie, he pointed to the lower part of the fuselage, where the cargo had been, and said, "Carry him into the shade."

They heaved him up again, with Jess hanging on to the edge of the group, her tears replaced now by a shock that looked etched in stone. Tom took in Freddie's oddly dumbfounded face, and noticed that he wasn't sweating, that his skin looked waxy but dry.

Shen briefly stopped next to Tom and said, "I'm pretty sure it's heat stroke, serious. The only way to keep him alive is using the water to sponge him down."

Tom understood what he was saying, that their water had already been squandered and become perilously low, that they would need a lot more the next day. But if Shen wanted Tom's permission, there was no question.

"There's a river. We'll find a way."

Shen nodded and said, "Good, but as long as you understand." Tom gave him a quizzical look and Shen added, "I think he'll die anyway." He didn't wait for a response, but headed into the fray, giving instructions for Barney to get water, telling the others to remove Freddie's clothes, to get something to fan the air around him.

Joel was in the thick of it too, sometimes repeating Shen's instructions, telling people to make space or help with one thing or another. Once, he peered out from the shade of the broken fuselage, past Tom and up the hill.

Tom turned in the same direction. The bonfire was still producing the faintest trail of smoke from somewhere within, but it wouldn't last much longer. Tom set off toward it, climbing the slope for the third and, he hoped, last time.

He could smell the bonfire before he reached it, a burnt chemical smell that seemed to cover the upper part of the slope. But he could also see from farther up the slope that the bonfire had been a more ambitious construction than it had seemed from down below.

There were suitcases to make up the structure of it, but layered on top were hundreds of items of clothing that had been found in the luggage. Much of it had burned, but some of the fibers had proved remarkably resilient, with even flashes of color still visible here and there.

Once he was on the ridge he poked at it with his foot, pulled a couple of suitcases about, creating enough disturbance that another billow of smoke rose up, but he saw it had done all the burning it would do. After that climb and in the late afternoon sun, he couldn't even feel any additional heat rising from it.

He looked at the main part of the plane where it lay wrecked and charred, and it had to be his imagination, but it already seemed to be merging with the valley floor. He could no longer see the blue of Charlie's shirt, either, no matter how much he stared. All those deaths, all those lost personalities, absorbed by this jungle and reduced to nothing.

He turned and let his eyes drift across the landscape, his real reason for coming up here, taking in the river, barely visible, the area where Naomi had been killed, the distant low hills and that tempting gap between them. They had no idea what that landscape had in store for them, what trials lay hidden in the undulating terrain between here and the cleft, but at least there were features, a direction in which to travel.

The sky was blue above but off to his left, what he thought was the north, there were clouds piling up on the horizon and although rain would have helped with the water problem, he could only imagine the extra strain it would put on the ramshackle camp below him.

There was no question, they had to leave, and there was only one thing that he could envisage delaying that departure. But even as the thought settled, a wailing scream pierced the air, rising up from below, long and distressing to listen to, and he knew that the obstacle to leaving had removed itself, because the person screaming was Jess.

CHAPTER 22

Tom left the smoldering remains of the bonfire and set off down the slope. If it had worked and attracted the attention of a passing plane in that vast empty sky, then it might have all seemed different.

As he reached the group he could hear lots of them talking in low voices, but Jess's near-hysterical voice rose above them. "No! I won't let you."

A calm, low response, the words just beyond Tom's hearing, then Jess again, her voice straining. "He's not being eaten. If you bury him, it's just—it's worse....No!"

He couldn't see Jess or Freddie, but then he heard Alice say, "Jess, we'll lay him in one of the luggage containers for now. We can seal it shut so nothing can get to him. He'll be okay in there until people come back here to get him."

There was silence in response, but he guessed Jess had yielded to that suggestion, because Joel said, "Then let's carry him to the slope. We'll do this right, Jess."

Tom drifted past, and found Shen and Barney sitting on the makeshift steps at the side of the plane. Shen's T-shirt was soaked with sweat, sticking to his lean frame, his face full of dejection. Barney saw Tom and gave him a helpless shrug.

Shen looked up and said, "For a little while, I thought..." He shook his head, as if thinking back over what had just happened. "But he just died, just like that, no—"

"Was there anything you could've done differently?"

Shen shook his head, clearly thinking through his actions and being too hard on himself. He certainly didn't realize that the rest of them, Tom included, probably wouldn't have even known what was wrong with Freddie, let alone how to attempt treating him.

Barney patted him on the shoulder. "You were really awesome."

"He still died."

Tom thought of Freddie and Jess, another couple of people who'd always been too easy to dismiss in a sort of visual shorthand—that odd-looking couple who were always joined at the hip—and it was strange to think he'd known almost nothing about them, that he'd never really heard either of them speak until Jess had called out on the slope, that he would never hear Freddie's voice now.

Maybe it wasn't Joel's fault, because even without his self-declared leadership, mistakes would have been made and lives probably lost, maybe more than had been lost already. But there was something obscene about the situation in Tom's mind, that they had been granted this amazing chance at survival and yet within one day, three people had died in such preventable ways.

He'd talked the night before about fate, and had genuinely believed that he'd seen it in Naomi's eyes, that it was all there, pre-written. But there had been nothing about Freddie and Jess that might have predicted this, just an insane decision by one person to build a bonfire.

And as he looked at Shen, with the same air about him as a doctor who'd worked heroically to save a doomed patient and failed, he understood that it was up to all of them, that they could blame Joel, or chance or destiny, or they could take control of their own lives.

For a couple of years after the death of Tom's parents, it had been a sort of recurring fantasy of his, thinking through ways in which he might have been there and managed to save them. Then at some point he'd come to accept that the fantasies were pointless because they were dead and he'd been a little kid, powerless to stop it even if he had been there.

Yet he was here now and he wasn't doing anything to save the people he was with. It was easy enough to sit back and blame others for those deaths in one way or another, but Tom was just drifting about like it had nothing at all to do with him, when in fact it did.

True, he'd never been a part of any group, and he doubted he'd be friends with most of them afterward. But Shen and Barney probably didn't feel any more connection with the others than Tom did, and yet they were still doing everything they could to help, to make that difference.

Seeing how much it meant to Shen, that he'd tried to save Freddie and lost him, made Tom feel like less of a person. Whether he'd wanted to be on this trip or not, he was here. He was the little boy he'd once imagined, being in the right place at the right time to save someone. He was here.

He looked at them and said, "I'm not leaving anyone else behind, not if I can help it. I'm sick of blaming Joel."

Still looking dejected, Shen said, "It's the right thing to aim for. I just don't know if we can do it."

"Tom can do it," said Barney.

Shen looked at him and nodded with what looked like unconditional acceptance.

And Tom immediately regretted what he'd said, because he knew that Shen had been right and Barney was wrong. Tom could try to keep everyone alive, and maybe it was the right approach to take, but he also knew that someone else would surely die. It was the nature of this environment. Someone else would die, no matter what Tom tried to do to stop that happening—it was really just a question of who and how and when.

CHAPTER 23

Jess stayed by the luggage container on the slope, remaining there even after darkness fell. There were questions about whether it was safe, but they decided that it was close enough to the fire to protect her from wild animals.

Their decision made little difference anyway because she wouldn't be moved. Nor did she eat, and only took a drink at the third attempt. But her half-presence and the loss of Freddie weighed heavily on the camp through the evening, the mood subdued.

Perhaps people were thinking about the next day too, though no one asked questions or asked if there was anything they needed to do. The bonfire and the hope of rescue seemed long forgotten.

Once again, Alice, George, and Tom took first watch by the

fire, though the novelty had worn off even for them. They were conscious too, of the day that was to follow, and they were all determined that tonight they'd stay only a few hours before waking Chris and Chloe.

Jess was still sitting by the container, but about an hour into their watch she appeared out of the dark like an apparition, moving past the fire without apparently seeing them. She almost could have been sleepwalking.

Alice said, "Are you going to bed, Jess?"

She nodded and drifted toward the stairs at the side of the plane.

Alice looked troubled somehow, perhaps by Jess's expression or her vigil over Freddie's body—or how suddenly she abandoned it.

"You think she's all right?"

George took a deep breath. "I guess so, but it must be tough, losing your boyfriend like that." He turned to face Alice, remembering that Ethan, her ex-boyfriend, was still in the wreckage on the other side of the hill. "Sorry, I didn't mean..."

She smiled dismissively. "Don't, it's not the same. Not even close. I can't imagine what Jess is going through."

As they'd talked, Tom had been listening, one ear trained on the night, and among all the sounds, there was one distinctive noise he hadn't heard—the hollow thumps of Jess climbing the makeshift stairs to the plane.

He reached for his flashlight and stood casually, not wanting to alarm them. "I'll be back in a minute."

"No worries," said George, and turned back to Alice.

Tom was about to climb the stairs himself when he heard the

unmistakable sound of someone walking through the under-growth into the dark of the jungle. It was the same natural path on which they'd found Naomi's shoe, and with a startling car-crash of thoughts, he understood immediately why Jess had finally left the slope.

He thought of going back to tell the other two, but she'd already gone some way and he didn't want to lose her. So he pointed the beam of light into the absorbent darkness of the jungle and followed after her.

He was glad he hadn't hesitated because within seconds the plane and the fire and all the others seemed far off. Just a dozen paces in and the world was reduced to the small pool of light in front of him as it danced across the bright green undergrowth, and then somewhere ahead, the more confused crashing of Jess, walking without the aid of a flashlight.

He wished he'd brought a branch or something to defend himself with, but it was too late now, and he had to hope that the unnatural glare of the flashlight would be enough to afford protection from the jaguar or whatever else was out here. And he tried not to think of how the light might also be attracting the other predators in this jungle, alerting them to something that was worth investigating.

He stopped walking, conscious that he could no longer hear Jess ahead of him. Briefly, the background noise of the jungle seemed to stop too, before flooding back over him. But there was still no sound of Jess.

He walked a little bit farther, halted, listened. For a moment he imagined he'd overtaken her, or worse, that she'd had a change of heart and turned back, leaving him out here on his own. He moved on again and saw something on the path ahead of him, the light picking it out even before he'd reached it—Naomi's sneaker.

This was the place. Naomi had died here, a simple fact that still seemed full of mystery—the person who'd needed to pee, who'd nervously asked if she could join Tom's escape party, her life snuffed out in this spot with a sudden raw violence.

The place where the undergrowth had been briefly flattened was no longer visible, the startlingly white shoe now the only reminder of what had happened here and the person who'd been taken. Yet her death was still here, it seemed, and he felt suddenly exposed, sensing that he was being watched from the darkness.

Still he stood for a second, and then heard the quietest voice, so quiet that he didn't realize at first how close she was. "Leave me alone."

He turned. She was standing just off the path amid the undergrowth, but almost within touching distance. He kept the flashlight low so that he could just barely see her, but the beam didn't dazzle her.

And it was disconcerting that she'd stopped in exactly this spot. Without a light, she couldn't have seen the sneaker on the path, couldn't have known that this was where the attack had happened. And yet perhaps in some subconscious way she had known. Maybe the trace of it, the energy of it, was still here in the atmosphere.

"What are you doing here, Jess?"

"Tom?" Obviously unable to see him in the darkness, she sounded faintly incredulous, and he wondered who she thought might have followed.

"Yeah, it's Tom." She didn't respond. "You want the jaguar to get you, is that it?"

She didn't answer directly, but said, "I'm not coming back. It doesn't...just doesn't..."

He could almost hear the storm raging in her head, the crash of too many shattered thoughts, and Freddie's absence at the heart of it all. He'd envied their intimacy, and maybe this should have been the moment his envy fell away, seeing what that closeness was doing to Jess now, but if anything, it only grew more intense, to see the truth of how much she had loved him.

And it was there in her voice as she said quite clearly, "Please leave me alone."

"Okay." He lowered the flashlight farther but didn't move, his own thoughts racing now, trying to think of a way to persuade her, all the time thinking they could both be attacked at any moment. He said casually, "You might have to wait a few days though."

"What?"

"When a jaguar feeds on something big, like a human, it won't feed again for three or four days. And they're territorial— one jaguar protects its area from others, so, I'm just saying you might have to wait."

There was a pause before her voice came back, barely a whisper, "You're lying."

"No, I'm not." But he was making it up and in truth he had no idea about the hunting habits of jaguars, and he could still feel the hair bristling on the back of his neck with the sense that they were both being watched, even now. "But I want you to come back with me to the fire."

"No. It's...there's..." Once again, the words dried up and fell away, and Tom knew he wasn't cut out for this, because he'd been on the receiving end of enough well-meaning chats in his own life, usually from people who had no idea. In truth, his knowledge of the uselessness of all those words of comfort was the only thing he had.

"Look, Jess, when I was little my parents died."

"I know."

Even that was a revelation, that someone like Jess had known this most basic fact about his life.

"I was too small to understand what people were saying, but it didn't stop them saying it, that I had to be strong for my mom and dad, that it didn't look like it would ever get better but it would, that it was a wound but one day it would just be a scar. And you know what, it was all the biggest load of crap. It doesn't get better. You lost someone you love and that never goes away. It changes who you are, the way you live your life. It never becomes good, it just becomes different."

Briefly he was transported, remembering a book his mom had often read with him when he was little, a book with a rabbit on the cover though he couldn't remember its name or even the story, in the same way that he failed to remember so many of the details from those years. And yet he'd loved that book and cherished even the fractured memory of it now, the memory of being enveloped in warmth, and the soothing sound of his mother's voice. He could feel tears welling in his eyes, though he couldn't remember the last time he'd cried, and suddenly standing there in the jungle he missed both of them more than he had in years.

"That's what they kept telling me today, that I had to be strong, that it was what Freddie would've wanted."

"What Freddie would've wanted is for both of you to walk

out of here. He didn't want to die, but if he'd had to choose, I'm pretty sure he would have chosen for him to die rather than you."

"I would have chosen me."

"I know. But that's why you have to come with me, Jess. I can't make it better, no one can. This is who you are now. And that's all I've got, no words of comfort—I just want you to come back."

She was motionless, seconds creeping past, and then finally she moved toward him. He was about to step back to let her onto the path, but she kept coming and put her arms around him, holding on to him, and was so quiet that it took a moment for him to realize that she was crying.

He should have felt better, he supposed, because he had persuaded her to live, for now, or allowed her to persuade herself, but he felt unaccountably low instead. Perhaps it was only because it had brought his own grief to the surface, and at some level, he'd never thought himself worthy of it—how could he be, and how could it be real grief, when most of the time he hardly remembered them at all?

CHAPTER 24

They walked back along the path in silence, and when they reached the plane she followed him back to the fire.

As he rounded the corner, Alice looked up. "There you are. We thought you felt sick or . . ." She stopped as she saw Jess. "Oh, hi, Jess."

"Hello." Tom sat down but Jess remained standing for a moment and said, "I got lost. Tom found me." She looked down at the fire. "Do you mind if I stay here for a while? I don't want to go inside."

"Of course not," said Alice. Jess sat across from them, on one of the piles of luggage. Tom had noticed out in the jungle how small she was—something he'd never seen before because Freddie had been exactly the same height as her—but sitting there now, she looked tiny. "Would you like something to eat and drink?"

She shook her head. "I might just lie down for a while if that's okay." She didn't wait for an answer, but curled up on the luggage.

Alice and George both looked at Tom, their expressions clear, wanting the full story. He smiled in response and shrugged, and then Alice mimicked his shrug, which made him laugh. When he looked again, Jess was already asleep, no doubt dragged down into the depths by the exhaustion of the day.

He turned back to the others then and said quietly, "She went out into the jungle. I think she had some idea the jaguar might take her."

"Oh God." Alice looked curious. "How did you know?"

"I didn't hear her going up the steps, so I went to check on her. Then I heard her crashing through the bushes. She was making so much noise, she probably scared the jaguar off."

George said, "Wow. You should've come and got me."

"Didn't have time. I didn't want her to go too far. Anyway, it turned out okay."

Alice said, "And you talked her into coming back." He nodded, hoping she didn't press him for the details, knowing that he didn't want to talk about those things again. But Alice nodded too, as if she knew exactly what that conversation might have been like. "I'm impressed. You should be proud. Anything could've happened to her." He smiled, and she said, "I'm serious, Tom."

"I know. Thanks." He glanced back across at Jess, who was sleeping peacefully. "Maybe it's stupid, but I just...had a moment, I guess, and decided if it's in my power at all, I'm not letting anyone else die."

George looked confused. "You haven't let anyone die. I mean, it's all so random anyway, like me leaving the football team."

Alice turned to him now and said, "Why *did* you leave? I remember Ethan saying no one could understand it."

"Yeah, they all tried changing my mind. And it made them mad that I wouldn't give them a reason they could make sense of."

"Maybe because you were so good."

"I *was* pretty good." He laughed, not taking himself too seriously, but then grew somber. "No disrespect to those guys, but I've got other dreams, you know—the athletic black kid doesn't always have to be on the football team."

Alice put a comforting hand on George's shoulder and Tom said, "Well, I'm glad you left."

"Thanks, I appreciate that. But I meant what I said just now. The people who've died since the crash, they might have died anyway, but if it's anyone's fault, it's Joel's."

Before Tom could reply, a low rumbling sounded across the sky, a long way off. They all stopped and looked up, because at first, it could easily have been a plane, but they faced each other again as they recognized it for what it was. Tom thought of the clouds he'd seen stacked up on the horizon and wondered if it was part of the same weather system, and if it was heading their way.

Finally, he said, "Maybe, but all the same, I'm not letting anyone else die, not if I can help it."

"You're right," said Alice. "It's what we should aim for, isn't it? Getting everyone out alive. Including us, obviously."

She laughed at the final comment, and yet it made Tom uneasy. He'd once again slipped into thinking it was only the others who were in danger, not him, not Alice or the other people he'd grown closer to. But now that she'd inadvertently planted the thought in his mind, he imagined the possibility of something happening to her, and was surprised by how terrifying he found that prospect.

Another rumble of thunder tremored across that distant sky, perhaps sounding closer, but still a long way off, and George raised his eyes to where the sky was still clear and full of stars above them, and said, "I would not want to be in this camp if it rains."

Tom understood what he meant—the kids were barely holding it together after two days of dry weather. It would probably only take some rain or some other random setback for it to descend into complete chaos. Tom looked up at the stars too, dazzlingly close and clear. But as beautiful as it was in that moment, he felt morning couldn't come soon enough.

CHAPTER 25

When, after three hours, they were finally faced with the prospect of going in and joining the others in the confines of the plane, they decided against it. Instead, they built up the fire and followed Jess's lead, bedding down on the piles of remaining luggage.

And with the crackling of the fire and the faint rumbling of thunder, Tom fell into a deep sleep, and woke when it was already light. He could hear movement and looked up to see Jess using the remaining pieces of wood to build up the fire again.

George and Alice were still sleeping and the cabin above them was quiet. Maybe it was just the exhaustion of the previous day or the fact that they'd become used to the racket of the jungle at daybreak, its constant noise already part of their daily rhythm.

"Hello," said Jess when she saw that he was awake.

"Hello." He sat up. "How long has it been light?"

"Only about ten minutes." She used the branch she was holding to poke at the fire. "Thank you. For last night."

He nodded. "You know we're leaving today?"

"Yeah." She looked up the slope to the container that held Freddie's body. "I might go and say good-bye now."

"Want me to come?"

"I'll be okay."

She walked away from the fire, still carrying the branch, and for a moment he wondered whether he should have told her not to try opening the container, but he didn't have to worry. When she got there, she only leaned against it with her head bowed, as though deep in prayer. Yes, she would be okay, but he'd told her the truth out there in the jungle dark—she would never again be the person she'd been two days ago.

All at once, people started to stir inside the plane. Alice awoke and sat up as Shen and Barney came around the corner.

Alice said, "Morning. Is it late?"

"No, only just light." He saw her glance in Jess's direction. "She's fine. She's just saying good-bye."

Alice shook her head, apparently left speechless by the enormity of what Jess was going through, but then she sighed and said, "I need to pee." She got up, exchanged greetings with Shen and Barney, and walked to the plane.

Somehow, Shen had managed to save and rearrange the food in such a way that there was something to cook and they all ate breakfast. The mood was better as they sat there eating too, a nervous energy but upbeat, perhaps because they knew there would be something to do today, and they would be heading somewhere, even if no one was sure where exactly.

The preparations for leaving took about an hour. Joel was in charge, making sure everyone had the right things in their backpacks, though he still needed key reminders from Alice—that waterproof gear shouldn't be left behind, that people should be wearing their boots rather than carrying them.

Joel also didn't seem to notice that there was a separate organization going on, as Shen and Barney worked methodically through the camp, taking down the mosquito netting, stowing key supplies in certain people's backpacks, trusting only Alice and George with the alcohol and first aid equipment, but distributing the food and drink items across the group.

Tom had been rooting around in his backpack that morning, for what he imagined might be his last change of clothes before they reached civilization, and hadn't noticed anything.

But Shen took him to one side as the group were getting themselves together and said, "There are a couple of lighters in the side pouch, and one of the knives. Barney's got the other one. Both flare guns and spare flares are under your clothes. Me and Barney have got some of the first aid supplies, the rest of it's with Alice and George, so is the alcohol. The boats have equipment stowed with them."

Tom nodded, but could see that Shen wanted more, some sort of approval, so he said, "I keep telling you, I'm not the leader. But I won't let you down."

"I know it." He smiled. "If I didn't, I would have kept one of the flare guns for myself."

Tom laughed, but it was cut short by Joel's voice rising up, saying, "Okay, it'll take four people to carry the cases with the two boats in. We'll take it in turns, but how about George and

Chris, Sandeep and Nick for the first section?" It wasn't a question, and they all nodded. "Now, we need to look at a route. Shen, you said the river's over there, right?"

"Actually, Tom said that, but yes. However, we're aiming for a break in the hills in that direction, so even though it means walking farther before reaching the river, that's the route we should take."

Joel smiled at him, a patronizing smile even after all that had happened, and said, "That's great, but we know there's a natural path in that direction."

Tom noticed Kate looking at him with horror, because, of course, it was the path on which Naomi had been taken by the jaguar, the path on which they would once again have to pass her abandoned sneaker. Only Tom knew that it was also the path on which Jess had tried to walk to her death the night before.

Tom said, "Actually, there's a better natural path in the direction Shen's talking about. There's a fallen tree across it at one point, but otherwise it's more open."

With an expression that suggested it was against his better judgment, Joel said, "Okay, so we'll head in that direction and see how we get on."

People started to put on their backpacks, but Barney said, "Oh, I've managed to find some poles if anyone wants them."

He walked over to the fuselage and picked up a bundle of poles, what looked like aluminum tubing from a tent frame. Tom couldn't help but be impressed, that he'd found them and thought to use them.

Not everyone saw it that way, and Nick said, "What good are they?"

The implied criticism seemed to wash over Barney and he just shrugged. "None at all really, I mean, unless you want something to knock branches out of the way, or cobwebs, things like that." He didn't need to say anything else—there was an immediate rush to relieve him of the poles, and it was funny to see Chloe in particular telling him he was "an absolute saint."

Barney picked up another pole of his own, then, smiling at Tom as he did so—it looked like he'd also found some heavy duty gaffer tape and had attached the other knife to the end of it, creating what looked more like a fishing spear than anything else. Standing there holding it, he really did look like a character from *Lord of the Flies,* and Tom wondered if anyone outside of AP Lit knew how *that* story ended.

CHAPTER 26

They set off in a long single file, like one of those old-fashioned expeditions to find the source of some river, usually carried out by pasty Europeans who were clueless about the environment. In that regard, they were just like one of those old Victorian expeditions—lost, poorly equipped, with no realistic idea of how they'd survive for more than a couple of days.

Joel was at the head of the column, but he'd conspired to make sure Shen was right behind him. He wasn't willing to relinquish his role as leader, but he'd finally figured out that Shen had all kinds of knowledge that might prove handy in the jungle—it was probably asking too much to expect him to see the same value in some of the others, like Kate and Barney.

Tom was at the very back, with George and Chris immediately ahead of him carrying the case with one of the boats in it. Just before entering the path, Tom looked back at the camp, at the torn tail-section, the fire still burning low, even though they'd tried to put it out, at the discarded items and the luggage containers still dotted up the slope, one of them containing Freddie's body.

He looked all the way up the slope then, to the forlorn remains of the previous day's bonfire, to the ridge that had first decided who died and who lived. His amazement remained undiminished—not a single one of them should have walked off that plane, and that was all the more reason that every one of them left should make it all the way home.

He turned and followed them into dappled and humid shade, listening to the conversations rattling back and forth along the line in front of him. They looked like an exploratory expedition, but they sounded just like a school field trip.

Progress seemed to be slow too, which he guessed was for the better, rather than have people collapsing with the heat. But a short while later the column stopped altogether.

Chris lowered the front of the carrying case to the floor, so George followed suit with the back and said, "What's going on?"

"I think the path's blocked."

George stepped to the side and looked ahead. "I think it's the tree. Tom said there was a fallen tree on the path."

Chris nodded but didn't seem to be listening and went a little way ahead to talk to Chloe.

George turned to Tom. "How big is this tree?"

Tom held his hand up, a little above waist-height. "I got up on it pretty easily." So had the jaguar, but he didn't share that. "Some of them might need a hand, especially with backpacks on."

George nodded but his concern was visible, that they could be slowed down this much by a fairly minor obstacle. Tom thought the same, wondering what lay ahead of them and whether they'd get better at dealing with it.

It was minutes before Chris came crashing back toward them, widening the path as he walked.

"Looks like we're on the move. I think Joel was just being careful—snakes, that kind of thing."

He reached for the handle of the case and the line edged forward, picking up speed, and when they got to the tree, Chris and George heaved the boat over with such ease that it was hard to guess what the problem had been.

Tom climbed up after them and looked along the trunk to the spot where he'd seen the jaguar, and he stared beyond, into the odd aquatic light beneath the canopy, thinking he might see it there, that if he stared long enough it might appear like things did in those books of magic pictures.

But there was nothing to see, so he jumped off the far side of the fallen trunk and followed the others. That seemed to be the nature of the jungle anyway, that most of its secrets were hidden from them, that Tom and the others were both there and not there, and every trace of their presence these last two days would soon be lost.

They walked on for over an hour with no further stops, their pace slow and steady. It wasn't difficult walking but the heat and the humidity and the relentless harassment from insects made it uncomfortable. It wasn't long before the conversations started to dry up, with only occasional strings of words drifting back along the line.

As they reached the hour mark, Chris said, "What if this path doesn't go to the river?"

George answered, "These paths are made by animals, so

chances are they'll lead to water. But we're heading in the right direction anyway."

"You think?"

"Yeah, and Shen knows what he's doing."

"Joel's leading," said Chris, and it sounded like he was aiming to set George straight, but in Tom's mind it also sounded like a word of caution, that they couldn't rely on Shen's good sense alone, because Shen wasn't in charge.

George didn't reply and they walked on in silence before the column started to slow again and then word came back along the line. They were stopping for a break up ahead, in a small clearing. It became obvious it wasn't much of a clearing, though, because there was some congestion, the people ahead slowing to a crawl as they waited to get into the resting place.

When Tom finally reached it, they looked like the stragglers of a defeated army, sitting around on a couple of boulders or on their backpacks. Chris dropped his end of the carrying case and immediately sat on it.

There was a small creek that had been running alongside their path but turned here and headed in the direction of the river. It had obviously flooded enough in the past that the vegetation had been pegged back from its banks. A few of the natural paths that threaded the jungle seemed to converge on this spot too.

Tom looked upstream, figuring it probably flowed close to the place where Naomi had been taken, then presumably up the side of the same hills on which their plane had broken its spine. There was barely a trickle of lifeless water in the bottom now, but looking at the steep and eroded banks was enough to show how fiercely it flowed during the rains.

Alice approached him and said, "Shen wants you and me to go with them to follow the creek to the river and check it out."

"Sure."

They stepped through the maze of resting bodies to where Shen and Joel were standing looking over the creek, Shen explaining something, Joel displaying the superficial level of interest Tom had seen in footage of politicians being shown around factories.

Shen turned as they reached them. "Ready?"

Joel was quick to add, "You don't need to come if you want to rest. I'm sure Shen and me can recon the river."

"I'm sure you could," said Alice.

The four of them followed the creek bed through a couple of bends, the air seeming to become more febrile, pulsing with life, the closer they got to the river itself. And when the strip of sleek muddy water appeared up ahead, there was nothing inviting or refreshing about it.

Shen climbed up the bank of the creek, onto a small point formed by its convergence with the river. They followed him, but it was instantly clear that they wouldn't be getting the boats on this river.

It was just about wide enough, but only a narrow channel looked deep enough, and it was strewn with rocks. A short distance downstream a tree had fallen across it too.

Tom checked his watch, estimating they probably had six or seven hours of daylight left. If there were no major obstacles, there was a chance they could make the distant low hills by the end of the day, but it was more likely they'd have to make camp somewhere tonight, rather than risk walking in darkness.

It was Joel who broke the silence, saying, "I always thought this boat plan of yours was crazy."

He'd addressed the comment to Tom, but Tom only looked back at him, and it was Shen who said, "We always knew the river might not be navigable."

"So what do you propose now?"

"We follow it until it is, then we launch the boats." He pointed downstream. "We're heading for a gap in the hills. Beyond them, there's a better chance."

Joel shook his head doubtfully, and looked at the sluggish water in front of them. "I have to say I'm not convinced, looking at this."

With remarkable good humor, Shen said, "There's one thing we can say with absolute certainty, Joel—rivers don't get narrower. So there's no alternative. It might take us a day to reach open water, it might take two, but we head downriver."

Joel nodded grudgingly, but looked at the banks with concern. "Could be awkward walking along here."

Alice did a double take. "Shen, didn't Barney say something about avoiding the river until we have to?"

"Of course. It's a focal point for predators, more risk of parasites, that kind of thing."

"That's what I was thinking," said Joel. "So we'll follow the river as far as we can, but from a distance." He turned to Tom. "Do you have anything to add, Tom?"

Tom shook his head and started back the way they'd come. He didn't care how they came to their decisions, or that Joel imagined himself as the leader of this escape, as long as they came to the right decisions, and kept heading in the right direction.

CHAPTER 27

Everyone was allowed to eat and drink. It wasn't enough, but they were already so exhausted by the heat that there were no complaints. Joel stood in the middle of the group and explained the problems they'd encountered at the river and what the plan would be from here.

Then he said, "We should swap the boat-carrying teams now, I think."

A murmur went through the camp, a few people volunteering, but George chipped in, saying, "I can do another hour, no worries."

"Me too," said Chris, and the other two agreed.

"That's appreciated," said Joel. "Okay, so let's get ourselves together and get on the move."

With an effort, people started to get to their feet. Chloe

seemed to stagger and sat back down again, laughing in confusion and shaking her head.

Barney was standing nearby and said, "Are you okay?"

She looked up and smiled uncertainly, a look that made Tom think of Freddie kneeling in a stupor on the slope.

But she climbed to her feet now and said, "I stood up too quickly. I'm all right, though."

Barney nodded, but looked at her closely, a look of concern on his face, and finally he smiled and said, "Would you like me to walk with you for the next stretch?"

"Would you mind?"

"Not at all. Let's take some of the drinks and things from your pack and put them in mine."

Tom smiled as he looked on. A casual observer might have thought Barney had a romantic interest in Chloe, but Tom already knew him well enough to know he'd have done the same for anyone. It was an even more impressive act of kindness in the light of the way Chloe had spoken to him just the day before.

Slowly, the column peeled away along the path, following Joel and Shen as they had before. For the most part, people kept the same position they'd had on the first leg, so that in the end, the clearing had only Chris, George, Tom, and Alice, the only person to break ranks.

"I think I'll walk at the back with you. Too much chatter farther up the line."

Tom said, "Then you've come to the right place—we don't do chatter."

She smiled and they set off. They didn't talk much, either, even when the path was open enough to walk side by side. The column also became quieter but progress was faster than it had been before.

They walked through an area that was deeply dappled in the shade of the canopy, and it was only when they emerged into a more open stretch that Tom saw the murkiness hadn't been caused by the trees alone. The sky had shifted away from blue to a hazy reddish orange.

Chris called back, saying, "I didn't think we'd been walking that long."

"We haven't," said George. "It's not the sun going down, it's something in the atmosphere."

Alice said, "Might be a fire from forest clearance."

Chris looked up into the sunset hue of the sky. "Could be a volcanic eruption. That'd be just our luck."

Tom turned to Alice. "I'd count surviving a plane crash *and* a volcano as pretty lucky, wouldn't you?"

"Pretty lucky, yeah, unless we're all killed in a tsunami."

Chris said, "You shouldn't joke about things like that—I had a dream that I was caught in a tsunami."

"Christian," she said in admonishment, though she was smiling, a clear affection still lingering from their shared childhood. Seeing her expression produced a pang of loneliness in Tom that he couldn't quite narrow down to specifics.

The sky continued to deepen as they walked, an orange mist hanging above them and, now and then, a faint acrid edge to it, suggestive of burning. Even from his place at the back, Tom could hear people talking about it, speculating, because burning still allowed for a lot of different possibilities.

Tom thought Alice was probably right, that it was the result of forest clearance, maybe hundreds of miles away, but there was definitely something eerie about it too. Even the jungle itself seemed to become more hushed as the ceiling of mist sank lower and wrapped itself around the treetops.

They stopped for a second time, but there were no clearings so they all sat where they were on the path. Drinks moved up and down the line, but no food this time.

Chris was sitting high on the boat's carrying case, so everyone looked up in his direction when he said, "You know, you'll probably all shout me down because that's what you do, even though I was right about the plane." There was a murmur in response, and he laughed. "Okay, I made up the stuff about the plane. But what if the plane didn't crash?"

Oscar called, "What!"

"Bear with me." Chris was showing a level of patience that suggested he was being serious for once. "Obviously the plane crashed. What I mean is, looking at this mist, maybe it's not just us, maybe something big happened, you know, like a meteor strike or a nuclear war or something, and our plane got thrown off course and we ended up here. But maybe it's not just us. For all we know, that's why no one came looking for us, because there's no one left out there."

Everyone was quiet in response, the last phrase left hanging there, because the way the world looked right now, it was all too believable that they would find it changed beyond recognition when they did get out.

It was Barney who finally broke the silence. "It's possible, of course, but the way the plane crashed suggests something much simpler. I mean—"

"But it's possible," said Chris, clinging to his theory.

"Possible. But highly unlikely."

The murmuring started again and Chris said, "You hear that? He's like a scientist, and he thinks I'm onto something."

Tom stood up and said, "Only one way to find out." He pointed at the boat. "I'll carry for a while."

"Me too," said Alice.

George did a double take. "Are you sure? We can get one of…"

"The boys?" She smiled. "If it gets too heavy, I'll let you know."

Slowly, they set off again, but they hadn't walked far before another halt was called. Lara had been bitten by something during the last rest and within twenty minutes her face had swollen on one side. Both Shen and Barney looked at it and put something on the bite, but Lara insisted she was fine and they set off again.

A little while later, up near the front, Nick lurched from the path and vomited violently into the undergrowth, and it seemed they'd have to stop again, but after a minute or two he was able to go on. Tom noticed too, that Mila, whom he'd seen limping the day before, was now using one of Barney's poles as a walking stick.

The whole column appeared to be weakening with every step, but they were moving in the right direction. They walked into deeper jungle, a ragged path climbing steadily uphill. Despite being bitten and harassed by insects, often unseen until they struck, despite the clinging and oppressive humidity, the constant whirring and buzzing of the landscape, the climb seemed to offer promise.

But then the column started once again to stagger to a halt. Tom was carrying the boat with Chris now, George and Alice bringing up the rear behind him.

As they slowed, George said, "We can't keep stopping like this."

Alice answered him, "I'm not sure we'll make the river before nightfall anyway, so I guess it's better to keep stopping if people are sick or tired, just to be safe, you know."

Unspoken, but there all the same, was the suggestion that they didn't want another needless death like Freddie's. This time, though, no one seemed to be ill. As they began to bunch up, it became clear they'd reached a natural obstacle.

Tom and Chris put the boat case down. Others had once again collapsed onto their backpacks, taking no interest in what lay ahead but flopping down lifelessly, some of them not even bothering to slap away the insects that landed constantly on their exposed skin.

Chloe looked sick from the heat and Chris went over to sit with her. George and Alice walked up to find out what was happening and Tom followed behind, to a point where the tree canopy seemed to thin out—though with the burnt orange sky, it wasn't much lighter there.

Almost immediately Tom saw the problem. A huge ravine cut through the jungle in front of them. He was amazed it hadn't been visible from their vantage point above the plane.

Where they were standing was about ten feet higher than the far side, but even that was probably forty or fifty feet above the bottom, and the two sides were at least thirty feet apart. The rocky bed far below was dry, though once again, the steep banks showed signs of the water that poured down here when the rains came. As it was, it looked like a fissure, as if the earth had been ripped apart.

Tom saw Joel and Shen, and made his way toward them.

Shen said, "Tom, help me out here. I think we should scout a place where we can get down and back up the other side."

The way the banks were overhanging in places, almost hollowed out, there was a good chance they'd collapsed here and there, offering a way down, but finding an entry point would be another thing.

"What's the alternative?"

Shen pointed over his shoulder, past Joel. A tree had fallen to form a natural downward sloping bridge to the other side. It seemed precariously balanced, but it was obviously Joel's choice.

Joel ignored Tom. "Shen, bro, we're running out of time, and people are too tired to be climbing down there and back out again. We've got a rope, so we'll tie it on this side. I'll carry it across to make sure the tree's stable and tie it over there as a guide. It's the only way."

Tom had to accept Joel's reasoning—they were in no shape as a group to get down into that ravine and back, and if he'd been alone he would have crossed the fallen tree without a second thought. But he wasn't alone, and the thought of trying to get everyone across it filled him with foreboding, especially when he thought of the kids who had sprains or were sick and suffering from the heat and hunger. It was at least a forty-foot drop, and if someone fell, the best they could hope for out here was that it would be a sudden death.

CHAPTER 28

It was another half hour before the group was assembled near the base of the tree, muscular roots twisting up into the air and out in all directions. And now that they were standing beside it, the challenge looked more intimidating: the tree sloped down to the other side of the ravine at more of an angle than they'd at first realized, and although the trunk was four or five feet across in diameter, the narrow path they'd have to take along the top of it looked hazardous.

It took Joel a couple of attempts to climb up onto it, but he looked unfazed when he turned to face them then and said, "See the foothold there, that's how you need to climb up—it's not hard once you know how."

Tom glanced at the people standing there, not convinced some of them would find it all that easy. Chloe in particular looked slightly dazed and he wondered if she'd picked up some kind of bug.

Joel tied one end of the rope to a huge, gnarled root, then set off along the trunk. He seemed to mask his own trepidation pretty well, though Tom could see how fiercely Joel was gripping the rope. It was also impossible not to notice that small clods of earth fell from the far edge of the ravine as Joel got nearer, dirt and stones clattering down into the void below.

Joel ran out of rope and tied it to one of the broken branches on the fallen tree itself before hopping the final couple of steps onto the other side. He jumped down, and as he landed he set off another small but noticeable landslide.

Mila, leaning heavily on her metal pole, stared down at the drop below them and said almost to herself, "I'm not sure I like the way the edge keeps crumbling like that."

Chris started to reply but the words never quite formed before Joel called over to them. "Okay, everyone, it's completely solid, and believe me, once you're on the tree, it's so wide, you don't even notice how high up you are." There was a murmur in response, what sounded like nerves rather than skepticism. "Shen, you come across first, then Nick and Sandeep with the first boat."

Any thought of how unsafe this bridge might be were cast aside amidst a flurry of organization. Shen started across immediately, and then Nick and Sandeep heaved the boat up onto the trunk and set off after him, gripping the guide rope and walking in baby steps to cope with the downward gradient and the weight of the case they carried between them.

Tom ignored the babble of organization and watched the far

side where the top of the tree rested, uneasy that the chunks of dirt continued to fall with every step Nick and Sandeep took. The whole side of the gorge seemed unstable.

Kate and Emma crossed with ease, their steps in sync. Chloe went over next, with Chris behind her, guiding her, but when she reached the end of the rope, even with only a couple of steps left to make, she froze and Chris didn't have enough room to get around her. Quickly Kate climbed back up and took hold of Chloe's hands, leading her the rest of the way.

Alice came over and said, "I'm taking the second boat with George. But we'll wait until the end, just because of the extra weight—George doesn't like how the side's giving way over there."

"Okay. I'll come over last. Once you two are clear I'll untie the rope and bring it with me."

She appeared troubled by that, and seemed to search for the right thing to say before settling on, "We have more rope. You could leave it so you'll have something to hang on to."

He smiled, touched that she was concerned, and said, "I'll be okay—it'll still be tied at the other end."

She nodded and was about to speak again when a shout came from the other side.

Oscar and Lara were on the tree, and he was screaming, "Hold on!" as a chunk of the opposite lip of the ravine crashed away in a small explosion of dirt and debris and the top of the tree pounded down into the newly formed gap.

Oscar and Lara were thrown off their feet by the impact but somehow managed to stay on the tree trunk, holding tight to the guide rope. Lara let out a small yelp of pain as she rubbed at her hip.

There was a small ripple of concerned comments from the

people around Tom, but then Joel's voice sounded, "Okay, you're okay, just keep coming along the tree—we've got you." Although Tom and the others could hear him, Joel raised his voice an extra notch as he called over to them. "The rest of you stay there for now. We'll check how stable it is."

George raised his eyebrows and said, "I think we already know."

They watched in silence as Oscar walked the final few steps, then Lara, limping slightly, and there were audible sighs of relief as the two of them jumped down off the tree. But there were still five of them on this side—Barney, Jess, George and Alice with the boat, and Tom.

Joel studied the ground, talking to Shen, who shook his head and looked more than once across at Barney, as if hoping for guidance. Joel kicked at the earth on the lip of the ravine, and when more debris tumbled away, he pushed at the trunk of the tree as if trying to prove how solid it was.

Tom heard Barney say, "Jess?"

He turned and saw that she'd climbed up onto the tree.

She smiled at Barney, then at Tom, a smile he understood and mistrusted all at once, and she said, "What Joel's doing won't tell us anything. I'm the lightest."

And with that she walked down the fallen trunk, hardly holding on to the guide rope at all. Halfway across she stopped and turned to look back at them, and Tom felt an instant sinking fear in his gut, that she was about to throw herself into the void. But then she shrugged, as though she'd only been trying to show them how easy it was, and continued on her way. More earth fell away as she neared the end, though the tree didn't move.

Joel didn't even notice her approach until the last few seconds and jumped back in shock, but then, as if it had been his idea, he shouted, "Great, we can do this. Barney, you're up next."

Barney crossed, and this time there was no further collapse. Tom helped George and Alice lift the boat up onto the trunk, then climbed up behind them and stood where the rope was tied to the upturned root.

He said, "As soon as you're across with the boat I'll untie the rope and follow."

The two of them set off, forced into the same baby steps the others had used carrying the boat case, trying to halt their downward momentum along the sloping trunk. The others followed every movement. The far side looked stable now, and yet still he sensed something was wrong.

He could feel some sort of movement in the trunk beneath his feet, and at first he thought it might be the vibration of George and Alice's steps, but it was more of a straining, like a rope creaking as it stretches to breaking point.

He knew George and Alice could feel it now too, because they were talking to each other, short hurried instructions, and they were picking up their pace over the second half of the crossing, and Joel was calling out, "Don't rush, guys—you've got this," but they ignored him and rushed on anyway, and Tom could feel it, the tension building beneath him, and then it exploded.

He felt himself lifting even as he heard the creak, like something splitting open. He vaulted clear as the tree shifted beneath him, and he pounded hard into the dirt, the impact made worse by his heavy backpack. He felt the air whoosh past him, heard a scream from the other side, a crash, and turned to look.

A whole chunk of the ravine's edge had just broken free and the tree tumbled into the chasm, the upturned roots appearing to launch skyward before crashing away, dust and debris filling the air. George and Alice were in the air too, and for a second Tom couldn't tell if they'd jumped or had been thrown, if they'd reach the other side or fall into the void.

Then they landed just past the edge, still holding the boat case between them and he knew they'd jumped, but the relief was short-lived. George was behind and as his feet hit the ground it crumbled beneath him and he tumbled backward, taking the boat case with him.

Alice screamed as she got pulled off her feet, but she was still holding the other strap, even though the combined weight of George and the case looked in danger of pulling her over the edge too. George was flailing below, colliding with the side of the ravine, holding on to the strap with one hand and struggling to steady himself enough to reach up with the other.

There was another jolt and George dropped another foot and Alice got dragged right to the edge, but still she gripped the strap, refusing to let go.

It was incredible that Alice was holding on at all, but then she screamed, "Somebody help me!"

A couple of people recovered from their shock and ran over, Chris responding quickest, grabbing hold of the handle with her and starting to haul it up. George's body crashed against the side again, setting off more small landslides, but he held on and as soon as he was close to the top, Oscar leaned over and took hold of his arm and they heaved both George and the boat case over the edge and scrambled away from any further possible collapse.

There were shouts of triumph now, and Tom found himself joining in, laughing with relief, because George had come so close to being killed, but he was okay. Tom glanced down at the tree, now lying wedged far below, but as he raised his eyes again, the jubilation on the far side fell away into silence and the others stared back at him, and Tom was glad he couldn't see all their expressions clearly from here.

Alice had been hugging George, but almost in response to the silence, she turned, saw Tom, and stepped forward, perilously close to the edge.

"We'll wait here!" It wasn't a suggestion, more as if she were stating an obvious truth. "You have to find a way down and across. If you can get down, we'll throw a rope down to you."

He looked down at the tree again, trying to see the rope they'd already lost, then back at the bedraggled group. Joel had been right—they'd have struggled to get down into that chasm. But it wouldn't be any easier for Tom, and they didn't have time to waste.

He called to them, "You can't wait. You need to carry on toward the river—" She was already shaking her head. "You have to move on! I'll be quick on my own. I'll find my way across and I'll catch up."

George stepped next to Alice, rubbing his hand as he shouted, "So a few of us can wait here for you and the rest can head on. We'll all catch up with them together."

It was tempting, but Tom knew it was the wrong choice. He'd laughed at their insistence on sticking together by the plane, but out here it was vital, because it was going to be tough enough getting through the jungle anyway without splintering into small groups. So he had to find a way of persuading George and Alice to leave him.

"I don't want you to wait. If you wait there I have to find my way back to you. If I'm on my own I can make directly for the river. You have to trust me on this—it's the only way. I'm better on my own."

Tom couldn't even see Joel but he heard him say, "Tom's right. We have to move on, and I'm sure if anyone can catch up with us, it's him." The words were hollow, meaningless, laced with something that sounded almost like satisfaction. He stepped through the group now and stood alongside Alice and George. "Is there anything we can do for you, bro?"

"You could stop calling me *bro,* but other than that, I'm good."

Joel feigned a smile, then turned away. His voice was almost the only thing audible above the jungle whirr as he organized and prepared the group for moving on.

As they started to head off, Kate came back to the edge and called, "Don't walk after dark, even if you think we're close. Better to build a fire and get to us in the morning." He nodded, but she looked troubled even as she walked away to join Emma.

Shen came back and cupped his hands over his mouth as a megaphone. "Head upstream. It's the opposite direction to us, and counterintuitive, but when I think of the landscape, I think you'll have a better chance of finding a way across. And it'll be safer."

Tom didn't want to think about what he might have meant by that final statement, so he said only, "I'll do that. Thanks, Shen."

George raised his hand in a wave and Tom responded

likewise. Then only Alice was left as the group traipsed slowly into the trees behind her.

"I'll be okay," he called, before she could say anything else.

She shook her head, and remained silent for a few more seconds before saying, "Promise me."

"I'll be okay, I promise. Now go." He couldn't say any more, finding himself slightly overcome. And he needed her to go, but felt a pang of loss when she finally turned and followed after the others.

Within seconds they'd disappeared into the depths of green. Still, Tom stood for another few minutes as their voices came back to him in ripples, and then there was silence but for the jungle, and he was alone. It was more than that—he'd spent half of his life alone, had shunned the company of his classmates, but this was different—it wasn't that he was alone, but that for the first time in his life, instantly, he felt lonely.

It was ironic, that a handful of those kids thought they needed *him*—to make decisions, to challenge Joel, to be a leader—but right now it felt like he needed them more. He wanted to be able to work on a plan with Shen or Barney, to have George and Alice to talk to, Jess to look out for.

He looked up at the thick orange sky clinging to the treetops, at the drop below him, at the jungle behind. For a moment, he felt overwhelmed, fearful without being sure what it was he feared, apart from that very same isolation he'd always reveled in. But it lasted only a moment, because he had no room for self-pity—he had made a promise, and he intended to keep it.

CHAPTER 29

Walking along the edge of the ravine was an impossibility. In places the vegetation grew right up to the lip and there was no way of knowing how stable the ground would be beneath it. So Tom had no choice but to turn back along the path they'd walked to get there.

He kept searching for paths heading off to the right, but the jungle seemed to be conspiring to send him back the way he'd come. They'd walked for many hours from the crash site, but Tom started to have an irrational fear that he'd end up back there, in the empty camp, with only Freddie's body in a luggage container and the other dead beyond the ridge for company.

The sky seemed to be getting darker, but he checked his watch and figured he still had two or three hours of daylight left. Those hours weren't much use, though, if he kept moving in the wrong direction and away from the others.

Briefly, his thoughts skipped to the rest of them, to Kate and Shen offering advice, George and Alice reluctantly leaving him behind. But he didn't want to think of them because it only reminded him how alone he was out here now. He probably wasn't in much more danger than he had been as part of the group, and yet it felt more dangerous.

He saw something that looked like a trail, or almost a trail, that would take him in the right direction. The vegetation had grown over the path, so it was harder to see what was underfoot, but he set off along it, making as much noise as he could with his steps, hoping to warn off anything that might bite him if disturbed or stepped on.

Twenty minutes later the path seemed to end in a dense thicket of a lush and knotted plant that he knew instinctively to avoid. He stopped, sipped at his water, swiped at an insect that landed on his neck, looked around, and finally edged around the plants before finding an even less promising trail. He thought he was heading the right way, but he seemed to be walking paths that even the large jungle animals avoided.

It became unnerving how much noise he was making crashing through the undergrowth—it might be warning off snakes but it was also making him deaf to the wider jungle beyond with all its other potential threats. Every few minutes he stopped and listened, letting the landscape's constant seething murmur wash back over him.

On one of those stops he heard a scream somewhere off to

his left and froze, feeling the chill even beyond the damp warmth of the T-shirt clinging to his skin. It had been a scream, but not human, and as his heartbeat settled back to normal speed he tried not to think about what it might have been or how close it was.

He pushed on, and briefly, when he saw a change in the light up ahead, he hoped he might be approaching more open ground, maybe even coming back to the edge of the ravine. Then his hopes faded as he saw that it wasn't a change in the light but some sort of mist. A few steps later, any remaining hope turned to dread when he realized that the mist was actually formed by dense clouds of cobwebs draped between the trees, blocking the way forward.

Tom edged toward them and could see now that they were bristling with life, thousands of spiders suspended within them. They seemed to stretch for thirty or forty yards along the trail, too, a continuous barrier of web and spiders. They weren't big, not as big as some of the spiders they'd already seen, but that didn't mean they weren't venomous, and there were just so many of them. He looked around, searching for another way forward, but this was the only path unless he turned back, and if he turned back now he doubted he'd ever catch up with the rest of them. He moved closer again, noticing the way the spiders nearest him seemed to twitch and respond to his approach, small jerking movements rippling through the pulsing cloud.

He took a step back, overtaken by a fear that the spiders might even leap from the web, then took out the knife Shen had left in the side pocket of his backpack.

He looked around for a branch that he could cut. Instead, he settled on a thick vine winding up a tree and cut it in two places.

He practiced using it to whip back the undergrowth, then moved back to the web.

There was another jitter of movement through the web in response to his approach, and Tom paused again, this time hit with a little regret. It was beautiful and ingenious in its own way, and if it weren't an obstacle he wouldn't damage it, but he had no choice.

He took a deep breath, then swung the vine to whip a hole in the web. It split down the middle, opening up a tunnel. Small bristling bodies seemed to scuttle in all directions, but it wasn't enough. All he'd done was penetrate a little way, the web ahead of him apparently no less dense and full of spiders that were visibly more agitated now in the face of his violence.

He couldn't stop—he knew that—and couldn't think too much about what he was doing, so he started forward, flailing the makeshift whip in front of him, the silk sticking to it, spiders flying through the air, maybe landing on him. He walked faster, too fast at one point, into a veil of web that stuck to his face and his hair and he felt something crawl rapidly across his forehead, over his ear, down his neck, but Tom was too fired-up, too adrenaline-fueled, to do anything but push on through the endless webs, swinging the cut creeper in front of him.

He was aware of so much agitated movement around him, of the web coating his skin and clothes, sticking so much that it felt like he was being trapped, slowly consumed. The spiders, in their own panicked attempts to escape the onslaught, seemed to jump and spring randomly, hitting him, landing on him, clinging, but still he pushed on, slashing a path with the cut creeper.

The first ending was false, a short gap of a few yards before the start of another colony. His heart was racing so hard now he wouldn't have been able to stop if he'd wanted to. He whipped an opening into the second colony and pressed right on into it, walking faster, whipping faster, completely covered now by the sticky spider silk and by the spiders themselves, scuttling across his arms, his face, his hair.

And then he crashed through the far side and ran another couple of steps and tossed the creeper aside and pulled his backpack free, dropping it to the floor. He didn't look down but slapped blindly across his arms and legs, his face and hair, and kept doing it like he was performing some crazy trance-like dance.

Finally, he looked down, searching for any remaining spiders. He thought he felt something on his back and yanked his T-shirt off and shook it and whipped himself with it, just to be sure. And only when he was convinced he'd got them all did he turn to his backpack and brush away the few spiders that still clung to it.

Tom stood then, catching his breath, looking back at the destruction he'd brought about. Despite the swath he'd cut through the colonies, the mist of web still hung draped between the trees and even overhead, so he was sure it wouldn't be long before the webs were rebuilt and there'd be no sign of him ever having been there.

He felt something move in his hair and quickly raised his hand, making contact, the spider falling onto his bare shoulder and then to the ground, and he jumped unnecessarily and brushed frantically at his hair again. And it was only then that he thought to check his hands and arms, making sure he hadn't been bitten, though there were no signs to suggest he had.

He nodded, making a physical effort to calm down again,

acknowledging that he'd gotten through it. He'd faced it, and he'd gotten through it. He pulled his T-shirt back on and looked ahead, where the trail looked a little more open. He could do this—he'd come through the worst, so he just had to keep going.

He picked up his backpack, took another sip of water, then searched the pack one more time before putting it back on. He set off immediately, but he was still skittish, still slapping at every small itch, reacting to every insect that landed on his skin as if he weren't fully convinced he'd managed to shake off all those spiders.

The trails became slightly more passable, and more numerous, and a couple of times he was able to veer back to the right, the direction he wanted to go. Then, half an hour after leaving the spider colonies behind, he found a small sloping clearing within the trees, not big, but perhaps big enough to set up camp.

He checked the time, thinking back to what Kate had said about building a fire, making sure not to walk after dark. He figured night would come with its usual speed in the next half hour or so.

It was already more than two hours since he'd been separated from the rest of the group and he wondered where they were now, how far away, how close to the gap in the hills and the promise of the river. It was a strange sensation to Tom, because he'd never cared much for any of them before coming here, and still didn't care for some of them now, but he hoped they made it, no matter what happened to him.

He looked around the clearing. He'd need to find some dry wood to burn, but this small area looked particularly lush and green. He moved around the edge, searching for anything that might burn easily, and he was too slow when he caught a sudden movement from the undergrowth below.

He felt the impact before he'd even seen it, his vision registering only after the fact, a snake, darting out of the green, striking his leg just below the knee with disturbing force, its head thumping against his calf. He jumped back, one step, then another, and saw the snake clearly now, at least five feet long, a flash of brown and black and yellow.

Tom jumped back a third step, but the snake coiled and struck a second time. It fell short but immediately reared up and lunged at him again, and as Tom tried to take another jump backward he stumbled, falling against his own pack. He rolled and scrambled to his feet even as he saw the snake tensing to strike a fourth time.

He grabbed his backpack and ran out of the clearing before he even knew what he was doing, and ran another twenty paces along the narrow trail before fear of running into some other unknown danger brought him to a stop. His heart hammering in his chest, he scanned the ground around him, imagining snakes everywhere now.

Then he looked down and saw the two small tears in the leg of his cargo pants where the snake had struck. Instantly, he felt unsteady on his feet, a different fear taking hold of him now. But he needed to know if he'd been bitten, even if there was nothing he could do about it.

He dropped his backpack onto the ground and sat on top of it, then pulled his pant leg up to the knee and looked down. He looked at it for a second only before closing his eyes and taking a couple of deep breaths, dread flooding his body in thick waves.

He shook his head, not wanting to see it again but knowing

he had to, and then opened his eyes. There were two neat puncture wounds on the side of his calf, his skin streaked with the blood that was running out of them.

"Stupid," he said under his breath. *"Stupid!"*

He suddenly felt sorrow, not just for himself, but for Toby, a kid he hadn't known, and yet Tom had been so quick to dismiss his death, to blame him for his carelessness. Tom had seen the reality now, the speed with which a snake could strike from a position of near invisibility. He thought of Toby falling, the viper lunging, and felt a surge of sadness for him, and shame that he had not felt it at the time.

At least Toby had been with other people, kids who'd tried to help him, who'd carried his dying body. It seemed fitting somehow, that if Tom was about to die it would be alone, and no one would ever know how or why. He didn't want it to be true, but at the same time, he couldn't help but think it was what he deserved. This was the end of his story, and he would end it on his own.

CHAPTER 30

Tom had thought about death a lot in the last eight years. And he'd often wondered if, when the time came, he might see his mom and dad—not in some afterlife, but in his final moments like he'd heard some people experienced, as if to reassure him that everything would be okay.

He sat there for a while, maybe only minutes, maybe longer, trying to slow his heartbeat, realizing it might never go back to normal again. He wished desperately for some sensation, some sign of their presence, so he wouldn't be alone anymore. An orphan anymore. And tears filled his eyes because he knew he'd been wanting that sensation for these last eight years, to know that they were nearby, watching over him.

For some reason, he suddenly remembered shooting hoops with his dad in the yard, and how his dad had never been much good at it. Then in the summer before the accident Tom had looked out of his bedroom window one evening and seen his dad pick up the basketball where it had been left on the ground and casually throw a perfect back-shot over his shoulder and through the hoop. Tom had been staggered at first, and more so when he'd realized his dad had only been pretending to be bad all that time, so that Tom could always win.

He smiled at the memory now, but was distracted by a fly homing in on the punctured flesh of his leg. Tom shooed it away and at the same time noticed his heart was no longer racing. He checked his watch but wasn't sure how long it was since he'd been bitten. He was afraid to hope.

Toby had gone into shock, that's what they'd said, but Tom's heart seemed to be beating normally now. The fly homed in again and Tom swatted it away. He got his water bottle and poured a little over the wound, wincing with the sting, and used it to wipe away the blood too.

Could the snake have been non-venomous? He could only wish he'd be that lucky, but by now he should've started to feel some symptoms. Still, he'd been bitten by a wild animal, and even if it wasn't immediately fatal, it could get infected. He didn't have the first aid kit, but he had his own antiseptic cream for blisters and minor wounds.

He stood awkwardly, treating the injured leg as if it was broken rather than bitten, afraid of moving it. And once he'd found the cream he lowered himself back down and rubbed it gingerly over the wound, cringing as his finger pushed through the congealing blood into one of the holes.

Once he was done he checked his watch again, knowing he

had to move, that the daylight wouldn't last much longer. If the snakebite didn't kill him, being out here alone at night without a fire absolutely would. But before he'd had the chance to act on the thought, he heard a noise somewhere on the trail ahead and immediately tensed, listening for more.

What else would this jungle throw at him?

There it was again, something moving toward him through the undergrowth. It wasn't a jaguar, he told himself that much, certain he wouldn't have heard a big cat approaching at all. It was probably a peccary or a deer.

Even so, he reached into the side pocket and pulled out the knife, then got back to his feet. He couldn't see anything, but the noise was still there, and it was definitely getting closer.

Finally he spotted some indistinct movement between the trees up ahead, little more than a shift in the light, and he gripped the knife tighter and his heart was beating fast again, though at least he knew why this time.

More noise, more movement, and quite suddenly she moved into view and he stared in amazement. His first thought was that they'd come back for him, but it was only one person.

Kate.

Kate had come back for him.

She saw him and her mouth formed into a broad grin and she laughed once and picked up her pace. Tom felt tears welling up again, but this time with a surge of joy and a relief greater than anything he'd experienced in the last few hours. She was laughing and crying by the time she reached him and they fell into each other's arms.

He held tight to her, and was comforted that she held as

tightly to him. Finally he pulled away from her, holding her at arm's length and looking into her face, still astonished.

"You came back for me."

She nodded, overwhelmed, then shrugged and said, "I knew I'd find you. I just couldn't stand the thought of you having to spend the night alone out here. Alice wanted to come too, so did George, but I knew I'd be better on my own." She looked over her shoulder. "You were heading the right way. I gambled on that: I was sure you would be."

"That makes one of us. I wasn't convinced, and I..." He shook his head. "We need to find somewhere to camp."

She nodded. "The edge of the ravine's only a few minutes back that way. We can camp there. And we'll catch up with them in the morning." She glanced down and took a step back, alarmed. "What happened to your leg?"

"A snake. It bit me. I found a clearing that looked like a good campsite, but then this snake came out of nowhere and bit me, and then kept coming at me. Even when I backed away, it kept coming after me." He found it hard to describe how it felt to get attacked and to think he might be dying, but maybe he didn't need to.

"Sit down. Let me look." He sat, grateful for her sure commands. As she crouched down to look, she said, "It came after you? What did it look like?"

"Four or five feet long, kind of yellow and brown and black— it moved so fast, I didn't get a good look."

"Wow." She studied the wound. "How's your breathing and your pulse?"

"Both okay now. Why did you say *wow*?"

"Any burning sensation around the wound?" She prodded the flesh around it.

"It hurts a little, but no burning. Why? What—"

She looked up at him. "It sounds like a fer-de-lance, which means you were lucky. I mean, *really* lucky. They kill a lot of people, and they're aggressive. There's a good chance that was what killed Toby."

"So why am I not dead?"

"Maybe twenty-five percent of the time, the first bite is a dry bite, no venom, like a warning shot. Looks like that's what's happened to you."

"You're sure?"

She nodded. "I think so. Otherwise the venom would have started digesting your flesh by now. That's why I asked about the burning."

"Wow," he said, dizzy with so many thoughts—of his parents, of thankfulness and relief, of never wanting to forget how lucky he'd been here today.

"Exactly. I've got some stuff to clean this better but let's make camp first."

She helped him to his feet.

"Kate, I…" He couldn't even sum up how grateful he was. "Just, thanks."

"You would've made it back on your own. I just figured you'd prefer some company. Isn't that what friends do?"

He smiled and laughed a little in acknowledgment. "I've never been much of a friend to anyone."

"Well…none of us is defined by who we were in the past."

She smiled at him in wonder. "We survived a plane crash, Tom. Whether we like it or not, *that's* who we are now."

He nodded and they headed back the way she'd come. Tom knew she was right too. They'd all been made new by that plane crash, and if they survived, if he managed to avoid any more snakes, these days in the jungle would be the days that defined the rest of their lives.

CHAPTER 31

Kate had been telling the truth: Tom had only been a few minutes away from reaching the ravine again, and at a place where the side had collapsed, forming a slope down into it.

It was tempting to camp for the night in the ravine itself, but it was obvious that the water, when it flowed through here, was sudden and violent. So they stayed near the lip and managed to find enough wood to build a decent fire.

As they took some of the remaining snacks from their packs, Kate said, "I noticed nuts and fruit on my way here. I didn't have time to collect any, but we should get some on the way back—we're running out of food."

He nodded. "How are the others?"

"I was only with them for about a half hour after we left you." She laughed to herself. "Joel, naturally, was against anyone else getting separated, but I didn't give him a choice this time." She looked at Tom now. "What was it like, being left on your own over here?"

"You mean besides being bitten by a venomous snake?" She laughed and he said, "Scary, even before that. The trails were all going in the wrong direction, so to get back this way I had to go into..." He shook his head. "I had to break through these colonies of spiders, like a curtain of web that was maybe twenty or thirty yards, thousands of spiders..."

"I've seen them! We saw them on vacation once. Like clouds of cotton candy."

"Yeah, so that was pretty wild. And just wondering whether I'd get back to you guys. And then there was the snake. What did you call it?"

"A fer-de-lance. It's a kind of pit viper. They kill so many people."

"And you think that could be what killed Toby?" Kate nodded, and Tom thought of him, of his stricken face as Chris had carried him up the hill. "I didn't know him."

"He was a jerk." She shrugged. "I know, you shouldn't speak bad of the dead, and I'm sorry that happened to him, really I am, but he was still a jerk. He used to make smart-ass comments about me and Emma all the time."

"Oh."

"Yeah, classic homophobic stuff—he was a little backward like that."

Tom glanced up at the orange sky hanging low overhead, and could tell it would get dark in the coming minutes, and was intrigued briefly that he'd already learned to detect that subtle shift. But there was something more pressing in his thoughts.

"But you two aren't together, are you?"

She gave him a crooked smile, an indication she'd slightly underestimated Tom, and said, "I guess I should have known that you'd spot that, for all your indifference." There was a teasing note in her voice but she grew serious again. "Emma's gay. I'm not. We've been best friends for so long, and I think it makes it easier for her that a lot of people think we're together—you wouldn't believe how many kids out there act like Toby, people who haven't woken up to the twenty-first century yet."

He nodded, impressed that friends would look out for each other like that, maybe even more impressed than by Kate's willingness to set off into the jungle on her own to find him. It probably said something about how screwed up his life was that he could understand taking a risk for another person, but the intricacies of friendship still seemed strange and a little confusing to him.

They sat in silence for a short while, as darkness fell and the world became reduced to the light from their fire and the constant seething of the jungle.

Kate used a branch to prod the fire then and said, "On the subject of relationships, you and Alice would be great together." He laughed, but simultaneously felt a buzz of happiness that he couldn't quite pinpoint. "I'm serious. I think she's liked you for a long time."

"I doubt that. But yeah, I think we have a connection. Who knows, maybe when we get back home...." The words dried in his throat and he changed the subject. "What about you? Is there anyone..."

"Not really." She continued to poke intently at the fire. "I was interested in someone, I guess, but...he was in the other part of the plane."

For some reason, Tom immediately thought of Charlie Stafford suspended up in that tree, and he could picture Charlie and Kate together without knowing why. It made him a little sad to think it could never happen now.

"I'm sorry."

"Yeah. I mean, don't get me wrong, he didn't know I liked him like that, and I doubt he would have been interested anyway."

"I don't see why not—you're attractive, you're smart..."

She smirked. "Don't get weird on me, Calloway!" He laughed, but then she said, "You know, part of it was, I always thought we've got so much time ahead of us, there's no rush. But look at us now." He nodded, thinking about what she'd said, and she added quickly, "Sorry, like I need to tell you about these kinds of things."

It took him a second to understand what she was apologizing for and when he got it, he smiled to show there was no need and said, "Actually, I wasn't thinking about my parents. I was thinking how you can't blame yourself for procrastinating. It's what we do, it's what separates us from every animal in this jungle, that we have a concept of the future, we plan, we dream. You know all these stupid memes about living every day like it's your last—well, we don't have to. That's one of the luxuries of being human."

"You're right." She waited a beat. "Although, in our present situation, I think our grip on that particular luxury might be a little bit shaky."

They both laughed, and then couldn't stop laughing, swept up by the relief and the happiness of being by this fire in this most unlikely of places. Sure, the next day could be their last, just like this one might have been, but they were still here, for now. Alive.

CHAPTER 32

They took turns sleeping for a few hours, and as soon as it was light they put out the fire before descending the collapsed side into the ravine. The sky was still a dense orange above them, and occasionally, as they walked along the bottom, they could get the telltale acrid smell that hinted at the origins of the pollution.

After a few hundred yards, they found a way out on the other side, and Kate led the way along the trail at the top, as familiar with it as if she'd walked it a dozen times.

They stopped to collect some fruit from a tree, papaya or some variant of it. Tom noticed another fruit-laden tree nearby and pointed it out, but Kate seemed unsure.

"I don't know what it is." She looked at the fruit in her hands. "I remember a guide giving us these when we were in Colombia."

"We might be in Colombia now."

She laughed. "Okay, when we were in Colombia on vacation."

They walked on but after a few minutes, Kate pointed to something littering the ground around a tree and said, "These are even better." She picked one up and handed it to him. It looked and felt like a coconut, only heavier. "We'll crack them open when we reach the others—brazil nuts."

He smiled and said, "And you said *I* should be the leader?"

"It's not my thing."

"It's not mine, either."

"Yes it is, Tom. You just don't know it. Come on, let's put these in our packs and move on."

"Yes, boss."

They walked on in near silence, though occasionally Kate would point out some animal or plant or tree and make a comment about it. And he could hardly blame Joel for not seeing the knowledge Kate had, because Tom hadn't been aware of it himself. Not even the brief preview in the jungle—when they'd found Naomi's sneaker—had prepared him for how adept she was in this environment.

When she walked in front he noticed the ease with which she moved and yet the complete awareness she seemed to possess, of what was around her, what was underfoot, what lay ahead. Kate and Emma had been ready to walk out of this jungle on their own, and seeing Kate now, he had every confidence they would have made it.

They stopped for lunch in a spot where a couple of trails met and there was enough room to sit on their backpacks. They shared a small pack of oatmeal cookies and the smallest of the papayas they'd collected, and it was only the juice from the fruit that made Tom realize how thirsty he was, but they held off on drinking any more of their diminishing water supply.

They sat for a little while afterward, oddly satisfied by the small amount of food and the relief of resting their tired legs. Kate opened her mouth as if to speak but then stopped and cocked her head to one side, and Tom looked off into the trees too.

Had they been hearing something? They'd become used to the background noise of the jungle, but faintly, above it, there had been something that sounded like voices, or certainly one voice.

It came to them both at once and Kate said, "Joel."

Tom nodded. "I never thought I'd be so happy to hear that voice. How far away would you say they are?"

"They sound close, don't they?" She looked along the trail as if trying to calculate, but then shrugged in defeat. "At least we know they're going in the right direction."

He smiled at her implicit confidence—there was no question in Kate's mind that she and Tom were headed the right way.

They set off a short while later, and over the next few hours they heard tantalizing snatches of what sounded like chatter somewhere ahead, and on one more occasion, Joel's voice rising up. But they didn't seem to get much closer and sometimes the voices even sounded more distant.

Kate said, "They're still ahead of us. I know they sound farther away all of a sudden, but that's probably just a trick of the geography."

"It has to be," he said, and saw that she appeared briefly unsure of herself. "Kate, we're moving pretty quickly, and they were slow even when we left them."

"You're right. I want to catch up with them before dark, that's all."

He checked his watch. "We have an hour or two. We'll do it."

He didn't know what he'd said, but she smiled at him, smiled for so long that he said, "What?"

"Nothing. Just…can we be friends when we get back?"

He laughed, a little embarrassed. "Aren't we friends now?"

"Well, yeah, but…" She shook her head, visibly trying to think of a way of summing up how new this was to her, that she might actually be friends with him. "Oh, who cares? Emma and me, we've always had a platonic crush on you, just because of the way you are in English, so aloof and hostile and noble all at once, kind of like that guy in *Brave New World*."

"The one who hangs himself?" She grinned and nodded, but then he said, "I never meant to be hostile."

"I know that. I know." She smiled again, a little sadly, and they walked on.

Ten minutes later, the trail skirted around a small rise and they got a glimpse of the hills ahead of them and what looked like the cleft that they were aiming for. It encouraged them, even though for the next half hour they heard nothing from the group they were pursuing.

But then they heard Joel again and, soon after, a few laughs and shouts. There was water flowing somewhere behind to the right too, the sound of rapids, but they focused instead on the noise ahead, because this time it did not fade back into the hum and whirr of the jungle.

They saw the other survivors before the group saw them. Kate and Tom crested a small rise and stopped, looking at the sight below. It was the point just before the river entered the gorge that split the range of hills, and the others were spread out across a rocky horseshoe beach that looked like it had been scooped out by the torrents coming downriver and hitting the narrow waters that entered the gorge.

Even from their vantage point, Tom could see that the river was running much faster here than they'd seen the previous day, but the eroded banks and wide beach suggested this was nothing compared with the way it was when the rains came.

Kate was clearly thinking along the same lines, because she said, "Not a bad place to camp, I guess. As long as it doesn't rain."

The people below were just starting to build a fire, so he guessed they hadn't been there long themselves. Maybe that's why they'd heard laughter, the joy of reaching any kind of destination after two days of hiking.

Tom noticed a huddle of people on one side of the beach and when someone stepped aside he could see Barney putting the finishing touches to what looked like a small improvised shelter with one of the mosquito nets hanging down over it. Maybe someone had been hurt or taken ill.

He glanced briefly around, trying to see who might be missing, and smiled involuntarily when he saw Alice crossing the beach carrying a couple of branches for the fire.

"Ready?" Kate asked.

He nodded, but said, "Before we go down there, you asked if we could be friends, and the answer obviously is yes, but I want you to know, I'll never ever forget what you did for me yesterday."

Sounding self-conscious, she replied, "You would've made it back on your own. And you would've done the same."

"Maybe."

Together, they started down the trail toward the new camp.

CHAPTER 33

Jess saw them first. She ran over to Tom and hugged him, and George and some of the others quickly followed, almost knocking him over. When he glanced off to one side he saw Kate in the middle of a similar huddle.

As the people backed off from Tom a little and started asking him too many questions to answer, he saw Alice, standing a few yards away, and she didn't move closer but smiled at him with such warmth that he thought maybe Kate had been right, that if they got through this, there could be something between them.

He took a few steps toward her and said casually, "How's it going?"

"Oh, you know," she said, just as casually, but then laughed and gave him a quick hug. "I never had a doubt."

Shen came over and said, "Good to see you back, Tom."

"Glad we caught up with you."

Shen frowned. "You would've anyway. I don't think we'll be moving from here for a day or two."

Tom immediately looked toward where Barney was still working, with Joel standing looking over the construction, almost as if he hadn't noticed Kate and Tom coming back into the camp. Tom could also see someone lying down under the mosquito net.

Alice said, "It's Chloe. She started to get sick yesterday. Barney made a sort of stretcher for her, but Shen doesn't think she's well enough to move for a while."

Shen said, "Yeah, it's some sort of fever. But I'm hopeful." He shrugged, belying how paper-thin that hope was. "We've been vaccinated against the worst diseases, but she needs rest badly. Everyone does; there are a couple of sprains here and there, a few people getting weak."

"What about our water supply?"

Shen's expression told Tom it wasn't great, but then he said, "I had concerns when Joel said we'd camp here, but there aren't any predators that we could see, and the water's flowing quite fast, so I think we'll use the purifying tablets, boil it for good measure."

Tom looked at the river. The rapids they'd heard on their approach seemed to be upstream of them now, though there were also large boulders just visible in the water downstream too, just before it curved out of sight around the edge of the hill. It was clear they'd have to get to the other side of that hill before launching the boats.

"What about food?"

Shen said, "You can go a long time without food."

Kate walked over and said, "We might be able to help with

that, won't we, Tom?" He'd forgotten about the fruit and nuts in his pack but before he could respond, Alice hugged Kate and he heard her whisper something. Kate smiled and said, "He would have made it back anyway. I think he'd already come through the worst before I found him. Even managed to get bitten by a snake."

Alice looked at him with alarm but he shook his head. "I'm fine. I'll let Shen take a look at it later, but I'm fine. Let's stick with the subject of food." Before she could respond, they took off their backpacks and started to empty their harvest.

It was only now that Joel came over and said, "Glad you could join us, Tom."

It was an attempt at understated humor so Tom smiled and said, "Well, I heard you were having a party."

"Yes." He smiled too, awkwardly, then looked down at the cache of food they'd harvested. "What's all this?"

Kate said, "That's papaya, and the things that look like coconuts are actually full of brazil nuts."

Shen and Alice were already crouched down inspecting them, but Joel said, "I'm not sure how wise that would be. You know, a lot of the things here might look familiar but could be poisonous. We were even warned about that, before leaving."

"Well, that'll be your choice, Joel. You can trust me and eat, or you can go hungry."

"No, I didn't mean to question—"

She didn't wait for him to finish but turned to Shen and said, "And if we're likely to be here for a day or two, tomorrow we can fish. I'll use one of the mosquito nets."

Joel looked skeptical, but didn't say anything and drifted off to oversee the fire. Emma called Kate and she went over to her and then Tom spotted Alice and Shen exchanging a glance.

He looked questioningly at them and Shen said quietly, "We should have been here hours ago. Joel kept heading in the wrong direction this morning. It took a lot to persuade him that we were going off course."

Alice added, "In the end, George climbed a tree to get a view, and then Joel had to admit we'd been going the wrong way and we needed to backtrack. It's been a tough day on everyone."

"It shows." He looked around the camp that was forming, a circle of backpacks and the two boat cases around the fire, the little makeshift hospital tent off to one side. Mila was sitting nursing her ankle, Nick looked pale and sickly, Oscar had crashed against his backpack, his hair sweat-slicked and plastered to his head. Yesterday had been rough for Tom, but he felt bad for the rest of them. "As long as we can eat and drink, a day recovering here might be a good thing."

Alice said, "We'll get to work on some food right away."

"Good idea," said Shen, and immediately looked around the camp, calling a few people to come over and work on opening the brazil nuts. He collected some packaged pastries from different backpacks and toasted them over the fire, a simple move that earned him effusive compliments. And with some food in their stomachs and a little rest, the mood became noticeably more upbeat than it had been just a short while ago. The presence of Chloe beneath the mosquito nets was the only reminder of how precarious their situation really was.

They were still sitting in satisfied silence around the fire when the sunset came somewhere beyond that orange mist, and total darkness descended.

Mila looked at Joel now and said, "So is this where we'll launch the boats?"

"We'll decide tomorrow," he said. "It's a good spot, and the river's wide enough, but we'll have to see what's downstream."

Shen didn't disagree but he looked at Tom, a wry smile just visible in the firelight. The gap was definitely more of a gorge and the boulders downstream had been visible even from the limited viewpoint of the beach, so Tom was certain they'd have to launch from the other side of the hills.

Maybe Joel had understood that too, but was putting off breaking the news until they were all a little more rested and had a new day ahead of them. Tom had to admire him at some level, because he had to be as tired as everyone else here and yet he was maintaining a veneer of calm composure, as if he were mentally carrying the whole group.

One by one they settled for the night. No roster was agreed to stay awake but soon there were only five who weren't sleeping. Barney was keeping a vigil by Chloe, a little way distant from the fire, using a damp cloth to mop her brow. Tom and Alice and George were still awake, and so was Shen.

They sat in silence for a while, but then Shen turned to Tom and said, "Do you think Kate will be able to catch fish?"

He masked it well, but the concern was clear in his voice. Tom knew Shen was worried they'd starve or die of thirst before reaching the outside world, that they were moving too slowly. At least that was one thing on which Tom could reassure him.

"If anyone can catch fish, it's Kate. She just understands nature, all of this—she's better than any of us out here. I only really saw that today."

Alice said, "It was amazing what she did yesterday. I wanted to go with her, so did George, but she was adamant she'd be better on her own. In the end it was Emma who told us to let her go, that she knew what she was doing, and I guess she was right: we probably would have just held her up, wouldn't we, George?"

"What? Sorry, I was thinking about fish."

They laughed, but then Shen said, "If we can catch fish we'll be okay, but I'll feel better when we get onto the river." He shrugged. "I think I'll get some sleep now."

He lay back against his pack and they went back to watching the fire in silence. But Tom was acutely aware of the others sleeping around them, the sound sleep of exhaustion.

Their situation felt fragile, as if at any moment something could snap and they'd all be cast into the void, but that fragility had been in the camp by the plane too—they just hadn't been able to see it as clearly. Perhaps Tom only saw it now because he'd been bitten by that snake, and he'd been away from them for a day. He was seeing them with fresh eyes and knew it was right that they wouldn't have survived if they'd stayed back at the crash site, but also that they wouldn't survive through many more days of living like this.

CHAPTER 34

The next morning didn't bring much to be optimistic about. The day broke with the same sickly orange pallor and as a group they weren't faring well. Oscar was sick in some unknown way. Lara was still limping from her fall on the tree. Mila was still using one of the poles as a walking stick. It created the impression of a camp under siege.

Joel broke the news early that they couldn't launch here so they would stay another day to recover before trekking over the hills. Rather than being disappointed, most of the group seemed relieved that they wouldn't have to climb over a hill in search of a better stretch of river. There was even an uplift in spirits as Joel organized people into collecting more wood and helping Shen with the water supply.

Tom said to Alice, "How are you this morning?"

She nodded and said, "You?"

"Okay. I think I'll climb the hill, see what the other side looks like."

She nodded again. "I'll come with you."

He was glad she wanted to come, a feeling that was still new enough to take him by surprise. Just a few days ago he'd felt he had nothing in common with any of them and couldn't have imagined himself bonding over two weeks in Costa Rica. Yet now, there were maybe half a dozen people he *had* bonded with and actually become friends with.

"We should tell Joel." She looked at him, one eyebrow raised, probably assuming he was joking. "Just to keep things cool," he explained.

Reluctantly, she said, "Okay, I'll tell him."

As she walked away, Barney came over carrying the spear he'd made out of the metal pole and the knife.

"Hi, Tom. I didn't get much chance to talk to you yesterday."

Tom looked across to the makeshift shelter where Barney had been tending to Chloe. Chris was there with her now. "How is she?"

"I think she'll be okay, but…"

Tom nodded and said, "I'm gonna scout over the hill, see what's ahead."

"Then you should take this." He handed him the spear. "Honestly, I really made it for you anyway."

"Thanks, Barney."

"My pleasure." He smiled and added, "Anyway, things to do."

Barney walked away and joined Kate and George, who were standing near the river. Tom watched as George held up a mosquito net and listened to Kate explain how they were going to use it.

Just then, Alice came back. "Joel wants us to wait a minute—he's coming with us."

"Let him," said Tom, and smiled.

The three of them set off, finding a way up off the beach and up the hill. The undergrowth was thicker, offering up no real paths, so Tom used the sharp knife-edge of the spear to clear the way in front as far as possible, trampling, too, conscious that they would all have to walk this same route at some point.

He wanted a vantage point, but wherever he had the chance to take a lower route around the side of the hill, he opted for that, once again thinking of the whole group making the same trek. And in the end, that took them to a kind of vantage point anyway, a small bluff on the other side that provided a view out over the tops of the trees that filled the slopes below it.

At first, the view wasn't promising. The land seemed to level out on the other side, nothing more than undulations and huge flat expanses, all of it green, an unending tropical wilderness stretching to the horizon under the sinking orange sky.

But Tom pointed to the river, wide enough below the gorge that from up here they could even see glimpses of flat open surface as it gently snaked away into the landscape.

Alice looked in the same direction for a little while before finally saying, "It looks like we're a long way from anywhere, though."

"But if there are settlements, they'll be on the river. It all looks the same from here, but…" She looked at him, and he laughed. "Honestly, I have no idea. But it's the way out."

Alice laughed too, but then Joel said, "Maybe not. Look over there." He pointed away from the river, to the left, where a narrow trail of smoke was rising up out of the blanket of trees.

For a moment, and only a moment, Tom felt his heartbeat kick up a notch, thinking maybe it was a village. Then the doubts started to creep in. He searched the landscape around the fire for the telltale line that suggested another river, but there was none.

It definitely looked like a managed fire, not some accidental bushfire or natural phenomenon, but he was full of misgivings about who might be responsible for a fire in a location like that. It would probably take a good couple of hours to walk there too, in the wrong direction.

Alice was apparently thinking along the same lines, because she sounded less than enthusiastic as she said, "It looks...remote. You know, it could be some tribe that's never had contact with the outside world before."

Joel looked dismissive. "This isn't one of your novels, Alice, it's the twenty-first century."

"You should try reading a bit more yourself—you wouldn't be such a jerk." He tried to laugh in mock outrage, but her ire was up. "Take a look at this jungle! Where do you think we are?"

"Well, I'm guessing the Amazon."

"Exactly. The Amazon, where there are still tribes that live in isolation, who probably don't like people crashing into their territory."

"It could be worse," said Tom. "We could at least try to persuade a tribe that we mean no harm. They could be rebels, drug gangs, who knows, and I couldn't see that ending well."

Joel looked exasperated. "Unbelievable! We have the first sign of other people, and you want to turn your back on it and sail down a river that might lead us nowhere." He pointed at the trail of smoke again. "These people will have food, maybe medical supplies, maybe a radio." Neither of them responded, though

Alice continued to shake her head gravely. "Look, I'm making an executive decision, and I intend to find out whose fire that is, but I'll make a compromise with you. Chloe can't be moved today anyway, so I suggest a small group of us goes and investigates the fire. We check it out, and if it looks unsafe, we back away unseen and return to the original plan."

Alice didn't look in the mood to compromise and said, "If it's a native tribe, I doubt we'd stand much chance of getting in there unseen."

"I'll grant that, but I still think it's a risk worth taking, and I think it's wrong to just assume that anyone who's out here automatically means us harm. But I have to tell you, Alice, I've decided, I'm going anyway."

Tom knew there'd be no persuading Joel now, and briefly he considered letting him go, letting the group split, but he still believed at some level that it was important they lost no one else. And instinctively, in his core, he knew that if they let Joel lead a group to that fire, the chances were high that another death would follow.

"Who do you want in this little reconnaissance group?"

Joel looked taken aback for a moment, perhaps thinking Tom would have put up more of an argument. "Okay. How about the three of us?" When neither of them objected to that, he added, "Maybe a couple more—Chris, Nick."

Tom nodded, glad that he hadn't mentioned Kate or George, Shen or Barney. He wanted them to stay behind, because he felt sure they'd get the others to safety if something went wrong. And as he exchanged another look with Alice, it seemed they'd both accepted that they would go along with it, but that they also both suspected there was a chance they'd never make it back to the river.

CHAPTER 35

When they got back to the camp, Mila was looking after Chloe. Kate and George and Shen were busy by the river, though it didn't look like they'd started fishing yet. Barney was sitting next to the fire, being watched by a couple of the others as he used a knife to take apart his backpack.

He looked up at Tom. "Hope you don't mind—I took the knife out of your backpack."

Joel sounded put out as he said, "I didn't know there was another knife."

Tom ignored him, replying to Barney instead. "I don't mind. What are you doing?"

Barney looked down at the deconstructed backpack. "It's a work in progress, but it occurred to me, what with the nylon and the frame, it makes the perfect basis for an oar."

Tom smiled, impressed by his ingenuity, his inventor's curiosity, but the smile fell away as Joel said, "That's great, although I'm hoping we won't be needing it." Barney's face fell in disappointment and Joel raised his voice to address the whole group. "We've spotted some smoke rising up on the other side of the hill, so some of us are going to investigate. Chris, Nick, I want you two to come with us." A chorus of questions rose up but Joel raised his hands to quiet them. "We don't know anything for now. It's definitely a human fire, but we need to check it out, to be sure it's people who might want to help us. I'm sure it will be, but if it isn't, we'll retreat back here and use the boats like we planned all along."

Alice offered a whispered correction to Tom, saying, "Like *you* planned all along."

Kate and George walked over, and George said, "I don't mind coming."

Kate added, "I'll come too."

Tom shook his head directly at them, even as Joel was saying, "No, we have enough people for now. We'll travel light, and we'll be back before dark."

Shen came closer now and said, "How far is this fire?"

"Not far, less than an hour's walk."

Alice looked skeptical. "I don't think so. I'd say an hour and a half at least, if the ground's easy."

"I agree," said Tom.

Shen nodded and said, "Then you should take your backpacks." Joel responded with a puzzled expression, making clear he thought it an outlandish suggestion, but Shen was deadly serious. "It sounds far enough that you could get lost. Of course, I hope that doesn't happen, but if it does, you should have your backpacks with you."

Alice said, "Good point. I'll take mine."

"Me too," said Tom, giving Joel no chance to argue.

As they prepared to leave, Tom approached Kate and George, and said, "I didn't want either of you to come." He looked over his shoulder to make sure Joel wasn't listening, but he was talking to Mila like some dignitary visiting a hospital. "I intend to come back, no question, but if something does go wrong, I know I can rely on you two and Barney and Shen to get everyone downriver."

"You have to come back," said George, so earnestly that Tom could only nod.

But Kate said, "You heard him, Tom. We need you back here, and I'm not coming looking for you a second time."

Tom smiled. He doubted they needed him as much as they thought they did, but he was touched that they felt like that. "I'll do my best."

There was some rearranging of the supplies in the backpacks as Shen made sure each group had a first aid kit and that the exploratory party had enough of the food and drink supply.

They set off then, with Joel in front, then Chris and Nick, and Alice and Tom following up the rear. They climbed quickly away from the beach, following the path they'd already cut and making quick progress to the bluff. The smoke was still rising up in the distance, a faint but steady ribbon against the sickly sky.

Chris smiled broadly and said, "This is it."

Tom wasn't sure what he meant but Joel nodded in agreement and pointed to the left-hand side of the bluff. "It looks like we'll be able to walk down that way, then we need to head diagonally—"

Alice interrupted him, saying, "What are you talking about?" He turned and looked at her. "Joel, once we're down there, we'll have no idea where this fire is. We need to walk along the top of this line of hills so we can see it. Then when it's more or less directly in front of us we can head straight down the hill."

To Tom's surprise, Nick said, "She's right."

Chris said, "To be fair, she usually is."

"Okay," said Joel, sounding as if it really wasn't okay at all. "It'll be harder work but if it makes you feel more confident, we can do that." He pointed at the spear in Tom's hand. "Mind if I use that, as I'm on point?"

"Sure," said Tom, and handed it to him.

They walked on, not quite along the top of the hills, but high enough up that they could occasionally look out through the tree canopies of the descending slopes and see the smoke in the distance. Each time Tom looked out he found himself relieved that the smoke seemed no nearer, because he sensed instinctively that they were heading toward something that was no safer than the jungle.

As it turned out, even Alice's estimate had been wildly optimistic—they'd been walking for over an hour before it finally seemed the smoke was directly in front of them, and it still looked some distance away. But it was within reach, and Tom knew they wouldn't turn back now, as much as he felt the urge to do just that.

"This is the problem," said Joel. "We're walking two long

sides of the triangle instead of one diagonal. We'd have been there by now if we'd walked the other way. Still..." He left the word hanging there, full with meaning, and set off down the slope.

Alice turned to Tom and said, "We could just kill him. No one would know."

Tom smiled. "You're forgetting, we're here to stop him from getting killed."

They followed after the others, and as the ground leveled out near the bottom of the hill they found their way back on to a path, but one that seemed different from those they'd encountered before. It was hard to pin down why, but this had the feel of a path that had been created by humans, and that should have given them hope, but instead Tom and Alice exchanged a glance that was full of foreboding.

It made Tom want to pause, because this felt like one of those moments, like the moment with Naomi in the plane or the strange atmosphere in the hours before Freddie died. That was how it felt now, like something momentous was going to happen and the channel was already open, that if he allowed himself time to think he'd be able to see through the fabric of time and know what was coming, what danger lay ahead.

But there *was* no time to think. They were moving on, and as he looked at Alice walking in front of him, he was determined on only one thing, that nothing would happen to her. He wasn't even sure why he felt it so strongly, but he felt it all the same—nothing could happen to her.

CHAPTER 36

They walked in complete silence now, hoping to approach the camp undetected. Tom studied the trees around him as he walked, searching for anything that might suggest they were entering tribal territory of some sort—he didn't know exactly what he was looking for, but he looked anyway. Perhaps he was hoping for some reassurance, but there was none to be found, and it seemed even the jungle was ill at ease, a bristling beyond the eerie stillness.

Every once in a while, Joel would stop and listen, but it was after almost another hour that they stopped for a drink and Alice said, "I can hear a car or something."

"Unlikely," said Chris, but Joel hushed him and they all stood alert.

Tom could hear it now. "Could be a generator."

Joel smiled, saying, "Told you."

Tom merely stared back at him, giving him nothing, and it was Alice who said, "You didn't tell us anything. So they've got a generator—that doesn't mean they're not dangerous."

"Agreed," said Joel. "But it also doesn't mean they *are* dangerous."

They moved on, and as they got closer they could hear the voices of several men, sounding like they were busy with some task. The group stopped again when they first spotted movement and the outlines of buildings ahead.

They moved forward a little farther, a position that offered a view but also enough cover that they were unlikely to be seen. There were three buildings, one like a large cabin or bunkhouse, another more like a small barn, and one that was partly open at the sides.

There were at least a couple dozen men in the clearing between the buildings, some of them heavily armed. Large sacks were being brought from the barn and passed on to the waiting men, the whole process being carried out with some urgency.

Tom and the others dropped back again and crouched down.

Joel said, "Okay, I think we need to be careful about how we go in. We don't want to do anything to spook them and—"

Alice smiled, in astonishment rather than humor. "You've got to be kidding." He looked at her, making a show of being confused by her interruption. "Joel, it's a cocaine factory."

"That's kind of a leap, Alice."

"No, it isn't. I've seen it on TV. The cocaine's grown and harvested in the jungle, then they fly it out from illegal airstrips. That open-sided building is where they process it. And that's probably a shipment going out."

He stared at her, as if trying but failing to find an argument, and finally said, "Okay, maybe you're right. But that doesn't mean they won't help us." Her mouth dropped open in disbelief. "Look, we'll let them finish what they're doing, let things calm down. Once the shipment's gone, if it really is a shipment, then we'll see how it looks."

Both Chris and Nick nodded in agreement.

Alice looked at Tom. He checked his watch and said, "We're already cutting it close if we still want to get back to the camp in daylight, but we can wait half an hour, see what happens."

Joel looked pleased and said, "So you agree it's worth a shot?"

"No, I think you're insane."

"So why are you willing to wait?"

Tom shrugged. "In the unlikely event they all clear out and leave a radio or something behind. Unlikely, but worth another half hour."

"You're both wrong, but we'll retreat a little way for half an hour, then see how the ground lies."

Alice didn't respond but also didn't wait, heading back into deeper cover away from the camp. They all followed, but even where they settled, they could still hear the noise of the generator and the shouts and talk and very occasional laughter in the camp.

The half hour was almost up when quite abruptly the camp seemed to fall silent. Even the generator shut off, but the talking stopped so suddenly that Tom became nervous, fearing they'd been spotted and were about to be ambushed.

Joel apparently didn't share his worries because he said, "Come on, Chris, we'll go and check out what's going on."

Chris nodded and looked at Tom as he said, "We're gonna get out of here. Fortune favors the brave."

They set off, and once the three of them were left, Nick shook his head and said to Tom, "You think you have all the answers, don't you? You think you're so cool."

Tom didn't like his tone, nor the suggestion that maybe Tom had been the topic of conversation among Joel and his cronies, and his voice had a challenge in it as he said, "Do we know each other?"

Nick, who seemed combative most of the time, looked unsure how to deal with Tom's hostility, and in the end he only said, "He'll prove you wrong."

Alice said, "Don't you mean me?" Nick looked confused. "You mean he'll prove *me* wrong. It was me who objected, but what, you think because I'm a girl, my point of view doesn't matter? It has to be about who's the most important boy in the group, is that what you're saying?"

"No, I... That's not what I meant. I—"

"Good. Because I don't know Tom that well, but I know he couldn't care less about any of that. All he's doing is trying to get us all out of here alive."

"So is Joel."

"Well he's not doing a very good job, is he?"

Nick looked ready to respond, but Tom heard movement and said, "They're coming back."

Chris almost fell at their feet in his eagerness to get back and report what they'd seen, but once there, he seemed uncertain what to say or maybe felt it was Joel's privilege to do the talking.

Joel crouched down again and said, "It's a go." Tom grimaced at the way Joel was talking, like he was part of some elite military unit. "There are only six or seven guys left, just the guys who look after it, probably, you know, like the farmers. So me and Chris, we'll put our backpacks on, walk into the camp from the other side, like we've come from the river."

Chris added, "We're gonna tell them our boat was damaged."

"If they seem helpful, we'll tell them there are more of us."

Alice said, "And if they don't?"

"We'll make a run for it, head for the river." Joel delivered the words with the relaxed air of someone who didn't believe for one second that this might go wrong. To support what sounded like a ludicrous backup plan, he said, "These guys are farmers, laborers, not rebels or anything."

He started to pull on his backpack and Chris followed suit as Alice said, "What, you're going now?"

"Fortune favors the brave," said Chris again, his eyes a little glazed with the prospect of what he clearly thought was going to be a triumph.

Joel nodded and handed the spear to Tom, saying, "Better leave this with you—don't want them getting the wrong idea."

Tom took it, even as he said, "I know we don't agree on much, but I'm asking you not to do this. You're putting yourself in danger, and the rest of us too. You saw the river. We can take the boats downstream."

"Sometimes, Tom, you have to take a risk, and this is a risk worth taking." He stood now. "Okay, Chris, let's roll."

And before anything else could be said, they strode off into the jungle.

CHAPTER 37

Tom and Alice and Nick moved up to their earlier vantage point, and now that there was less activity they had a better view of the small camp beyond. The barn was closed and the open-sided building looked deserted. The bunkhouse door was ajar and they could just hear what sounded like a radio inside, playing scratchy, indistinct music. The smoke they'd seen was rising up from a narrow metal chimney on the roof of the bunkhouse.

For the first time, Tom also noticed that there was a dog chained up at the side of the main building. Behind it was a low addition to the bunkhouse, perhaps housing a generator, and large jerry cans of what he guessed was gasoline stacked beyond it.

The dog was lying with its face flat on the ground but it sprang to its feet now and peered into the trees. It growled and let out an uncertain bark. Then it barked again.

A man appeared in the open door of the bunkhouse and stepped onto the small deck that ran along the front of it. He said something in Spanish to the dog, which wagged its tail in response and barked again, staring at the trees. The man turned to stare too.

He was heavyset with thinning hair and a mustache, wearing a grubby tank undershirt and what looked like green soccer shorts—Tom could buy Joel's assertion that he might be a farmer, but he also didn't look like the kind of person Tom would want to tangle with. There was a meanness about him, a dangerous edge to the way he held himself, alert but completely without fear.

The man saw or heard something now, and called a few inaudible words to the dark of the open door. A moment later, a couple more men came out, one younger, the other old with a thick mop of white hair. Both had guns, and the younger one handed a revolver to the first man.

Alice mumbled something under her breath in response to the sight of the guns and the looks of fierce uncertainty on the faces of the men. But there was no time to say anything else because Joel and Chris came crashing out of the undergrowth on the far side of the camp and into the clearing.

The dog barked again but the first man shouted and it cowered away to the side of the building.

Joel raised his hand in a wave and called out cheerily, "*¡Hola! ¡Buenos dias!* Can you help us?"

"Hello," called Chris, also with a wave.

The younger guy laughed in apparent disbelief. The older man turned and walked back into the bunkhouse. The first man, the one with the mustache, continued to stare, his expression unflinching. Before Joel and Chris had reached them, three more men had emerged from the door, none of them armed, which at least suggested they didn't see the newcomers as a threat.

Joel started to talk again as he reached the men, though Tom couldn't hear his words, just the distinctive, slightly domineering tone of his voice. Chris was adding comments, pointing off into the trees as he did so, overplaying his part.

And it was already obvious that they were wasting their time. The man with the mustache was stone-faced, then amused. He said something over his shoulder and the other men laughed. Joel laughed too, apparently unable to see that the men were mocking him, and that there was menace in their mockery.

The man pointed questioningly to the backpacks, and Joel's voice once again hummed across the distance as he took off his backpack and handed it over. Chris did the same and two of the other men started to look inside them.

Joel reached out, pointing to his own backpack in an attempt to explain something, but whether he moved too quickly or the mustache guy was just tiring of him, it was immediately obvious he'd made a mistake. The man struck out with sickening speed, a blow with the back of his hand that knocked Joel's face sideways.

Alice cursed again and Nick said, "No, no, no," as if by repeating it he could make things go into reverse. Chris stepped back in shock, but that just brought a more urgent response. The first man—the leader, without a doubt—barked out a brief command. The others dropped the packs and grabbed hold of Joel and Chris.

Chris sounded panicky as he shouted, "Say something, Joel!"

But if Joel responded, they didn't hear it from their hiding place, and it produced no effect.

More instructions were given and the two boys were pushed, with kicks and shoves to prod them on their way, across to the barn. They were taken inside, one of the men emerging again almost immediately, but not the others.

A couple of minutes crept past, silence beyond the closed barn door. Tom strained to listen, not certain that he wanted to hear what was happening in there, but listening anyway.

Then the door opened and the other two men came out, laughing with each other. Tom tried to work out what that laughter might mean, if there were any hints within it as to what might have happened to Joel and Chris. For a moment he imagined them both dead in there, killed silently with a minimum of fuss, their deaths no less random and swift than the viper bite that had killed Toby.

The boss said something to the younger man and there was a brief discussion before the younger one went back to the barn. He came out again with a small crate to sit on, closed the door, and settled down—guard duty, thought Tom with relief. They weren't dead, not yet.

The other men carried the backpacks into the bunkhouse and the camp once again fell into stillness and silence. They weren't dead. It was something to hold on to, but they were locked up, and that made the decision about what to do next even harder.

Tom checked his watch, then gestured to Alice that they should move back to a safer distance. He didn't bother to tell Nick, figuring that he'd be smart enough to follow.

And once they were away from the camp, Alice said, "I knew it. What do we do now?"

Tom shook his head, because although he'd been equally sure of this ending badly, he hadn't given any thought to what they'd do when it did. It wasn't as if they could rescue them, but they couldn't just leave them, either.

Alice said, "They won't escape." Her anger flared up, and she looked furious with Joel and Chris and even herself. "This was so stupid! What a stupid, stupid thing to do!"

"Joel said they weren't heavily armed, but they looked it to me." It was Nick, and they both turned to him now. His lip was trembling slightly. "We have to leave." He caught their expressions and added defensively, "You said yourself, it'll be dark soon. We have to think of the others. If we get out of here, we can get help, but it's not like we can do anything ourselves."

Tom said, "You think we should leave?" Nick nodded, his face full of nerves and fear. "These are your friends."

"That's not fair. It's not about that."

Alice said, "I'm not leaving Chris. I just can't."

Tom looked at her, understanding her entirely, seeing the way she was resisting her own helplessness, determined to find a way, determined not to have to face his family and explain why she'd had to leave him behind.

He'd thought earlier about not wanting anything to happen to Alice, but he realized now that this was happening to her too, that losing Chris would be traumatic for her, no less than being seriously wounded herself. It only doubled Tom's resolve.

He looked at his watch, then said, "It'll be dark in less than an hour, so we can't walk back in the light anyway. We'll move back to our vantage point, and just see what happens, see if they're left unguarded at all." Nick's lip was trembling violently now and he was shaking his head, so Tom added, "We don't do anything to endanger the three of us, that's without question. I'm just saying we wait and see. Agreed?"

After what felt like a long time, Nick nodded. Tom turned to Alice and she agreed too, gratefully, because she hadn't yet been forced to accept something she could never accept.

"Good," said Tom, though he knew that his air of certainty and control was a complete sham, because deep down, he understood that there were only a limited number of outcomes here, and he didn't like any of them.

CHAPTER 38

Nothing much seemed to happen for quite a while. The tinny music continued from the bunkhouse, together with laughter and occasionally raised voices. There was the smell of cooking too, of meat, the aroma gnawing away at their own hunger.

But the air of normality only created a more heightened sense of unease. The atmosphere seemed volatile, and the mood of the men sounded more and more unstable, as if at any moment they might explode into violence.

One of the men came out with a plate and a bottle of beer, giving it to the young guy on guard duty before heading back inside. They watched the young guy eat, and so did the dog. When he'd finished, he walked over and tipped the scraps onto the floor before taking the plate back into the bunkhouse.

There was shouting and the young guy came back out, calling

back an angry response but looking chastened. The mood in the bunkhouse sounded ugly now. The guard sat back on his crate, looking miserable.

Now that Tom looked at him, he guessed the guard wasn't much older than them, but his olive complexion and sleek dark hair were matched with a soldier's solid physique. Then there was the gun that he handled, in the relaxed and confident style of someone who'd learned how to use it a long time ago.

So even if the others drank themselves into a stupor, Tom didn't like their chances of overpowering the guard. And given the way they'd shouted at him, presumably for leaving his post, it looked more and more likely that no opportunity would arise, and that sooner or later they'd have to accept they had no choice but to leave them behind—and hope.

More time elapsed, and once again, with nothing really happening, Nick became more agitated. He whispered, "This is pointless." They looked at him. "They're probably already dead."

Tom had been increasingly sensing the pointlessness of it himself, but if anything, Nick's doubting only strengthened Tom's determination to find a way, and he said firmly, "You don't guard dead people."

"Anyway, we're staying," said Alice. "But feel free to walk back on your own, any time you like."

"I'm not saying that. But...we can't just sit here forever."

That was a truth Tom couldn't deny, but he said, "They think Chris and Joel are on their own, so they're not expecting anyone else, and they'll have to sleep sometime."

The three of them fell back into silence, and they stayed like that until darkness fell. As ever, nightfall brought a subtle shift in

212 I KEVIN WIGNALL

the seething soundscape of the jungle and an immediate increase in the number of mosquitoes harassing them.

A light came on in the bunkhouse and then the door was closed, but in the darkness the sounds from within, raucous and drunken, still came clearly across the jungle to them. The guard went into the barn and came back out almost immediately, carrying a lantern that he lit and placed on the ground next to him—within seconds, moths spun out of the dark and crashed frantically into it.

The noise within the bunkhouse rose in peaks, falling away again, and then the door opened and two men stepped out. Even in silhouette, Tom could see that one was the man in charge. He wasn't sure if he recognized the other, but he didn't like the slightly drunken swagger of either of them.

The boss was eating a huge piece of meat, what looked like half a chicken, but he saw the dog now and teased it, holding the meat just beyond the reach of its chain. He dropped it on the ground then and laughed as the dog struggled in vain to reach it.

The two men headed across to the barn, talking to the young guard, and Tom felt his stomach tightening into a ball of vicious energy, because he didn't like how this was looking at all. Whatever they had in mind, they looked fired up with alcohol and cruelty.

The guard stood in response to them and the boss laughed and patted him on the cheek. The guard knocked his hand away halfheartedly and walked back to the bunkhouse, closing the door behind him, briefly dulling the chorus from within before it started up again.

The other man picked up the lantern and both of them

walked into the barn and closed the door. Tom wasn't sure if he could hear them laughing about something, or if that was just the sound carrying from the bunkhouse.

Then he heard Alice, almost mumbling to herself before the words formed together and she said, "I don't like this, Tom. I don't like it at all."

Tom hardly heard her. He was staring at the sliver of light around the doors to the bunkhouse and the barn, at the dog trying to get to the food that was in the dirt beyond its reach, and he could hear the noise coming from the camp, and the dog straining at its chain, and indistinct words from both Nick and Alice, and the constant chatter of the jungle and the troubling silence of the barn.

Something bad was happening, right now in that barn, at the hands of those men, and there was no time left to wait. He had said more than once that he wouldn't let anyone else die, and it was easy and immature to say, but the time had come to put those words into action.

He was here, and the time was now.

CHAPTER 39

He pulled his backpack toward him in the dark, adrenaline flooding his bloodstream so instantaneously that he had to hold on to something to stop his hands shaking. He found the flare guns, loaded them, even with his fingers fumbling, slipped them into his belt, and grabbed hold of the spear.

"If something happens, get back to the camp, get the boats to the river, and go."

He stood.

"No, wait..." It was Alice, but there was no time.

"You heard me. If you have to, you go."

And he set off through the undergrowth, breaking into a run even as the thoughts and ideas assembled, the possibilities, the things he could and would have to do. As he reached the clearing, his thoughts suddenly crystalized and the nerves fell away and he felt an odd sense of peace deep within himself.

The dog saw him first, backing away from the meat, growling, uncertain. It let out an exploratory bark, but the noise from elsewhere was loud enough that no one would hear. He had to save the dog, he knew that, even in the middle of all the things he had to do—the dog had done no harm to anyone.

He moved silently toward it, picked up the meat and held it out. The dog hesitated, still growling, but edged forward and snatched the meat from his hand. With its mouth full, Tom moved in, scratching the top of its head even as it growled possessively at him. He reached over then and released its chain and the dog jumped away from him and carried its prize off into the shadows.

Tom moved on to the jerry cans. He put his spear down, then opened the first can and poured the fuel in a line along the side of the bunkhouse and onto the decking. He ran back, got another and opened it, leaving it on its side near the bunkhouse door, the gasoline glugging out across the timbers.

He got his spear, retreating then beyond the far corner of the barn. He could hear the voices of the two men inside, playful and malicious, and he thought he heard Joel once, weakly, a plea of some sort.

But he didn't want to listen. He hoped he wasn't too late, but he didn't want to listen. He took the first flare gun from his belt and aimed it at the remaining jerry cans at the side of the bunkhouse. He fired, and the flare shot out into the darkness with a noise like tearing paper, arcing and spinning toward its destination.

Tom expected an explosion, but not *this* kind of explosion. It was instant and astounding, a blast of light and heat and wind, knocking him backward onto the ground, filling the sky with a brief blinding flash and flying debris as the bunkhouse blew apart and disintegrated.

He scrambled back onto his knees, only certain he was still holding the spear when he leaned on it, almost like a walking stick. The barn door flew open and the leader burst out of it. He saw Tom kneeling on the ground and ran toward him.

Tom didn't hesitate, time slowing down as the bulk of the man careened toward him. Tom pushed himself up, climbing to his feet, and before he was even upright, he thrust the spear forward, into the man's stomach, pushing harder as it met resistance, fat and muscle and bone, pushing until they crashed into each other, a shattering blow, and Tom could smell the man's sweat and the beer and meat on his breath.

They spun around each other, as if performing a choreo-graphed street dance, and the man fell onto his back in the dirt, the spear pushed up at an angle into the top of his stomach, under his ribs. The momentum sent Tom stumbling over him toward the open barn door, and even as he tried to right himself, he pulled the other flare gun free and turned to face the barn.

He saw Joel and Chris, their hands tied to a beam above their heads. He saw the other guy standing by them, holding a machete, looking confused, panicked.

He saw the gun in Tom's hand and said something urgent in Spanish, holding his hands out in submission, and Tom fired. The flare tore in a short haphazard trail across the barn and blasted into him, a scorch-black explosion into his stomach, and the man screamed and fell backward, and he kept screaming for a few seconds more as Tom ran into the barn.

Chris was bruised around the eye. Joel's T-shirt had been torn off and was lying like a rag on the floor. They were both talking but the roar of the explosion was still in his ears and Tom couldn't hear them or make sense of what they were saying. He ran over to the man on the floor, dead now, his flesh still burning and sulfurous, and pulled the machete from his hand.

He cut Chris's ropes first, then Joel's, and they were still talking but he ignored them and said, "Follow me."

He ran back out, and for some reason thought to retrieve Barney's spear, but it was wedged so deeply into the dead man's body and was so slicked in blood that he left it. Across the way, what little remained of the bunkhouse was burning furiously, a bonfire that no longer even resembled a building.

Tom turned away from it, blinded for a moment, the darkness beyond looking total and uncompromising, but then he spotted a flashlight beam in the distance, merely a pinhole against the velvet backdrop of the jungle.

He headed for it, vaguely conscious of Chris and Joel running behind him, and of the deeper roar of fire farther back. At last, the beam of light moved and came toward them and they nearly ran into each other.

Chris was still pulling the remains of the rope from his wrists, babbling and distraught, saying, "No way, no way, that was… What were they gonna do to us?"

Joel had been quiet but said, "Shut up, Chris."

"He cut your shirt off!" He turned to Nick, who looked as shell-shocked as if he'd been in the barn himself. "They were…

That wasn't good. If Tom hadn't come...Man, thank you so much, always. They were acting so weird."

More urgently, Joel said, "Chris, just shut up!"

"It's true, you know it is."

"Christian," said Alice, using his full name, but reassuring this time, and he turned to her and she put her arms around him, calming him instantly.

Nick looked at Tom and said, "I'm sorry—the things I said earlier."

Tom shook his head. "It doesn't matter."

Joel said, "Thank you. What you just did was...heroic."

Tom nodded, accepting the thanks, but hardly feeling like a hero. He turned back to face the burning camp, trying to take on board that he had just killed at least half a dozen people. The two he'd killed directly hardly seemed real, but he kept thinking of the guard who'd been nearly their own age, and he'd had no choice, he was sure of that, but he still couldn't fully comprehend that he'd ended that kid's life.

He caught movement in the shadows between the camp and where they were standing and he tensed, his hand tightening around the handle of the machete, but he relaxed again as he saw the dog come trotting with a light step toward him. Its tail was wagging and as it reached him it nuzzled his leg and he scratched the top of its head. At least he'd saved the dog—he wasn't sure why, but that really mattered to him right now.

CHAPTER 40

They found their way back to the remaining backpacks and Nick gave Joel a T-shirt. Joel thanked him, subdued, diminished in some way by what he'd just experienced. Tom's T-shirt was wet with blood and he pulled it off and threw it away before getting a fresh one from his pack.

Alice kept glancing at Chris, wanting to be sure he was okay, but she had a solid determination about her now and she said, "We should use one flashlight at a time, in case the batteries run out. The river's that way and the hills are there, so if we head roughly in that direction, the third side of the triangle Joel was talking about, we can't get lost without coming to the river first. Agreed?"

"Agreed," said Nick.

She nodded and said, "I'll carry the flashlight. Tom, you've got the machete, so we'll take the lead."

Chris said, "I'll take your backpack, Alice."

She looked ready to object but saw something in his eyes and nodded. Joel said, "I can carry yours, Tom, if you don't mind."

Tom wasn't really sure what that was all about but he shrugged and said, "Sure."

They prepared to set off, but almost as an afterthought, Alice said, "Oh, Tom." He turned toward her and she hugged him, tightly, her head against his, and she whispered close to his ear, her voice full of emotion, "Thank you. Thank you."

He nodded, though she couldn't see, and he found his throat tightening with emotion too, perhaps only because he couldn't remember the last time he'd encountered this kind of total gratitude. In fact, now that he thought of it, he wasn't sure he'd ever done anything before in his life that had meant this much to another person.

She pulled away then and said, "What about you? Are you okay?"

"I'm fine," he said, because he did feel fine, though he knew he probably shouldn't, and that something had changed within him in the last fifteen minutes, whether he fully knew it yet or not. "I just killed a whole bunch of people, but I'm fine."

"You did what you had to do, and you saved two people."

"And a dog."

She laughed. "And a dog."

They set off through the jungle, and the dog went with them, sometimes scouting ahead, responding to scents and sounds they couldn't detect themselves, occasionally becoming alert or growling before coming back to Tom.

He didn't have the time to think much during the walk back,

because walking through the jungle at night, even with the aid of a flashlight and a dog, required full concentration.

Only once did anyone refer again to what had happened, and that was when Chris said, "You don't think they'll come after us? Those other guys?"

"I doubt it," said Alice. "Even if they heard the explosion, they'd probably think it was soldiers or another gang. I don't think they'd turn back with a whole load of cocaine."

Joel added, "They wouldn't know where to find us anyway." His voice seemed to have regained its confidence and authority, but none of them responded and they walked on for some time in almost complete silence.

When the ground started to climb, the undergrowth also became thicker. Tom walked in front, holding a flashlight in one hand and the machete in the other, but progress was slower and the dog stayed behind him now, walking alongside Alice.

Tom was just reaching the point of suggesting they might need to backtrack and try a different route when Alice pointed and said, "Wait, shine the light up there, to the right." He aimed the beam in that direction. "Is that the bluff we stood on today?"

"It might be." And the more he looked, the more sure he was that they were standing below it.

He pushed on, the dog barking once, in exuberance it seemed, perhaps picking up on his change of mood. He was more certain when they finally got onto the bluff itself, even seeing it in the unfamiliar dark, and then they found the beginning of the path they'd trampled and hacked to get there.

Now that they knew where they were, they stopped for ten minutes and had something to drink. The dog explored the area around the bluff. No one spoke at first and Tom felt a sense of peace falling over him, realizing only now that he hadn't quite relaxed since leaving the cocaine factory.

But they were within reach of getting back to the others now, and Joel's voice floated out of the dark, saying, "We probably shouldn't tell the others too much about what happened this evening. It might upset some of them."

His thinking was fairly transparent, and Tom could detect some humor in Alice's voice as she said, "You mean, we don't need to tell them you messed up?"

But Joel's voice came back forcefully. "We didn't mess up, we took a risk, for the sake of everyone else, and maybe that risk didn't pay off, but that doesn't mean we were wrong to take it."

"We'll have to agree to disagree on that, Joel, because I think it's the most stupid thing you've done, and that's saying something."

For a moment there was no response, and then he said, "All I've done from the minute we crashed is try to help everyone, and that's what Chris and I were doing when we walked into that camp. I just think it could upset people if we tell them too much about it."

Alice sounded furious as she said, "Fine."

There was another pause, and Tom sensed Joel was waiting for him to respond, so in the end he said, "I don't care either way. But we should go."

They started walking again, a different silence now, a sense that the five of them were once again divided into factions. Given what had happened, or what Tom thought had happened back there in the camp, he was just puzzled that it hadn't dented Joel's apparent air of control or his desire to be seen as the person making all the key decisions.

It didn't matter though, none of that mattered, not in the grand scheme of things, and if the events of this evening hadn't revealed that particular truth to Joel, then nothing would.

CHAPTER 41

The dog reached the camp before them, rushing ahead, producing a brief scream from one of the girls, then excitement from all of them.

Mila said, "It's Joel and the others!"

That produced more excitement and by the time they descended back down the slope onto the beach they were all standing, the fire behind them. The reunion was chaotic and loud. Lara grabbed hold of Alice, a couple more crowded around Joel and Nick and Chris. Kate came up and hugged Tom before stepping back and laughing a little to herself.

As she went back to the fire, Shen and Barney and George came over to him and George said, "I knew you'd come back."

Tom nodded, but looked at Barney and said, "I lost your spear."

"But gained a machete. And a dog."

"Yeah," said Tom, laughing. The dog was looping manically around their camp area as if following a trail. It reached Chloe's net-covered bed, and Tom said, "How's Chloe?"

"Better," said Shen. "She won't be ready to move tomorrow, but she's a lot better, definitely over the worst."

"Good."

Then he smiled as Joel's earlier suggestion to keep quiet got cast aside, Chris saying to Oscar and Sandeep, "Just insane. Seriously, me and Joel got tied up. I mean, I don't even wanna know what they were gonna do to us. But then Tom came in like Vin Diesel and killed them all. Seriously. Just blew this guy away with a flare gun right in front of us. It was…" The other voices fell away until everyone was listening to Chris and then he realized and stopped. He looked at Joel and said, "Sorry."

Joel shook his head, as if to say it didn't matter, but everyone else was looking at Tom now.

Oscar said, "You killed people?"

He sounded intrigued, even awestruck, and the faces of the others seemed split between horror and fascination. Tom didn't think any of those responses were appropriate, but nor was he sure what the correct response should have been. The one thing he knew for sure was that he didn't like those stares—he'd just started to feel he belonged, with some of them at least, and now he felt like an outsider all over again.

But it was Alice who answered anyway, saying, "It wasn't like that. Chris is exaggerating again."

To his credit, Chris shrugged and said, "Okay, maybe, a little. But I was the one who said the plane would crash."

That brought some laughter and lighthearted derision, all of which Chris took gamely on the chin in his attempt to undo his revelations of a minute before. It seemed to work to some extent, in that people kept talking to him and Joel in the same way, but Tom caught a few more intrigued stares in his direction and it was clear that none of them believed Chris had exaggerated entirely.

Tom turned back to the others and said, "What's the food situation?"

Shen nodded, as though he'd been waiting for the question. "It took a while to develop a technique, but Kate managed to catch a couple of fish. We cooked them over the fire this afternoon. She thinks we'll catch more tomorrow."

"We will," said George. "Now that we know how to do it. She's a natural."

"I know it," said Tom.

"And we're lucky there don't seem to be any anacondas or caimans on this stretch, so the fish are plentiful."

"How do you know there aren't any?"

"We don't know for sure, but we were there all afternoon and no thirty-foot snakes or alligator-type things came flying out at us." George laughed. "It's good news, anyway. It means we can save the remaining snacks until we're in the boats."

"Yeah, sure, and the sooner we get in those boats, the better."

George looked at Tom for a moment and asked, "What really happened back there?"

Kate came back over as Tom started talking. "Pretty much what Chris said. It was some sort of cocaine factory, drug cartel, or rebels. Joel thought the two of them could just walk in there and tell them they were lost. Alice tried to warn them, but..."

"But what was that he said about you killing everyone?"

Tom thought of the young guard emptying the scraps of his dinner for the dog, thought of him trying to act tough in front of the older guys. He thought too of the white-haired man, and for some reason wondered in retrospect if he'd been the cook—he wasn't sure why he thought that, and it hardly mattered because they were all dead.

"It wasn't really the way Chris made it out to be. I blew up the bunkhouse with five or six of them inside. The other two were in the barn where they had Chris and Joel tied up. One almost ran into the spear. The other one I shot with a flare gun."

"Wow."

"Yeah, wow," said Tom. "I didn't really think about it at the time. I just didn't have much choice."

George had the same look on his face that Oscar had shown earlier, a mixture of intrigue and awe, but he put it into words. "I guess we're all wondering what we would've done in the same situation. I like to think I would've done what you did, but who knows?"

Again, Tom was struck by the fact that they thought he was brave or a hero, when he didn't feel like he'd been either.

"Yeah, well, the truth is, I'm not even sure *I'd* do it again. None of us knows, not until it happens."

George accepted the point but Kate said, "No, Tom, I think you'd do it every time. You might not know it, but it's who you are." She smiled mischievously, adding, "I mean, if you did it for Joel, you'd do it for anyone."

"Maybe." But he was grateful for her mild teasing, grateful that Kate also seemed to think no less of him for what he'd done.

It was left at that and little by little the camp settled down again. The only real difference was the dog, which various people fussed over, though it always came back and sat next to Tom. Julia had never let him have a dog, but he was glad for this one now because, for all the bad things that he'd done back at that camp, at least he'd also done this one good thing too.

CHAPTER 42

Tom was woken at first light by the dog growling. He opened his eyes, saw that same stained-orange sky hanging low overheard. The dog let out a bark and growled again. Tom heard one of the girls, half-asleep, saying, "What's he barking at?"

Tom thought of the men from the camp and jumped up, but the dog was facing the river, growling, running forward toward the water before retreating again. He stood, rubbing his eyes even as the others were also getting to their feet.

His first thought was something in the water, a caiman or anaconda, but as he approached he couldn't see anything, and in fact, the dog seemed to be focusing on the opposite bank. Tom stared over there, but again could see nothing at all.

Tom scratched the top of the dog's head and he calmed for a moment and settled by him, but then jumped and barked again.

Kate was nearby now and said, "What's he barking at, Tom?"

"Not sure. Something's spooked him. Maybe a jaguar or something."

She came over and said, "Well, I'd rather have a spooked dog than a jaguar."

Unexpectedly, Chloe's voice emerged from the other side of the fire, saying, "Did I hear a dog barking?"

They looked and saw she was sitting up under the nets. A few of the others headed over to her, so Tom faced the river again. The dog had calmed down and appeared relaxed now, but Tom still stared into the undergrowth on the other bank, wondering what it had detected in there.

He only gave up looking when he heard Joel in pep-talk mode, saying, "Okay, everyone, let's have a good day today, a chance to recover, and then tomorrow we'll head over the hill and launch the boats."

Tom smiled, amused by Joel's need to take ownership of their deliverance. He also sounded as though the events of yesterday had already been forgotten, and maybe he had already managed to put them out of his mind.

Tom envied him for that. Joel had acted stupidly and something terrible had nearly happened to him and Chris as a result, but in the end they hadn't suffered any serious harm, and the trauma of being a captive would diminish in time and become a boastful story about a lucky escape in the jungle.

The real price of Joel's stupidity had, as always, been paid by others, and Tom was one of those now, because he had killed people. He could remember their faces so clearly, and he had an uncomfortable feeling he'd never forget them—the two men in the barn, the old man with the white hair, the young guard.

He turned back and faced the camp, the group coalescing around the fire now. Chloe was on her feet and being helped to the fire by Barney and Mila—she looked a lot better, but Shen's assessment was probably right about her not being ready to travel today.

They were all talking again too, animated, as cohesive a group as they'd been immediately after the crash. And standing there near the water with the dog lying nearby, Tom briefly felt about as far removed from them as he ever had.

But just then he realized someone was looking back at him—Alice—and when he made eye contact she smiled, even laughed a little, finding some amusement in the sight of him standing at a distance again. And Tom smiled too, thinking maybe his days of being an outsider were over, that he'd made connections now, perhaps even become part of a jigsaw puzzle of sorts.

As if to prove that, Kate walked over to him and said, "We'll need a couple of people to keep a lookout while me and George are fishing. It takes a lot of concentration, so someone else needs to look out for predators."

"I can do that."

"I thought you would." She looked at the river. "With any luck, they'll be sick of eating fish by the end of the day."

"Where'd you catch it yesterday?"

"Over here, I'll show you."

And with that, Tom edged back into the group, and the day progressed with some sort of normality. Kate and George proved adept at catching fish, one disturbing them and chasing them into the net held by the other.

Most of the group ended up watching them, their spirits rising with each catch. The only person who seemed at all subdued was Chris, who sat next to Chloe for most of the day, talking quietly, neither of their voices audible above the general excitement and the occasional playful barks of the dog.

Late in the afternoon, not long before the sun would be setting somewhere behind the opaque orange mist, Shen skewered the fish onto one of the poles and started to cook it over the fire. The dog joined the rest of them in watching it cook, knowing he would be in for the scraps, but then quite abruptly, he became alert and turned away to look at the river.

He growled and took a cautious step forward. Tom stood, turning to look in the same direction, and the dog took that as his cue, leaping forward with a couple of aggressive barks.

The group fell silent, and then Chris said, "What is it, Tom?"

Tom shook his head, but the dog was still growling, still fixed on the same stretch of undergrowth on the far bank. Tom picked up a stone and pitched it across the river, aiming for the focus of the dog's stare. It hit the undergrowth on the far side, and there, briefly, was a flash of color and movement as something leapt away and into the depths of the jungle beyond.

"Did you see anything?"

"I'm not sure," said Tom. "Maybe a big cat."

Chloe said to no one in particular, "It's awesome having a dog around."

The dog turned and went back to watching the fish, which Tom took as proof enough that he'd scared off whatever had been over there. He went back and sat down himself, but he sensed it was right for them to move on, the mysterious watcher on the other bank just one more indication that this was not their environment, that they weren't meant to be here.

Darkness fell as they were eating, almost unnoticed because of the dim twilight they'd become used to and the distraction of the food and the fire.

But a short while later, Mila said, "I'm glad it's dark. That orange sky freaks me out."

"I know what you mean," said Emma. Then, to the group, she said, "Do you think something major might have happened? I mean, the people you saw in that camp, were they acting normally?"

Alice said, "I think so. I haven't spent that much time around cocaine producers."

A few of them laughed, but Emma said, "It just all seems a little weird."

No one laughed at that, and a short while later thunder rumbled in the distance and the mood became more somber still. Those things, the strangely lit sky, the threat of distant storms, seemed to sum up that they were still traveling through an unknown, with no idea how far they were from safety or even if it was out there at all.

Within an hour, they started to settle and sleep where they could. Joel made a point of saying he'd keep first watch, so Tom slept too, the exertions of the previous day and night still catching up with him. The thunder continued to rumble in the distance as he fell away, never coming much closer, like the sound of a distant battle.

CHAPTER 43

Tom woke and immediately held his watch to face the fire—it was just after four in the morning, another couple of hours from daylight. At first he thought no one else was awake but then he noticed Shen nearby, sitting on his backpack, staring quizzically at the sky.

He understood why when the night suddenly lit up, bringing the surrounding jungle close before sending it rushing back into the dark. Tom waited for the thunder, but it didn't come.

He sat up and looked at Shen, who smiled and said, "It's been like that for an hour. I can't hear any thunder at all, but the sky looks stormy, and the river's louder."

Now that he'd said it, Tom also noticed that the river seemed to be running faster behind them.

"Just louder, or higher too?"

"I hadn't thought of that." He reached for his flashlight and got up, walking to the water's edge. Tom followed him, looking down at the light where it fell on the swiftly rippling surface. Shen seemed troubled. "There must be a lot of rain falling high in the hills."

He walked along the bank to the end of the little beach closest to the gorge entrance, keeping the light on the water, and again, Tom went with him. The water was already lapping up over the far edge in little waves. Tom thought of the way the beach had been carved out, the ravine they'd crossed, the forces with which they'd been shaped.

Almost to himself, Shen said, "I knew this was a mistake."

He was talking about the decision to camp here, although if they'd left that day it wouldn't have seemed like a mistake at all and they'd have remembered it only as a great place to recover and catch fish.

Tom said, "We have to get off this beach. Start waking them."

Tom stayed where he was, listening to the river, as Shen walked over to the fire and said, "Everyone, we need to move off the beach." It was met with grumbles and moans, but also with a few people moving and asking what was going on. "It's not raining here, but it's raining in the hills, and unless I'm mistaken, this beach is about to flood."

That got everyone's attention and a dozen flashlight beams started crisscrossing and dancing around the camp, people moving, the dog looping happily around them. The dog quickly found his way to Tom, who scratched the top of his head, but he still listened intently, unable to shake his uneasiness.

He heard Joel saying, "Shen, bro, are you sure about this?"

The night lit up, illuminating the beach, and revealed several tiny streams of water working their way from the edge. Tom looked across at the camp, caught like a tableau in that moment of light, a confusion of bodies and backpacks and clumsy movements.

And then beyond their chatter, beyond the rippling water beside him, beyond the jungle itself, he heard a noise, almost like a distant plane, and he wondered for a fraction of a second if their stricken plane had sounded like that as it made its final descent into the jungle. But this was not a plane, and it was coming toward him and in one terrifying moment he understood immediately what it was.

"Everyone! Move! *Now*!"

The dog barked and Tom ran himself, scooping up the backpack and machete with one hand, grabbing the handle of one of the boat cases with the other and dragging it across the rocky shore. The noise was deafening now, in his own ears at least. It was raining in the hills and a wall of water was barreling toward them.

His urgency spread like a contagion and there was a lot more concentrated activity going on around him, the flashlights all pointing in the same direction as they climbed up onto the higher ground above the beach.

Tom heard the fire hiss as he climbed the bank. He turned to see the flames being extinguished as the first water lapped over the fire in the darkness.

Then he heard one of the girls shout, "Barney, no!"

Barney called back from somewhere below, "I'm okay!"

The night lit up again and Tom saw Barney on the beach,

dashing away from them, the water already halfway to his knees. But in that splintered second of light, Tom saw what Barney was heading for, the other boat case, and he knew he was right—they needed both boats.

Tom threw his backpack and machete down and jumped into the shallow water. The lights were trained on the beach now, and Tom could see that George had also gone back and all three boys reached the boat case at once and started to haul it toward the higher ground.

Another surge of water came, the level suddenly reaching Tom's knees, pulling hard at his legs. He saw Barney stumble, but before Tom could even react, George reached out and took hold of Barney's arm, righting him.

They were pushing hard but the current was against them and the roaring upstream suggested they weren't in the worst of it yet. He heard shouts from the bank, sounding muffled and distant even though they were only a few yards away.

Another swell of water came, pulsing and pulling so power-fully that for a moment Tom could only plant his feet and hope to hold firm. As soon as it eased, they pushed on again and this time they reached the bank, and the lights danced again as hands reached down to pull the three of them and the boat onto the higher ground.

They were still catching their breath when the roar intensified and the flashlights focused back on the flood as something like an ocean wave surged and crashed through the horseshoe of the beach. Water sprayed up as it broke against the bank, making everyone take another involuntary backward step.

More lightning flashed and now they could see how the water

had completely engulfed what had been their camp until a few minutes ago.

Joel said, "Barney, that was a crazy thing to do. Brave, I'll give you that, but we could've lost you."

Barney said, "We need that boat."

"Of course we do," said George. "Quick thinking, Barney—we would've been in trouble without it."

"Thanks."

"Point taken," said Joel in an oddly petulant tone. "Now, is everyone okay?" He got a slightly dejected chorus of positive responses, then said, "Anyone got any idea of the time?"

"Just after four," said Tom.

"Okay, well it's a good hour or so over the hill to the other part of the river. Why don't we get ourselves organized, then walk up to that bluff we stood on?"

Chloe or Mila—Tom wasn't sure which—said, "What, in the dark?"

"It shouldn't be a problem as far as the bluff," said Joel. "We cut the path back as we walked, so it's pretty open, and we have our flashlights. We can rest there until it gets light and that way we won't have so far to walk to the river."

There was no real response after that, because the plan seemed set in stone. For once, Tom even agreed with him, because it was an easy path, one they'd already descended in darkness, and it was better to be moving rather than standing here waiting for the sun to come up.

It was only when they got themselves organized that Alice said, "What will this do to the river on the other side?"

Shen answered, "I think this section floods here because the gorge is pretty narrow, so with a more open flow on the other side I doubt it would break its banks so easily. If anything, a faster current might help us."

Joel added, "We'll have to give it a try anyway—the river's our only realistic option for getting out of here. We've known that all along."

Tom smiled. He would've liked to see Alice and Shen's expressions. Aside from Joel talking as though the river escape had always been his plan, he was ignoring one other obvious route, because those cocaine smugglers had been heading somewhere, even if it was just a remote jungle airstrip. And as unlikely as that option seemed right now, they'd have to consider it if going down the river proved impossible.

He guessed they'd find out about that soon enough, though, because after a little more organization, they set off in a long nocturnal column, up the hill and toward the bluff on the other side. Every five minutes or so as they walked, the jungle lit up around them, throwing startling shadows. After each lightning flash, there was another flurry of talking, often about the lack of rain or thunder.

By the time they reached the bluff, there was probably only another half hour of darkness left, but the weather finally broke and a steady rain started to fall. That produced another flurry of activity as people reached for waterproof gear, then searched for spares they could give Joel and Chris.

Daylight came, finally without the orange hue, but the sight from the bluff only served to subdue them even more. The jungle seemed to stretch out forever in front of them, rain-soaked and featureless except for the muddy brown of the river snaking off to their right.

But whatever the others thought looking out at that view, Tom felt a frisson of nerves and energy, a slight elevation in the adrenaline flowing around his bloodstream, a desire to move on and find out. It felt like many days had crawled past since he'd first imagined this escape, and this was the ultimate test of Tom's plan.

If it succeeded, Joel would take the credit, and Tom didn't mind that so much. But if it failed, there'd be absolute certainty, in some minds at least, about whose fault it was.

CHAPTER 44

They walked the last leg with the rain falling constantly, water seeping and steaming through the jungle floor around them, forming into tiny streams, so that in the end it appeared the river was coming to meet them.

The riverbank was raised, so they didn't see the water until they were almost on it, and then before anyone could speak, the dog barked furiously and bounded down the bank. There was a splash and flurry of movement in front of them, the unmistakable outline of a caiman slipping beneath the surface.

Tom searched the murky water, trying to see if it would reappear, but Shen was standing next to him and said, "It was one of the smaller species, which is a good sign." Tom looked at him. "Black caimans are the ones we have to watch out for, but if there was a black caiman here it probably would've eaten that one."

Joel came to the bank. He looked briefly at Tom—an oddly unfriendly look that Tom couldn't quite work out. Far from acting friendlier toward Tom since the cocaine factory rescue, Joel seemed to be becoming steadily more resentful. To Shen he said, "So it's safe? To launch the boats?"

They all looked toward the river where the dog was busily patrolling the water's edge, apparently baffled by the caiman's disappearance.

"Nothing's coming after the dog and the water's flowing fast, but not dangerously so. It's wide enough too, though we'll have to make sure we keep to the middle, to avoid getting snagged. That's where Barney's oars should help." When Shen got no answer, he turned to face Joel. "So yes, I'd say it's safe to launch the boats."

"Great. In which case, why don't you and Barney open them and get them pumped up." He glanced at Tom again before turning to the group. "Chris, Nick, Sandeep, Oscar, you help Shen and Barney with the boats. Everyone else, check your backpacks, see if there's anything that can be left behind."

Shen looked puzzled. "The boats are going to be pretty big."

"Even so, everyone, check your packs."

People started to move, though with the exception of Shen and Barney, none of them seemed to have much idea what they were supposed to be doing.

Alice walked over to Tom and said, "I notice he didn't ask any girls to help put the boats up."

"He didn't ask me, either."

"Probably for the same reason. Scared of you, scared of girls."

Tom laughed and they watched as the boats were opened for

the first time. They were yellow octagonal rafts, big enough that they had to be moved onto the sloping bank, touching the water's edge. As their scale became apparent, Tom noticed a couple of people picking up discarded items and putting them back into their packs.

Once the boats were fully inflated, Joel pointed one by one, saying, "Okay, my boat, I'll take Chris, Nick, Chloe, Mila, Oscar, Lara—"

Lara looked put out. "Oh, I thought I'd go with Alice."

He sounded like a teacher in response. "We're all going to be together anyway so it doesn't matter which boat you're in. Sandeep's in the other raft and he's not complaining. We're just dividing the group, not worrying about who's friends with who."

Alice and Tom exchanged a glance, acknowledging the lie of Joel's last comment, given that he'd made sure all of his friends were with him in his boat. Or all but one, anyway.

Despite Joel's comment, Sandeep looked just as put out that he'd been assigned to Tom's boat, and Tom didn't get it, either, because he'd imagined Sandeep being good friends with Joel. His dad was a professional golfer and Sandeep had won a couple of amateur trophies himself—Tom only knew this because he'd overheard someone at school explaining once why Sandeep dressed like a middle-aged man.

So maybe it was just Tom's prejudice—automatically linking Joel with a kid who played golf—and maybe they weren't such close friends. Tom didn't mind this arrangement, anyway, and would have more or less chosen the people he'd been allotted, especially because, with the exception of Lara, his raft contained most of the people who'd originally asked to leave with him.

"Okay, let's get launched. Everyone who's in my boat…"

Joel headed down to the water's edge and the others duti-fully followed him, while he dished out instructions. He seemed incredibly eager to get on the water, and Tom wondered if it was just that he wanted *his* boat to be in the lead. Sure enough, within a couple of minutes they were on the river and being pulled out into the current, even as the rest of them just watched.

Shen stepped forward and called, "Keep in the middle of the channel!"

Joel waved, though it was unclear whether he'd heard, and the raft slipped out of view.

They stood there for a second, and then George said, "Okay, they're gone, let's go back to the plane and wait to be rescued."

Laughing, they started getting their things into the raft, lift-ing it out onto the water, and climbing aboard one by one. In their group, a few words were exchanged, but no orders, and no one took charge. They still managed to launch the boat as quickly as Joel had launched his, which Tom saw as a vindication in some way.

The dog had paced manically up and down the bank the whole time, but as soon as Tom climbed in, he jumped over the side and stumbled into the middle like a drunk, earning another collective laugh. Then George pushed the raft and jumped aboard in one fluid movement, while Sandeep and Barney started to row as they drifted quickly into the middle of the channel.

The raft immediately felt more robust than Tom had expected, the sides higher too, designed for being adrift on an ocean rather than a river. He'd thought the octagonal shape might make it difficult to handle, and he imagined it spinning like a top downstream, but the flow of the river was strong enough that Sandeep and Barney found it easy to maintain a central course with their oars.

There was a slight bend ahead, and the other boat had already disappeared around it before they'd launched, but as they approached it themselves they could hear the unmistakable chatter and laughter. And as they rounded the bend, Barney started rowing furiously.

It was soon clear why. Joel's boat had become snagged against a branch or root that arched out into the water, and it took some quick maneuvering to stop the second raft from ramming into it. Chris and Oscar were working hard to free it.

Shen shouted, "Any damage?"

"It's fine," said Joel. "We'll pass you on the next bend."

Kate turned incredulously to the rest of them. "Did I hear him right? He thinks it's a race?" She shook her head, full of contempt.

Shen said, "I'm sure he didn't mean it like that." He looked at the river ahead of them, smooth and open, but containing any number of dangers in the miles ahead, and added, "I hope not, anyway."

Sandeep looked back for a second. "Should we try to wait for them?"

A collective "No!" came straight back at him and he laughed and went back to using the oar to keep their boat steadily mid-river.

The river seemed to be made up of long stretches that were more or less straight, punctuated with shallow meandering turns, but the turns were frequent enough that for the next hour or so they never once saw Joel's raft. It had to be reasonably close behind them, but they couldn't even hear the others.

The rain stopped, and the humidity became even more intense. They took off their waterproof gear and dropped it into the bottom of the boat.

The number of flies and other insects buzzing around them rose steadily. The jungle was dense and unchanging. It hummed and whirred on either side, but there seemed to be an eerie peacefulness on the water itself.

The dog soon learned to stand and move comfortably among them, and seemed transfixed by the riverbanks, as if he alone could see the secrets hidden within that lush dark green. Occasionally he would bark, his nose pointed at a particular spot on the bank, and they'd all stare in vain and speculate on what he might have seen.

The clouds broke up, the first patches of blue appeared, and within no time at all, the sky had cleared and the heat became total, as if it were inside them, a part of them. They became deaf to the sounds of the jungle now and floated on in a muted silence, and whenever someone spoke, a couple of the others would jump in shock at the sudden noise.

A couple of hours in, Shen shared some of the few remaining drinks and food. They were down to snacks now—nuts and cookies—but they savored them like a feast. Tom opened his pack of cookies, took one for himself and gave the other to the dog. Alice gave the dog something, then a few more people.

The dog went from person to person with ludicrously grateful eyes and Tom laughed and said, "Well, at least the dog won't starve."

There was more laughter, not from their boat, but from upriver. It was the first time they'd had any indication the other boat was still behind them, a joyful laughter that Tom could easily imagine being a response to a joke from Chris.

Alice said, "That's a relief."

Jess nodded in agreement. "I was getting a little worried about them."

Sandeep turned briefly to look at them all. "Joel's not stupid—I know he can be a bit of an ass, but he's not bad when you get to know him better. His dad gives him a really hard time, like nothing he does is ever good enough. That's why he's always pushing himself."

It immediately made sense to Tom and he felt a small wave of sympathy for Joel, but Kate was apparently unconvinced and said, "I heard that too, and any other time I'd feel for him, but out here, it's our lives on the line."

Sandeep said, "And he knows that—he's trying to look after everyone."

Kate laughed bitterly and said, "Like he looked after Naomi and Freddie?" Her face immediately filled with horror and she turned to Jess and said, "Jess, I'm so sorry, I didn't mean..."

"It's okay," said Jess, a calmness about her that Tom thought deceptive, a calmness that hinted how far she still had to go. But then she took him and everyone else by surprise. "Freddie could've stopped when he was feeling sick. Joel kept telling us what to do, but none of us had to listen to him. We should've all been more like Tom."

To his shame, others nodded in agreement, but he knew it was untrue. Maybe some of them should have been more like him, but the one person who shouldn't have was Tom himself.

He shook his head and said, "No, maybe some of us should've been more like Joel. He was so desperate to be leader, we all let him do it, but I could've stepped up and didn't. Alice could've, Shen, or George, all of us together. The reason he made so many mistakes was that none of us wanted to take responsibility."

Barney turned and said, "The only thing necessary for the triumph of stupidity is that smart people say nothing."

Kate did a double take. "That's amazing, who said that?"

"I did," said Barney. "Actually, I'm paraphrasing Edmund Burke, but, you know."

Kate stared at him for a second or two, transfixed, yet one more person who seemed to have seen Barney with fresh eyes, then said, "Would you like me to take over with the oar for a bit? You've been at it a long time."

"Willingly."

"I will too," said Emma, and moved to take the oar from Sandeep.

For the next half hour or so, the two girls handled the oars with the dog standing between them, facing ahead. Once again, there was only silence behind them, and even on the straighter stretches of river, Tom could see nothing of the other raft when he looked back.

They entered a stretch with a different kind of silence, something so unsettling that they all looked around, spooked, as if expecting to see something, or someone, staring back at them from the dark within the overgrown riverbanks.

And then the dog started to growl.

CHAPTER 45

The dog faced forward, head lowered, tail down, producing a constant low growl that sounded almost like an outboard motor. They looked at each other in confusion, because there was no threat visible, but they were all too unsettled to make a joke about it.

And then the boat exploded.

Tom flew up and out and then into the river, water going up his nose, filling his ears, his clothes immediately waterlogged, dragging him down against the current.

He surfaced, amazed to see the boat intact—it had felt as though it had been destroyed. Everyone on board was shouting and he glanced about quickly and saw two other heads in the water—Emma and Sandeep—then the dog, and a backpack floating on the surface.

Emma started to swim back to the boat, grabbing the pack and taking it with her, even as Kate shouted, "Leave the pack! It doesn't matter!"

But she took it anyway, maybe because she hadn't heard with everyone gabbling, asking panicked questions, no one with answers. Could it have been a caiman? But Shen or George had said they were unlikely to attack the boats. They'd also said it was important no one ended up in the river, and Tom was acutely conscious of the murky water beneath him now, and all the dangers it might contain.

Tom saw one of Barney's hollow metal poles floating nearby and reached out for it. His fingers made contact, but at the same time, his foot also touched something big and bulky beneath him.

Tom recoiled in alarm, then kicked out, making contact, then again, harder, a fierce kick, and this time his boot slid over it and he felt a searing pain along his calf as if it had been torn open, but he kicked again and again until his foot kicked against clear water.

Then he heard George shout, "Guys!" Tom turned and saw him standing in the boat, looking down into the water. "Black caiman. Big. Get back in the boat!"

Tom started to swim, still clutching the pole, and as he looked ahead he could see them dragging Emma over the side and back in, then the backpack she'd managed to save. He couldn't see the dog and felt a moment of panic, but it had somehow managed to swim to the far side of the boat and Barney and Alice pulled it aboard now.

Tom heard something like a whimper behind him and spun around in the water to see Sandeep frozen, treading water but unable to act. He'd read once that the people most likely to die in an accident or a terrorist attack were those who froze, and now he could see why.

"Sandeep! Swim!"

Sandeep looked at him, nodded but did nothing, and said helplessly, "Don't leave me."

"Swim to me! Do it now."

Behind him, George shouted, "You have to swim too, Tom. I can't see where it went!"

A couple more shouted Tom's name, but he only looked at Sandeep and shouted again, "Swim to me!"

Sandeep nodded, but this time started a nervous crawl, his eyes darting about everywhere. He'd almost reached Tom when he glanced to his left and let out a cry of fear and Tom looked too, and saw the dark shadow in the water, moving fast toward them.

He kicked out again, and simultaneously heaved Sandeep by the shoulder, pushing him in the direction of the boat and screaming at him, *"Swim!"*

Sandeep finally swam away, splashing wildly, the others shouting encouragement, and Tom kicked once more at the shadow below but his foot met no contact and he saw the caiman rising up toward him. He stabbed down toward it with the metal pole, once, then twice, hitting something, then a third time.

The pole jammed into something, not fleshy, but locking firmly into place, and he was propelled through the water toward the boat for a few yards, from so powerful a force, it felt like it might lift him right out of the water as long as he held on to that pole, or as if the pole itself might snap.

As soon as the momentum slowed, he pulled his arm back and stabbed urgently again with the pole, four or five times in quick succession. The final thrust met no resistance, but even as he drew back to jab again into the depths, he felt something latch fiercely on to his arm. He tried to turn and strike back, but he was against the side of the boat, and it was a hand on his arm, the others heaving him out of the water.

Only now that he could feel his own waterlogged heaviness being hauled free of the river did the panic of what he'd just done set in and he kicked out again as if imagining the caiman might try one more time for him.

George said, "We've got you. You're clear," and it calmed him immediately. He fell into the boat and took a moment or two to see that they were all there, and that Jess and Barney had already started rowing fast. George shook his head and said, "Man, you're just the gift that keeps giving." He whooped and the dog barked in response and everyone laughed with relief.

It was only then that he noticed Alice staring down with horror at his leg. He looked down himself, saw the leg of his cargo pants torn and bloody, the exposed skin beneath slicked with blood.

He looked up and met her eyes, saying, "It's okay. I've got another pair in my backpack."

She laughed a little, but it was weak laughter and the smile fell away as Shen said, "I need to dress that, and I need to do it fast."

Tom nodded, and Shen unlaced Tom's boots and pulled them off. Tom undid the cargo pants and lifted himself up to push them down but immediately grimaced as the wet material started to move over the damaged skin, snagging at it.

Shen said, "Stop. I'll use scissors to cut them free."

He reached into his backpack for the first aid kit, opened it, but kept looking between the contents and Tom's leg. He cut the material then and peeled it away from the wound, sending another stinging pain through him.

Everyone else watched, although he noticed a couple of them avert their eyes when his lower leg was revealed. Shen, on the other hand, sighed with what looked like relief and nodded to himself before turning back to Tom.

"I still need to clean it and dress it, but it appears to be an abrasion rather than a bite or claw wound. And it probably helps that it's not the same leg as the snakebite." He reached back into the kit as he said, "This is going to sting. A lot."

And he wasn't kidding. It felt like a fire tearing through his leg, such a white heat that it was as if he could feel it actively burning the germs away. He clenched his teeth, his eyes watering, and when it subsided slightly, he laughed at the shock of how much it stung.

He looked back at Alice, who was smiling now, nodding, relieved. Then he looked at Kate, who was helping Emma find dry clothes, though Tom could feel his T-shirt drying in the sun even as he sat there. And then he saw Sandeep where he was still slumped against the side of the boat, staring back at him.

As soon as they made eye contact, Sandeep said, "Sorry."

"Don't be—you didn't do anything wrong. You okay?"

He nodded, looking overwhelmed, and Alice turned to him and said, "Which is your backpack, Sandeep? You should change out of some of those clothes."

They all went silent for a while, with Shen dressing Tom's leg and Barney and Jess rowing. It wasn't until ten minutes later, when they were sure the danger was behind them, that Emma said, "I just hope the others are okay."

George said, "They'll be okay. Tom gave that thing such a beating, it won't be attacking anyone anytime soon."

They laughed, even though they knew it wasn't true. The other boat was coming, probably too loud, already declaring itself to the caiman that was waiting below. And there was nothing any of them could do about it. They rowed on, away from danger, but they all remained silent now, listening, hoping.

CHAPTER 46

They didn't hear anything from the other boat, but it was a long while before anyone spoke about it again.

Finally, Barney said, "Oh, well, no news is good news."

It was met with subdued laughter, but little by little they started to talk again, and perhaps Barney was right. If the caiman had attacked, they would surely have heard screams or a commotion. They would have heard something, just as Joel and the others might have heard the noise of their own boat being attacked.

A little while later, they rounded a bend and found a smooth, flat rock sitting in the middle of the river like a giant stepping stone. It was easy enough for them to push into the channel to one side of it, but they passed more in the next twenty minutes, as if they'd entered into some new geological area. It meant they had to be more vigilant, but they made steady progress.

They followed another bend, long and sweeping and with trees overhanging on both shores, and when they came into the next straight section, Shen looked ahead with concern. There were more stones worn smooth, but his eyes were focused beyond them, where the river seemed to disappear into a blur.

"It looks like we're merging with another river." He immediately put his finger to his lips and everyone remained quiet. He listened intently, then looked forward again. "Try to move the boat closer to the right bank, not right into it, just closer. And it might be a good idea to have fresh rowers." George took over and Tom was about to, but saw Alice preparing to move and nodded in deference to her.

Whatever Shen had noticed, Barney had picked up on it too, and without exchanging a word, the two of them were incredibly alert all of a sudden, looking ahead, at the water beside the raft, at the banks, cocking their heads and listening. It was almost as if they were mimicking the dog, and the dog in turn studied their every move.

Tom could see there were more rocks in the river up ahead, and although he was sure a channel would open between them, from here they appeared to form a wall. But there was something more disturbing, in the slightly hazy quality of the air just beyond those rocks—he could just see a strip of the river they were about to join, the vegetation on its far shore, but it was as though he was looking at them through a veil.

Then Alice pointed and said, "It looks like rapids up ahead."

Shen nodded. "Keep bearing right." He put a hand on Barney's shoulder and stood, struggling to keep his balance as he looked ahead. "I don't think it's much of a drop at all, but it's still too much of a risk. I think there's a little bit of a point where the rivers meet, enough for us to beach."

He lowered himself back into a kneeling position as Emma said, "But didn't you say we had to avoid the river's edge?"

There it was, barely beneath the surface, the unease they'd all had since the caiman attack, the full awareness of how dangerous the river could be.

"Yes. Yes, I did."

Tom smiled at her. "It's daylight, and we have the dog. I'm sure we'll be safe."

That seemed to reassure her, but Tom figured the real issue would be whether they were able to get to shore. There were no decent landing spots here, and they didn't want to go ashore too soon anyway, but if they left it too late, they might have no option but to tackle the rapids.

He looked over the side of the boat where the current was visibly faster. He'd already put on his other pants, but seeing the change in the river, he automatically reached for his boots and put them back on too.

"Keep bearing right if you can," said Shen.

"Trying," said George without looking back. He was on the left-hand side, rowing hard. The river surface looked flat and sleek, but it was clear the currents were strengthening, and George was struggling to take the boat where he wanted it to go.

Within minutes, the river changed. The water started to foam and bubble around the rocks and boulders. The surface rippled and folded in on itself as the constant downward flow pulsed toward the barrier of the rapids. Despite that, Shen risked standing again, once more using Barney as a support, looking ahead to the shore.

He pointed, almost falling over in the process, and said, "Just before the rapids, there's an open section, almost like a little beach."

Alice called back, "You'll have to direct us!"

"You need to move left ahead." There was a boulder, bigger than the others, sticking up high out of the water. "But from there we can push for the right bank."

He lowered himself down again and George and Alice took the raft around the boulder, but immediately struggled to control it as the current seemed to fling them downstream, gaining speed. And then there were more rocks ahead and the hiss and crash of the rapids themselves began to fill the air.

George rowed harder, so hard that Barney's workmanship looked in danger of failing, the oar looking flimsier and more ragged each time it came out of the water. They moved right, but not enough. They'd picked up too much speed, the shore sliding past, just out of reach, the boat funneled relentlessly toward the rapids.

George shouted now, "We won't make this!"

Emma looked at the bank and said, "But we're so close!"

"We're going too fast!"

He was right. The momentum was growing every second, pulling them on, the rapids frighteningly close now, looking increasingly unavoidable.

The bank, still dense with vegetation, was close enough that Tom probably could have thrown his backpack ashore, if not quite close enough to jump that distance himself. But he also understood why George and Alice were struggling to close down that gap, because the water was streaming past the side of the raft now, splashing up with the collision of speed and force.

Then Tom remembered the anchor. He pushed his backpack aside and grabbed it. Shen saw it at the same time and looked briefly undecided about the best thing to do with it.

Tom didn't give him the chance but knelt against the back wall of the raft and shouted, "I'm throwing the anchor in!"

He got some response from the rowers, lost in the increasing noise around them, but as he got ready to throw it, Shen said, "You need to tie it off."

"No time!"

He wrapped the end of the rope around his hand and threw the anchor into the water behind them, slipping his other hand into the grasp line that surrounded the raft.

That was a precaution that paid off—the anchor reached the riverbed and snagged, pulling his arm, then his body, pulling him so hard that the wall of the raft was in danger of buckling.

Someone shouted, "Whoa!" as the boat slowed dramatically, but Tom could tell it wouldn't be enough. The anchor had caught on something but it was already becoming slack in his hand, only its own weight in the water pulling them back.

"That helped," said Alice. "Do it again."

He pulled the anchor back and threw it again, but this time there was no purchase, no jolt in the raft's progress.

George shouted, "Running out of time!"

And Tom knew now that he didn't have time for another exploratory drop. He looked to the shore, the roots of trees gnarled on the banks. It was worth a shot, but he'd need both arms, he knew it.

He called back, even as he was heaving the anchor in again, "Everyone get down! Someone hold my legs!"

He felt someone grab his injured leg and he winced with pain, but immediately, Kate said, "Not there. Like this!" She put one hand on his thigh, another around his ankle.

The anchor came free of the water. Tom pulled it close, grabbed hold of the anchor itself, slimy with whatever it had dragged through.

George shouted something else, maybe just his name, sounding panicked, but Tom focused only on the weight and feel of the anchor in his hand, the rope in his other hand, the trees on the bank with their roots twisting and jutting down into the water.

He hurled the anchor, throwing so hard that his shoulder jarred with the effort. It arced toward the bank, reminding him for a moment of the flare, tearing across the barn and into the torso of that man. It disappeared in among the trees and plants, but again, seemed to gain no purchase, for a second or two at least.

The jolt came, though, and when it did it still caught him unawares, slamming him into the side of the raft, forcing Kate and Sandeep to cling more tightly to his legs. His other shoulder felt almost as if it had popped out of its socket. He heard people fall and tumble behind him as the raft ground to a halt. The water crashed up against it and spilled inside, not enough to cause a problem, but enough to know the anchor had snagged on something and the raft had as good as stopped dead.

The dog barked, excitable, and the raft drifted toward the

bank. They were still a little way from the beach that Shen had spotted, but this close to the vegetation, the current was slower and he knew they were out of danger now.

"Everyone okay?" He got a gabble of responses. "If I let this go, can we take it down to the beach?"

It was Alice who replied, saying, "Let it go."

He released the rope, seeing for the first time that it had burned the skin away around his hand and wrist, and the raft moved smoothly on but at a manageable speed this time, and within seconds, George and Alice had brought them alongside the small beach.

George jumped out, then Sandeep, then the dog. The rest of them climbed ashore and pulled the raft up behind them. Everyone was out of breath. Only the dog dashed around, scouting with enthusiasm around this new terrain, his silence reassuring everyone that—finally—there was nothing here to fear.

CHAPTER 47

The beach was only just big enough to hold the raft, the bank rising up around them and back into dense vegetation. There was a thin strip continuing along the riverbank, like a perilous footpath, maybe another twenty paces to the narrow point Shen had seen.

Once the boat was secure, Shen set off along it and the others followed, and soon they all climbed up the bank onto the point, filling it, the bruising rapids to their left, and a much wider river in front of them. The far bank was still a mass of vegetation, and there was no question they were still in the middle of the jungle landscape they'd seen from the bluff, but this river was big and wide enough that it filled them with a quiet hope that they were getting somewhere.

No one spoke at first, but then Shen said, "We should get

back to warn the others if we can." Everyone nodded and started back to the small beach and the raft, but Shen turned to George and Alice. "Really good job there."

"Thanks," said George.

"Yeah, thanks," said Alice.

Shen turned to Tom and smiled, shaking his head before saying, "I completely forgot about the anchor."

"Let's just hope we don't need it again."

Shen nodded, glancing out at the wide sweep of river that lay ahead of them, and they both followed the others along the water's edge.

Once back on the beach, they all waited and watched. The roaring noise of the rapids removed any hope of hearing the others coming, so they studied the water on either side of the prominent boulder that obscured the middle of the river from view.

Tom had imagined the other raft could only be ten or fifteen minutes behind them, and they'd taken nearly ten minutes exploring the point, so he expected them to appear any second. When they didn't, he looked at his watch, then five minutes later, then another five.

Barney said, "They should be here by now."

Kate said, "What about the caiman?"

"We would have heard something," said Shen, with no confidence.

"I think so too," said George.

Tom thought of the other raft, noisily approaching that stretch of river, none of them realizing the danger that was lurking in the water beneath them. Worse, if the caiman had attacked and the boat had been destroyed, as their own so easily could have been, probably only one of them would have been killed to begin with, the others scrambling to a hostile bank or swimming helplessly downstream. And Tom and the others could do nothing except wait, but he hoped the first sight of them wasn't going to be a body.

He checked his watch again, and then Jess, the shortest in the group, said, "I see them." She pointed to the gap between the bank and the large boulder.

It was a moment or two before he saw the welcome flash of yellow as they passed another rock farther upstream, the boat looking undamaged. The others spotted them at the same time and there was a chorus of agreement as relief spilled out of them. Tom guessed they'd probably rowed past the caiman without even knowing it.

But then Alice said, "I just hope they see us in time."

They all started shouting and waving, even though the other raft was hidden by the boulder now. The dog barked too, the whole group producing enough noise that the others would probably have heard it even over the hiss and moan of the rapids.

The raft appeared. Joel and Nick were at the front, both rowing furiously, not in an attempt to change course or slow down, but toward the rapids, apparently intent on running them. The others were all out of sight, low down inside the raft.

Both Joel and Nick saw them on the riverbank, the yellow of their own raft no doubt like a beacon, but Joel only laughed, probably thinking they'd run aground by accident and this was a chance for his boat to take the lead again. Nick looked a lot less happy and was shouting something, his words lost to those on the shore.

Getting no response, he pulled at Joel's arm now, knocking him off balance so he fell backward into the raft. And Nick started rowing even harder, the suggestion that he'd understood even if Joel hadn't. He was on the left-hand side of the boat and with only him rowing, the boat edged toward the beach, but it was obvious it would never make it in time.

Nick screamed something, his voice audible above the rapids, even if they couldn't make out the words. It had some effect, because Joel scrambled back up but seemed unsure what to do. In the end, he got behind Nick and started rowing on the same side, but the raft was out of control now, already passing the beach, gaining speed.

It spun on, heading for a rock almost in the middle of the river. Nick saw the rock, approaching fast, and shouted again, then turned, his eyes locking on Tom and the others as they stood there watching. He shouted something, but no words reached the shore.

The raft slammed into the boulder, coming to a stop with a violent shudder. The back lifted out of the water and for a moment looked as if it would tip over. All the people on board screamed, the noise strangely reminiscent of theme parks. Backpacks catapulted into the air, and so did Nick.

He flew upward in an incredibly graceful arc, like someone bouncing off a trampoline onto a lawn. Tom followed his flight, his progress seeming to be in slow motion, but there was nothing slow or graceful about his landing. He accelerated downward, smashing onto another boulder, a brutal, buckling impact, his leg snapping sideways before he ricocheted off and disappeared into the water.

Seconds passed in stunned silence, seconds in which Tom kept seeing that moment of impact, the way Nick's body had flailed like a puppet, the snapping of his leg. And now he was gone. He'd been so afraid in the jungle when Chris and Joel had been taken captive, yet it had ended for him here, stupidly.

He was gone, but they kept their eyes on the water, and there was a collective gasp when his head bobbed back to the surface, already far downstream, his lifeless body being pulled out into the current of the wider river. The shock in the group was palpable, but no one spoke.

And then, miraculously it seemed, Nick raised his hand out of the water, a pitiful wave before he was dragged out of sight.

Behind Tom, someone said, "He waved!"

"I don't think it was a wave. I think it was just his body moving in the current."

"It was a wave," said Tom.

And that meant he was alive.

He looked out at the raft wedged up onto the rock. It appeared undamaged as far as he could tell, and everyone else aboard seemed shaken but otherwise unhurt. So they had to go after Nick, there was no other option, as broken as he was, even if he was dying or already dead by now—they couldn't leave him.

He ran to their raft, grabbed the spare rope, and handed it to Sandeep.

Before saying anything to him, he turned to the others and said, "Carry the raft along to the point, get ready to launch it."

Emma said, "Tom, we can't save him. He's gone."

"We're going," said Tom, with such conviction that everyone moved to pick up the raft and started along the narrow strip of beach. He turned back to Sandeep. "Throw the other end of this rope to them. Don't go in the water yourself. As soon as they've got the rope, you can help pull them over here. Then follow us. Once we get Nick, we'll get to the bank and wait. If you haven't followed us within an hour, we'll come back, even if we have to walk. Got it?"

Sandeep nodded, looking afraid and uncertain, but equally afraid of disobeying instructions that had been issued with such determination, and he said only, "Nick's gone."

"No. He isn't."

And Tom didn't wait for an answer but set off after the others. He didn't know why it mattered so much, maybe because of that stupid promise he'd made, or maybe only because Nick had doubted him, but he wouldn't accept that they'd lost him, not while there was any hope left at all.

CHAPTER 48

The others had already reached the small point by the time Tom caught up with them, and were carrying the raft over to the bank of the larger river. Nobody spoke, not now, and in silence they got the raft into the water and climbed aboard. Once again, George was the last on, pushing the raft from the shallows and jumping in at the same time.

The current immediately pulled them out into the river, but Alice and Kate started rowing, like competitors in a race for which there was no apparent finish line. The others scanned the expanse of water ahead of them, even though Tom knew most of them probably thought there was no chance of finding Nick now.

Maybe they were right, but Nick had still been conscious on the other side of the rapids—he'd waved, and if there was any chance of reaching him, they had to at least try. It didn't matter who it was—he was hurt, and alone, and he needed their help.

After a minute or two, Barney pointed ahead and there was a moment of hope before they realized it wasn't Nick. There was another moment then, of fear that it might be another caiman, before they got close enough to see it was part of a tree that had fallen and been swept downriver.

They rowed on. Kate began to tire and George took over, renewing his partnership with Alice, and between them they seemed to increase the raft's speed. Tom would have offered to take Alice's place, but she seemed in no danger of tiring, a determination that was visible from behind in the movement of her back, her shoulders, the way her arms dug the oar into the water.

Still there was nothing. Tom could see in the faces of those who weren't rowing, even in Shen's face, an increasing sense of hopelessness. And looking at the size of the river, thinking back, seeing Nick's leg snap under his body, even Tom began to doubt.

But Nick had waved, he'd been alive, and they had to focus on that. As long as he was afloat, there was still time.

Kate seemed to pick up on Tom's thoughts, because she said now, "Is Nick a good swimmer?"

No one answered, presumably because no one knew, and because they'd all seen what had happened to his body on those boulders.

And then the dog barked and they all rose to attention and stared forward.

It was Jess again who pointed. "Yes! It's him, it's him!"

She was right, but without pausing, George said, "He's not waving."

Only Nick's head was visible above the slick surface of the water, and he was facing them, but he didn't wave. Alice and George managed to find even more speed from somewhere, angling the raft at the same time, so their position in the river shifted, moving them onto a collision course for Nick.

When they were only a short distance away, they stopped rowing, then put the oars back in to slow themselves down. And still, Nick appeared unresponsive.

"Maybe he's just exhausted," said Emma.

George shouted, "Okay, get ready, we're on him!"

George dropped his oar back in the raft and leaned over so violently, it looked like he was trying to dive into the river himself. He grunted and strained with the effort then, the side of the raft crumpling under his body weight. Tom jumped up next to him, grabbing hold of the first thing that came to him. As it cleared the water he saw it was Nick's leg and he almost dropped it in response before realizing this was the good leg.

Between them, they heaved him over the side and now that he was out of the water he screamed. The other leg hung down at the knee, sickeningly limp, as if it had snapped clean in two and might simply fall out of his pant leg into the river.

As they lay him down on the floor of the raft, he screamed even louder, a sound so disturbing that everyone but Shen recoiled slightly. Shen jumped forward, moved the broken leg—another piercing scream—gave some short, sharp orders, got the medical kit, and got two or three people working for him.

And still Nick screamed, but Shen glanced back at Tom and said, "Screaming is good."

Tom guessed he meant it was better than silence, and now Tom handed the oar back to George and said, "Get us to the shore as soon as you see a safe place. I said we'd wait for the others."

"Cool," said George, and started to row.

Tom sat back against the side of the raft. The dog immediately stepped over legs and slumped down next to him, putting his head on Tom's lap, perhaps seeing Tom as a safe haven in the midst of all that distress.

After a few seconds, Tom closed his eyes, falling into some inner peace with the dog beside him, as Nick's screams steadied and Shen and the others moved about him, jostling the raft, and the rhythmic rowing of the oars carried them gently onward.

None of this is real, he thought. It felt like he'd imagined all of it, or maybe he'd died in that plane crash and these were the inventions of his brain's final moments. He had not been face-to-face with a jaguar deep in the Amazon jungle, or with snakes and caimans and spiders, he had not saved people, killed people, he was not sitting here with this dog resting his head on his lap.

And yet he knew all those things had really happened, and in the light of that knowledge, it seemed like it was the real world that was a dream, and that his life before coming here had been his mind's creation. It was the same for all of them, and whatever happened, what Kate had said to him would be true, that the tragedies and triumphs of these last few days would be the foundation of their lives from now on, the things that had happened beforehand reduced to insignificance.

He heard Alice say, "What about over there?"

"Looks good," said George, their voices bringing Tom back to the present. He looked ahead and saw the stretch of rocky shore where the jungle was raised up and back on a steep earthen bank.

A few minutes later, they were at the river's shallow edge and George jumped out again. They climbed ashore, secured the boat, and were mindful of the dog, watching him for signs that there might be something to worry about—the dog, for his part, found lots of interesting things to sniff but nothing to growl or bark at.

Shen stayed behind, still working on Nick in the boat, and Nick himself was quieter now, moaning but not screaming. The others stood in a huddle nearby, some watching Shen, some talking, comforting each other, still in shock.

Tom stood some way distant, looking out at the river, at the width of it, wondering how long it might be until it yielded a settlement of some kind, knowing they needed it now more than ever. After a short while, Barney walked over to where Tom was standing.

He crouched down and petted the dog, then looked up at Tom. "I think he'll be okay. I mean, we'll need to get somewhere soon, but it's better than it might have been." He stood again. "You saved him, Tom. I know we all helped, but it was you."

Tom said with a laugh, "He doesn't even like me. But I couldn't leave him, you know."

"I know, like you couldn't leave Sandeep, or Joel and Chris. It's who you are. I mean, I know I'm probably not *cool* enough to be your friend, but I think you're the best kind of friend there is, the kind who steps up when it really matters."

Tom looked at him. "Barney, you're more than cool enough to be my friend. And I couldn't think of anyone I'd rather be in a plane crash with."

"Except Alice?" He had a sly smile, similar to the one he'd

had a million years ago when he'd talked about Miss Graham having the hots for Tom.

"Yeah, maybe. And Kate, of course, and Shen, George, the dog…"

Barney laughed, but was distracted, pointing as he said, "That was quick."

It was the other raft, mid-river, still some distance away but close enough to suggest they'd moved quickly. Chris was at the front with the one remaining oar, working from side to side. He saw them on the bank and started to work his way laboriously against the current.

Sandeep tied the rope onto the grasp line, then coiled it, ready to throw. Tom moved along the bank and got ready, studying the boat. The others all looked in a state of shock, though he couldn't see Joel's face and couldn't hear him, either.

Sandeep threw the rope and Tom caught it and held it fast, though Chris's rowing had pretty much done the trick anyway and the raft came ashore almost on top of the other one.

They clambered out quickly and as soon as they saw that Nick was in the other boat, their attention was all on him.

Joel walked over too, but instantly, Nick screamed at him. "I told you! I *told* you. I could've been killed. We all could've!"

Joel shook his head in response. "It didn't work out, Nick, and I'm sorry about that, but we had to give it a try."

"No! We didn't." He pointed at George. "*They* didn't!"

"Nick, I can see you're angry now, and I understand that, but—"

Alice walked up to Joel and said, "Enough!" She looked at him. "I think you've said enough, and this isn't helping. Nick needs to rest." Joel looked exasperated, as if he was being unfairly treated, but he moved away and didn't speak again. Alice turned to Chris. "How many backpacks have you got?"

"Two."

"We need to check how much food and drink we have left."

Chloe looked confused. "We haven't got anything left. Maybe something to drink, but no food. We ate it earlier."

Alice looked astounded, but Shen called from the boat, saying, "So we should check our supplies anyway, see what we *do* have."

Shen involuntarily looked out at the river, and Tom knew what he was thinking, that they needed to find a settlement soon, not just because of Nick, but because feeding themselves out here, let alone producing safe water to drink, would be almost impossible. It was a moment they would have faced anyway, but by finishing their supplies and losing their backpacks, the other boat had almost definitely brought the end a day closer.

CHAPTER 49

It was only when the remaining supplies were arranged on the floor of the other raft that Tom realized how hungry he was. But now that he felt the gnawing hollowness in his stomach, he was actually astonished that it had taken so long to hit him, because they'd hardly been eating enough—he credited Shen with concealing that truth.

Shen had briefly left Nick and joined the rest of them, but even he looked dejected. "We should stow it all away again, divide it out later."

Kate said, "I can't fish here without a rod. I guess I could scout for food, but that won't help with water, and it'll take time too."

Oscar looked confused and said, "I thought we were camping here. Shouldn't we build a fire?"

Shen shook his head. "No. I think it's best to move on while we can."

Joel had been quiet since the argument with Nick, but he glanced up at the sky and said, "I understand what you're saying, Shen, but Oscar's got a point. We've probably only got an hour of light left, and this looks like a good spot—we don't know when we'll find another one."

Shen nodded, but he was preoccupied with looking at the river as he replied. "It's wide, so we can keep to the middle, use the remaining flashlights to make sure we don't drift off course or run into something."

Joel looked taken aback. "You know, you're all really good at criticizing my decisions, and I'll admit some haven't worked out, but you're talking about drifting downriver in the middle of the night, when caimans and anacondas and all kinds of other things go hunting, and we'll be in pitch black. Sandeep told me what happened to your boat even in daylight, so you have to know it's ridiculous. *No.* I appreciate your efforts, Shen, I really do, but I won't let you do this."

Shen's voice remained measured. "I'm talking about getting Nick to a hospital, I'm talking about finding a village before we start to starve, before we're forced to drink unclean water, before people start *dying.*"

"I want those things too, and one more night won't hurt. But a night on the river might. I see where you're coming from, Shen, but I've made my decision."

Shen simply stared back at him, apparently unable even to formulate a response. Tom looked on, astonished, because he knew Shen wouldn't have suggested traveling through the night if he didn't think it was a matter of survival, and not just for Nick.

Joel turned away from Shen and called out, "Everyone!"

A few people had drifted here and there on the narrow beach, but they all turned to face him now.

Without much conviction, Shen tried to intervene again. "Joel—"

Joel ignored him, his voice taking on the familiar tone as he said, "I've given it some thought, but I don't think it's safe to stay on the river after dark, so we'll camp here tonight and move on at first light. Start looking for firewood, but be careful."

A good number of them started scouring the driftwood on the bank right away. Shen shook his head, and both Alice and George looked at him with concern, then at Tom. But then Joel looked at Tom as well, and smiled—a smile that seemed oddly victorious. Tom wasn't sure what victory he thought he'd won, except that people were still willing to follow his orders, even with Nick lying broken in the bottom of the raft.

Tom noticed Barney was looking at him too, a searching, expectant gaze, almost as if he was reminding Tom of what he'd said about the kind of friend he was, the kind who stepped up. And Barney was right to look at him like that—in the beginning he could have played the outsider card, but not now. These people were his friends and they wanted him to do what he should have done all along.

Sandeep, holding a few pieces of driftwood, called, "Where are we building the fire, Joel?"

But before Joel could answer, Tom said, "Nowhere. We're not staying."

Joel turned to him, still with that smile. "It's already been decided, Tom."

"Yeah, it has. We're moving on, for all the reasons Shen talked about."

"Really?"

"Yes, really."

"Well, I have no intention of arguing with you, but let's see what the others think, shall we?" He raised his voice again. "Everyone listen! Tom wants to be in charge all of a sudden. So you all have a decision. You can sail downriver in the pitch black, unable to see obstructions or if you're about to be attacked by a caiman again, no idea where you're going, or you can camp by the fire on this bank and head out at first light. It's your choice. Are you in Tom's boat, or are you in mine?"

For a moment that seemed to stretch and distort, no one said anything, and Tom wondered if he'd misread those expressions or the general mood of the group.

But then Barney put his hand up and smiled as though it should have been taken for granted. "I'm with Tom and Shen, naturally."

"Me too," said Alice.

"And us," said Kate, speaking for her and Emma.

Jess put her hand up, and George smiled at her and said, "I think the people from our boat plan to stick together."

Joel shook his head, a look of derision on his face. "So predictable. Okay, it's decided—this is where we separate."

"Hold on." It was Chris. For the first time, Joel's confidence looked shaken. "I don't think we should split up. Just—I don't. And, the thing is—"

Chloe said, "Chris?"

"Sorry, Chloe." He pointed at Tom. "But this guy saved my life. He saved yours too, Joel."

"You don't know that. You don't know what would have happened if—"

"Yes, Joel, I do. And that's enough for me. Where Tom goes,
I go."

Joel turned to Tom with a look of venom as he said, "Is this
what you want? Now that all the hard choices have been made, *you*
want to be leader."

Tom shook his head. "You just don't get it, do you, Joel? We
didn't need a leader. We're just a bunch of kids lost in the jungle. All
we needed was to listen to each other. If we'd done that, three people
might be alive now who aren't."

"You can't blame me for those people dying!" He stepped forward aggressively. "I didn't kill anyone!"

Tom stood his ground, looking confident enough that Joel
stopped his advance a couple of paces away.

"No, you didn't kill anyone. I did, we all did, because we
let you do all the talking. But that stops now. We're moving on.
We're tying the boats together and we're moving on."

Joel looked ready to object again, but he glanced around at
the other faces, then shook his head, a mocking superiority that
seemed paper-thin now.

"Fine! Have it your way, but I want everyone to remember,
when this goes wrong—and it *will* go wrong—that I objected."

Sandeep dropped the wood he'd been holding and said,
"What do we need to do, Tom?"

"We need to tie the boats together. The one with Nick can go
at the back. Shen should stay with him, maybe a few more…"

"I will," said Chris.

"Me too," said Mila. Chloe raised her hand to volunteer as well.

Tom nodded and said, "That might be enough. We'll be more crowded in the other boat, but it's more important that Nick can lie flat. You can ask Shen and Barney if there's anything else you need to do. But let's go as soon as we can—Nick needs to be in a hospital."

Everyone started moving, all with a purpose, taking instructions from Shen and Barney, moving the other boat around and tying them together, spreading out the remaining packs.

Alice walked past Tom and muttered, "Nicely done."

He laughed a little, and more as George gave him a friendly shoulder shove and said, "About time."

Then the dog barked and Tom turned to see that Joel was walking along the narrow beach toward the trees.

Kate followed his gaze and said, "I came after you, Tom, but I'm not going after him."

Tom smiled at her but then shook his head, baffled, wondering whether Joel wanted to be left behind, or whether he planned to go missing long enough to stop them from leaving before dark. Whatever the case, it made Tom angry.

He walked along the beach quickly, the dog keeping pace with him, reaching Joel at the top of the bank as he headed into the dappled dark of the trees.

"Hey!"

Joel stopped, but took his time turning, and said, "I need to pee, or do I need your permission for that?"

"If that's all you need, then go ahead, I'll wait." Joel looked askance. "You're coming with us, Joel, even if I have to tie you to the boat."

"You think you're such a big hero, don't you?"

Tom wasn't in the mood to navigate Joel's damaged ego. "Just water the flowers and let's get out of here."

"I can wait," said Joel, and jumped back down the bank and walked toward the boats. Tom reached down and scratched the top of the dog's head, then followed.

CHAPTER 50

Within fifteen minutes, they'd set off again. At first, the atmosphere was awkward and tense, people talking as if there hadn't been an argument, that Joel wasn't sitting silent and stony-faced against the wall of the lead boat. But then they seemed to genuinely forget that he was there and the conversations flowed more naturally.

The river remained wide and flat, the banks lush and over-hanging the water, with dark depths that looked as impenetrable as ever. Maybe because they were a reasonable distance from either bank, the dog seemed more relaxed and only barked or growled a few times.

Barney worked on building a stretcher for Nick, using the frames of backpacks, and despite the limited space, the others were keen to help. Even when there was nothing they could do, they watched him working, fascinated by his progress.

An hour in, and sensing that darkness would fall soon, Alice divided up the remaining snacks and they ate. Tom shared his with the dog again and so did the others in his boat.

For the first time since leaving the riverbank, Joel spoke. "Our last food and you're giving it to the dog."

No one responded, except by making a more visible fuss over the dog. Alice smiled at him and said, "We haven't even given you a name, have we? What can we call him? Tom, what do you think?"

"Something Spanish, I guess."

Emma said, "What's Spanish for dog?"

No one answered, and then Joel said, *"Perro."*

He sounded so grudging that Tom almost laughed and stopped himself only by repeating the word. *"Perro."*

Immediately, the dog's ears pricked up and he looked at Tom, and everyone else laughed. For a few minutes, people took turns calling him that most basic of Spanish names, and so he officially became Perro.

They rowed on, and after another half hour, the jungle seemed to become heightened in some way, as if in anticipation, and then darkness fell with its usual speed, enveloping them and reducing the world to nothing but the rafts they were sitting in.

They didn't know how much life was left in each of the remaining flashlights, so they decided to use one at a time, with someone just behind the two rowers, moving the light from side to side. The beam rarely reached the dense cover of the jungle, so they had only the reassurance of the water all around them.

It was impossible to hear their progress. The noise of the jungle and the gentle splashing of the oars in the water were constant and uniform, producing the illusion that they were simply suspended in the night.

Those who weren't rowing or holding the light slept on and off. Tom didn't. He took a shift with the flashlight, then took over one of the oars, and kept at it for a few hours, the concentration and the building muscle fatigue helping to take his mind of his hunger. He couldn't even remember now when he *had* last slept.

Finally he heard someone move behind him, and Sandeep's voice came out of the dark, saying quietly, "Tom, let me take over. You've been at it for hours."

"I'm fine," said Tom.

"Even so, get some sleep. Let me do this."

Tom handed him the oar, then felt his way blindly to where Sandeep had been sitting.

Sleep came quickly, but almost as instantly, the dreams came tumbling in on the back of it, confused and jagged. He was kneeling, holding the makeshift spear, and a body fell onto the point and he rammed it up and forward, feeling the resistance of gristle and bone, hearing it, but when he looked up he saw the young guard's face, not the older man's. His subconscious jumped track then and he was in the barn, holding the flare gun, pulling the trigger, but Alice was there, screaming at him to stop and he couldn't understand why but then the flare tore through the barn and burst into Chris's stomach where he hung from the ropes that bound him.

Tom woke with a shudder, his entire body taut, his heart thumping violently. He relaxed again as he remembered where he was, saw the gentle beacon of the flashlight beam swaying back and forth, heard the sound of the oars.

His breathing settled again, and Alice's voice came softly out of the dark, saying, "Are you okay?"

She was sitting right next to him, and he didn't know whether she'd been there all along or whether she'd moved there while he slept.

"I'm okay."

"You jumped like you were having a bad dream."

"Yeah, I was dreaming. It was all mixed up, but…it wasn't good."

"About what happened in the cocaine factory?"

"Yeah."

She didn't answer, but then he felt her take hold of his hand and squeeze it, and that was answer enough. He was absurdly grateful for that human contact.

She didn't let go and after a little while she said, "I'm always here if you want to talk about it, but if you don't, that's okay too."

"There's not much to talk about. But I keep thinking of that kid who was guarding them…"

"I keep thinking about him too. He didn't look much older than us."

He nodded, though they couldn't see each other in the darkness, reassured somehow that her thoughts were aligned with his.

"I'm sure he still would've killed us, I'm sure they all would, but that doesn't help much."

"No." There was another pause, like a held breath, and then she said, "I just hate to think what might have happened if you hadn't gone in there when you did."

He thought of Chris and Joel tied to that beam, the bruise

around Chris's eye, Joel's bare torso and torn T-shirt, thought of the look in the eyes of the men he'd killed.

"Yeah," was all he said, and neither of them spoke for a while.

Finally, Alice said, "You should try to sleep again. I'm here."

He knew what she meant, that she was holding his hand, as if offering a way back from the dreams that might come.

"Thanks," he said, and closed his eyes and allowed sleep to come back in on waves. And this time the dreams did not follow and he slept soundly.

CHAPTER 51

He woke, or half-woke, to the sound of Chris in the other raft, saying, "So weird. I always need to pee first thing, but this morning, not a bit."

Even still lost on the edges of sleep, Tom smiled, and more as Chloe said, "Well, that's a relief for all of us."

Closer, Barney said, "It's because we're all dehydrated."

Tom became conscious of Alice's hand still in his. He opened his eyes and looked around. It was daylight, but he was already becoming familiar enough with the subtle tonal shifts that he could tell it hadn't been light for long. Alice was sleeping next to him, and most of the others were still asleep but they all started to stir now at the sound of voices.

Alice woke and released his hand and stretched.

"Morning," said Tom.

"Good morning," she said, smiling before a little frown crossed her face. "I feel like something died in my mouth."

With a comical flourish, Barney handed her a tube of toothpaste. "Multipurpose—it'll also ward off the hunger."

She took it, smiling. "You're a genius, Barney."

Tom glanced forward to where Kate and Jess were rowing, then at the river around them. It looked no different, as though they'd traveled no distance at all since darkness had fallen. They seemed to be at the start of a long shallow bend to the right, but even that was a repeat of the section they'd been on when the sun had set.

Everyone was awake now, everyone except Perro, who was curled up contentedly in the middle of the raft. A couple of tubes of toothpaste were being passed around, and then the remaining drinks.

Alice said, "How's Nick?"

It was Nick's own voice that came from the bottom of the other raft. "I'm doing okay."

"Good," Alice called back, even as Shen gave her a grave look, contradicting his patient's assessment of how he was doing.

Ironically, though, despite their situation being marginally worse, the whole group seemed in better spirits this morning, most of them chatting amiably, Chris and Chloe even bickering in a good-humored way. Only Joel seemed oddly quiet, a satisfied expression on his face that was hard to fathom.

Tom took some of the toothpaste Alice offered him, happy that it had freshened his mouth but pretty certain it had only made his hunger worse. He looked forward again, where the shallow bend was revealing one slight change—the river seemed to be opening even wider as they rounded it.

He said, "Would either of you like a break from rowing?"

Jess turned with a smile. "We haven't been doing it long. We took over from Sandeep and Barney."

He nodded, but then Kate, who was on the left, cried out, "Oh, my God!" She started rowing harder, half a dozen quick strokes, before stopping, craning her neck. "Oh, my God! A town! There's a *town*!"

She started rowing again, and so did Jess. Chris grabbed the oar in the second raft and rowed on the left too. Tom could see that the bank was high and open on the right-hand side beyond the bend, and then he saw what Kate had seen from her kneeling position.

There were wooden jetties and boats tied up, and buildings above a steep bank, not those of a native village, but colonial-style buildings, what looked like a customs house, a church with a flight of wide stone steps in front of it descending to the river. On either side of the bigger buildings were smaller houses, the roofs just visible from the water, but neatly set out, with palm trees rising up here and there.

They had no idea where they were, even which country they were in, but the appearance of the town was surreal. A few days before, Barney had joked about a beach resort being beyond the low hills, and the sight of this white church tower seemed no less extraordinary.

They rowed on in a blur, making an incoherent commotion between them, waking Perro, who joined in with excited barks. And when they reached the stone steps, probably put there hundreds of years earlier by Spanish conquerors, George jumped across the gap with the rope and found a post to tie it off.

They scrambled ashore, stretching their legs as they stood on the steps, dazed for a moment, unsure what to do next. Then the focus shifted to Nick, and Shen started giving instructions to get him onto the stretcher.

Nick cried out as he was lifted from the bottom of the raft, then shouted painfully, "No! No! Leave me here!"

But Shen ignored him and a few seconds later said, "All done. You're okay. We're taking you ashore."

He gestured for Chris and George to pick up the makeshift stretcher and the whole party followed them up the steps. It was only when they reached the top and stood before the church and the small settlement that stretched back from the river that Tom realized Joel wasn't with them.

Before he could say anything, Shen walked over to him and said, "Good job. You said you wouldn't let anyone else die, and you didn't."

"Thanks, although I'm not sure I can really take the credit. Luck played a part, and so did everyone else."

"You make your own luck—it's been proven, scientifically, and you made it for us." He smiled and held out his hand. "Either way, it's been an honor."

"Likewise," said Tom, and shook his hand. Barney came over and they shook hands too. Tom thought it was funny, how Shen and Barney simultaneously seemed younger than everyone else but also much older and wiser, but he valued both of them for it, and was pretty sure they'd played a much bigger part in getting everyone to safety than he had.

The church door opened and Tom turned, feeling a sudden wave of nervous anticipation—after more than a week on their own, they were finally about to encounter an adult, someone who'd take control of this insane situation.

And then he saw that it was Joel coming out of the church and Tom couldn't help but laugh.

Joel shook his head, acting as if the last twenty-four hours hadn't happened. "It's still early. Maybe we should just walk along this street here, see if we can find anyone in the houses."

He didn't wait for a response but started along the wide dusty road that ran alongside the church, toward the houses that sat behind picket fences in various states of repair. The rest of them followed.

Alice fell in beside Tom and said, "Surprise, surprise, he's up in front again."

"We're all safe now. He can do what he likes."

They walked on and saw a child's bike leaning on one of the fences, though there were still no people to be seen.

Alice looked at the bike and said, "It's weird, isn't it, the way it felt like the whole world had changed when we were lost? You know, people talking about meteor strikes and things like that, but this is it—nothing's changed, nothing at all."

Tom nodded, smiling, but he was actually wondering if perhaps the world *had* changed, and changed completely, but that they were the only ones who could see it. And if each of them inhabited a world of their own creation, perhaps that was the truth. All he said was, "We haven't seen any people yet."

Before she could answer, they heard Joel saying cheerily, "*¡Hola!*"

Tom had a disturbing flashback to him walking into that camp, but then he saw up ahead, a large woman standing on a porch with a small child next to her.

"*Hola.* Do you speak English? *¿Inglés?* Uh...*habla inglés?*" She shook her head, looking at the entire group with suspicion. "*¡Inglés!*" Joel repeated louder, as if she simply hadn't heard him.

She said something to the child, who nodded and ran off, out of a side gate and along the road. If this was their deliverance, it seemed to Tom that it wasn't going to plan. Then things took another turn as a vehicle approached along the dusty road, an SUV, and even some distance away, the lights on top burst into life and then went out again.

Alice said, "You think the police here are likely to speak English?"

The car stopped and Joel approached even as the policeman opened his door and climbed out, looking curious but unhurried.

Tom said, "Let's just hope we find out before Joel gets himself shot."

She laughed, and he had been joking, but within seconds it didn't seem that way. Joel talked and the policeman stared at him in unhappy confusion, but then Joel seemed to reach out and the policeman slapped his hand away and put his other hand on his gun.

Alice gasped, "Oh my God, what is he doing?"

Tom shook his head, but stepped through the group and called out, "*¡Señor!*" And as he uttered that word, one of the few he knew in Spanish, it reminded him of something from the morning of the crash, a Spanish name, someone he'd never known. He slipped off his backpack and reached inside, into the pocket of his torn cargo pants, and smiled when he found the thick paper still folded there.

He took it out, the boarding pass that belonged to Miguel Fernandez, who it already seemed had died in another age. The policeman still had his hand resting on his gun, but he looked at the pass in Tom's hand and reached out cautiously to take it.

Joel stared at Tom. "I had this covered—you know, you don't have to—"

The policeman glared at Joel and pointed a warning finger, the meaning of which was clear enough that Joel took a nervous step back.

Once he was satisfied that his point had been made, the policeman looked down at the boarding pass again and studied it for a second. Then the truth sank in and he looked up at Tom with astonishment and said something in Spanish.

Tom nodded, and gestured to the whole group.

The policeman made the sign of the cross and shouted something to the woman on the porch, who responded by letting out a little cry and throwing her arms up in the air. She rushed to the gate and started to pull some of the girls in and toward her door, gesturing then for the boys to follow with the stretcher.

The child came along the road, running, a priest running alongside him. And the priest shouted something good-humored to the policeman, who in turn pointed him toward Tom as he replied.

The priest gave Tom a look of total shock as he said, "I'm Father Francisco. You were in the plane that disappeared?"

"Yes. We're the only survivors. We crashed in the mountains more than a week ago. We came downriver, in rafts. I think we've traveled a long way. We don't even know what country this is."

"Then let me be the first to welcome you to Brazil. But where you crashed is a mystery. You came all this way by river?"

"We walked through the jungle first."

The priest looked at him, with dark laughing eyes, and he took hold of Tom's shoulders and said, "It's a miracle. It's nothing short of a miracle."

And Tom nodded, because right now it felt like nothing less.

CHAPTER 52

Nick and some of the others stayed in the woman's house. The rest were taken to the priest's rectory where they settled in the large sitting room, still cool at this time of morning with two fans spinning lazily on the ceiling above them. The priest's housekeeper brought them coffee and cake, the sticky sweetness causing a euphoric silence.

It was only as they sat savoring the cake that Tom looked around and saw that they'd once again separated into the same two distinct groups. With the exception of Shen, who'd stayed to look after Nick until a doctor could get there, it was pretty much the original escape party sitting around Tom now.

They weren't inclined to speak, but the housekeeper started cooking ham and eggs and as the smell reached them from the kitchen, George began to cry. Kate put a hand on his shoulder but he laughed through his tears and said, "I've been dreaming about bacon for so long!"

And they all laughed and talked now, even beginning to laugh over some of the events of the last few days, now that they were safely behind them. Father Francisco popped in several times to check on them, though he mainly just fussed over Perro.

After everyone had made their tearful calls home, Shen arrived. A couple of people jumped up and hugged him, making him clearly embarrassed. He shrugged and said, "A doctor arrived, and a local politician, so I left."

Barney smiled. "You're a welcome addition."

"Well, I'd rather be here. And...well, the politician speaks English, so Joel and the others were telling him what happened, only, not the way I remember it."

Alice glanced at Tom but then said, "Who cares? We all know what really happened. That's all that matters."

There was a sense for a while too, that their little group really was all that mattered. They heard voices as people came to the main door of the house and spoke to the priest or the housekeeper, and they heard vehicles outside, and on two occasions helicopters flew low overhead and seemed to land somewhere not too far off.

But the friends were left alone, talking and laughing, sometimes lulled into silence. And Tom was there, one of them. He'd joked with Miss Graham that two weeks wasn't long enough to get to know him, and yet here he was, feeling closer to some of these people than he ever had to anyone.

It was late morning when Father Francisco came in again and said, "I have news. After lunch, you'll be going by boat to a bigger town. There you can have medical checks and stay the night, then fly home."

Tom noticed Alice's face fill with unease at the mention of flying, and he was unsettled by that because she'd seemed to take everything so much in stride, but then that only reminded him that he didn't really know her that well, not yet. That would be his senior year, becoming a real friend to these people, becoming the sort of person people wanted as a friend.

"What about Nick?"

It was Shen who'd asked, and Father Francisco smiled uncertainly before saying, "Oh, you mean the injured boy. Yes, he's fine, he'll leave after you, but arrive before. He'll be going in the helicopter." He looked down now at Perro, who was sitting next to him, leaning on his leg. "Does your dog have a name?"

"Perro," said Tom.

"Ah, Spanish. In Portuguese we'd say *cão* or *cachorro*, but Perro is a nice name." He frowned regretfully. "You know, it's going to be very difficult to take him with you."

"He's been our mascot," said Kate. "Tom saved him."

"A dog is a good friend to have in the wilderness. My own dog died a month ago. He was thirteen, so quite old, and I thought maybe I wouldn't have another, but…"

Tom smiled, looking at the way Perro's head rested against the priest's leg, as if they'd always been together. In a selfish way he wanted to face the difficulties and take him home, but he knew somehow that this was why he'd saved him, so that he could find a home like this, where he'd be loved.

"I can't give him away, Father: he's not mine to give. But would you be willing to look after him for me?"

"Nothing would make me happier. You know—" He stopped as a knock sounded on the door. He listened for a moment, and then the housekeeper called to him. "Excuse me for a moment."

After he'd gone, George looked at him with mock outrage. "I can't believe you're giving our dog away. Who made you leader?"

Tom deadpanned, "You know, *bro,* I made an executive decision."

Alice shook her head. "You should've checked with Joel first. You know he's only like this because he wants to *help* us."

Just then, Father Francisco appeared in the doorway and said, "Tom, could I have a word?"

"Of course."

"In private."

"Sure." He got up and followed the priest out, and Tom was aware of the room falling into concerned silence behind him, until Alice called Perro back. They went into the priest's messy study, but without sitting down, Father Francisco turned with a troubled expression.

"It seems one of the helicopters we've heard flying over is a local TV crew. The reporter and the cameraman just came here—that's why I was called to the door." Tom nodded, not sure why it was a problem or what it had to do with him. Even with the little distance that already existed between the present and their ordeal, he could see that there'd be massive media interest in this story, that they'd all be famous for a while once they got back home. The priest could see his confusion and shook his head regretfully. "They asked for you, specifically. They wanted to talk to you about the cocaine factory."

"I see."

He saw that Joel and the others had already talked to the reporter. Or to the politician. The important part was that they'd talked, and would continue to talk, because that was what they did.

And because of that, Tom also saw so much more, the way in which this journey home would never quite come to an end. There would be official interviews, and press interest, and endless speculation. They would never quite make it back to the real world, because this would be their new reality, and part of that would be the cocaine factory and what he'd done there.

"So...it's true, what they were asking about?"

Tom nodded. "Two of the boys in the other house, they were caught, and...there's no way of making this sound good so I'll just say it. I killed them all. I don't know, maybe half a dozen men. I killed them all. It was the only way I could see to save Joel and Chris."

"But how? You're just a boy yourself."

"I blew up the bunkhouse. The two who were with Joel and Chris, one of them basically ran onto the spear I had, the other I shot with a flare gun."

Father Francisco stared at him, barely able to conceal his astonishment. "And how do you feel about that?"

Tom thought of the young guard, the final evening of his life spent sitting on watch, miserable, probably imagining a better future for himself. "I don't know what else I could've done." A pause, then he remembered the one good thing to come out of that situation. "It's where Perro came from."

The priest put his hand on Tom's shoulder and said, "It's a shame you'll be leaving soon, but when you get home, it's important you have the chance to talk about this. I don't mean to the media, I mean to a counselor or a doctor...even a priest."

"I will. Thanks."

"And you need to prepare yourself for the press to lie and exaggerate. Even just now, one of the reporters said he'd heard you were completely out of control and dangerous."

"Maybe I was," said Tom, though he could easily guess that it hadn't been the reporter exaggerating about him. "I had to save them, that was all."

"It sounds to me that you were very brave. But you'll need a different kind of bravery now."

"I understand. Thank you."

He left the study, feeling dejected, seeing now how easily his actions would be misinterpreted by the outside world, no doubt with the help of Joel and some of the others. He bumped into Alice, who'd clearly been looking for him.

"What is it?"

He shook his head dismissively, trying to downplay it as he said, "A reporter wanted to speak to me. About killing all those people at the cocaine factory."

The anger was instant, and so powerful it looked for a moment that she might storm right out of the house to go looking for Joel. "I can't believe it! What a stupid jerk!"

"We don't know it was him."

"If it was Chris, I'll be even more furious." She fixed her eyes on him. "What you did in that cocaine factory was the most heroic thing I've ever seen in my life. Don't you forget that. They don't get ownership of this."

Tom nodded, and said, "Come on. I don't want it to ruin the mood. We're here. We made it."

"Okay." But she hesitated, then she hugged him and kissed him on the cheek, then held his face in her hands and kissed him for real before stepping back shyly.

"What was that for?"

"Just. Because." Her forehead furrowed. "Why? Don't you—?"

"Oh yeah." He kissed her back and then they laughed as Perro barked from the neighboring room.

They went back in to join the others and told them that the reporter had wanted to speak to Tom. And even as he was still buzzing with the thought of that kiss, there was a nagging doubt in his mind, a fear that this might actually mark the beginning of the end of the friendships he'd made in the jungle.

He was sure they all saw it differently, but in Tom's mind, this first hint of intrusion from the press told him everything he needed to know about the weeks and months to come. In the face of that barrage, it was hard to believe these bonds could ever survive the return to their normal lives.

He didn't want it that way, of course, but he could so easily believe that he'd be no more a part of their lives in the coming year than he had in the previous one. It didn't matter what Alice said—Tom would always be *that person,* not the one who'd saved, but the one who'd killed, who'd been out of control, the one people whispered about, pointed at, the one who caused rooms to fall into silence.

He was almost surrendering himself to that fate when George

stood up and said, "I need to say something." They all stopped to listen. "You know, most of the people I counted as my best friends until a month or so back, they died in that crash, and they were good people. But this last week, you guys have shown me what real friendship is, and that's you more than anyone, Tom. I don't care what stories get out, I'll tell the truth to anyone who'll listen. I'm proud to count you as a friend."

"Me too," said Kate, immediately, and a chorus of voices joined in.

Tom smiled and nodded, but couldn't speak, suddenly overwhelmed after everything he'd been through, and he was relieved when George came over and almost crushed him in a bear hug. And he thought again of what Kate had said to him alone out there in the jungle—*this is who we are now.* Maybe that was true, he thought, with a feeling of unfamiliar warmth, and a hope for the future—this is who we are now.

This is who I am now.

EPILOGUE

It's called the butterfly effect, and it's the part of chaos theory that everyone loves. The idea is that a butterfly flapping its wings can cause a hurricane on the other side of the world. Not directly, of course. It's not like the wings disturb some air and that disturbance disturbs more air and so on until it grows into a hurricane—that would just be stupid.

What it really means is that everything is incredibly complex, with millions of tiny factors built into almost every occurrence, and if you remove just one of them (the beat of the butterfly's wings), then it might happen differently, or even not at all.

So, a few years back, some jerk named Pedro Herrera started dating the daughter of his boss at the law firm where he worked. When the relationship turned sour because Pedro was being a jerk, things started going wrong for him, and he got fired soon after. At first, he accepted grudgingly that it had been his own mistakes that had done him in, but as time went on and his life spiraled downward, he convinced himself that his ex-girlfriend had persuaded her father to fire him for no reason.

He became obsessed with revenge—not against her father, because he was a powerful man—but against his ex. He wouldn't do anything major—he wasn't a psycho or anything—but he'd make her suffer for the wrong she'd done him. Pedro was the butterfly, and his bizarre decision to seek revenge was the beat of his wings.

His ex-girlfriend was Gloria Olivares. She'd moved and changed her number, but he found her new address, learned her new number, and started a subtle but determined campaign of harassment, phoning in the middle of the night and saying nothing when she answered, letting the phone ring until her voicemail message sounded but leaving no messages, sending mail-order deliveries, often including cryptic notes that might or might not refer to private details of their relationship.

Except Pedro, being a jerk, had tracked down the *wrong* Gloria Olivares. This Gloria was a laboratory technician who was mystified by the cryptic notes and increasingly terrified by the campaign of harassment.

She started to suffer horrendous migraines brought on by the stress, and after taking too many days off work, she began to fear she might lose her job. So she started going to work even with the migraines, and after one particularly stressful night, she accidentally mixed up two lab results, a cancer-free biopsy and a malignant growth.

So if it hadn't been for Pedro and his twisted but mistaken campaign, Gloria wouldn't have messed up at work and a pilot named Javier Quevedo—who'd lost both parents to cancer, and whose wife had been killed the year before in a street robbery—wouldn't have received test results telling him the terrible news that he had terminal cancer.

Even then, if Javier had insisted on a second opinion, he would have found out it was a mistake, and he wouldn't have sunk into a dangerous depression of his own, and from the bottom of that depression, his mind would not have found its way to the catastrophic decision that he would make his plane disappear in the Amazon jungle and never be found. Life had treated him with nothing but cruelty, so he would play a cruel joke on life in turn, and that would be his legacy. The pilot of that Malaysian plane had done it, and so would he.

That was Javier's plan, anyway, and he researched it thoroughly. Of course, if he'd researched a little more, particularly about the unique thermals in the valley system where he'd chosen to crash, he would have succeeded in taking the plane down whole, the mystery would have been complete, and nineteen people would not have survived.

And if nineteen people had not survived the crash, two of them—Alice Dysart and Tom Calloway—would never have spoken outside of their English class, would never have come to know each other as anything more than someone to debate with over Shakespeare. They would probably never have seen each other again after high school, and they definitely wouldn't have remained part of a close-knit group of friends who'd traveled those jungle paths together.

And that's the butterfly effect. If some jerk called Pedro Herrera hadn't set out on a misguided attempt to take revenge on his ex-girlfriend, two hundred and twelve people would not have died, and Alice and Tom would never have ended up together, or gone on to live the lives they lived after the crash.

ACKNOWLEDGEMENTS

I want to thank Jenny Bak and the team at Jimmy Patterson Books for helping to make this novel the best it could be, not least the publisher himself, James Patterson, whose support and enthusiasm for storytelling has played a big part in getting *When We Were Lost* into your hands.

Thanks also to Penelope Burns and everyone at Gelfman Schneider/ICM Partners, who got behind this story right from the start.

I also want to thank Owen and Lucy, who gave crucial linguistic advice, even if they don't remember giving it.

And finally, my thanks go to you, the reader, because without you, authors are nothing. This book is the butterfly, but *you* are the beating of its wings.

ABOUT THE AUTHOR

KEVIN WIGNALL was born in Brussels, Belgium, and spent most of his childhood living on military bases around Europe. A prolific writer, his many novels and short stories have inspired filmmakers, musicians, and other artists. He's based in England and spends a lot of time traveling, though he doesn't like flying (which may or may not have contributed to the idea for this story). *When We Were Lost* is his first book for young adults, and is in development in Hollywood as a feature film. Find updates at kevinwignall.com or follow him on Instagram at @kevin_wignall.